A JOLLY FELLOWS
BY
Frank Richard Stockton

A JOLLY FELLOWSHIP

Published by Milk Press

New York City, NY

First published circa 1902

Copyright © Milk Press, 2015

All rights reserved

Except in the United States of America, this book is sold subject to the condition that it shall not, by way of trade or otherwise, be lent, re-sold, hired out, or otherwise circulated without the publisher's prior consent in any form of binding or cover other than that in which it is published and without a similar condition including this condition being imposed on the subsequent purchaser.

ABOUT MILK PRESS

Milk Press loves books, and we want the youngest generation to grow up and love them just as much. We publish classic children's literature for young and old alike, including cherished fairy tales and the most famous novels and stories.

CHAPTER I.: WE MAKE A START.

I was sitting on the deck of a Savannah steam-ship, which was lying at a dock in the East River, New York. I was waiting for young Rectus, and had already waited some time; which surprised me, because Rectus was, as a general thing, a very prompt fellow, who seldom kept people waiting. But it was probably impossible for him to regulate his own movements this time, for his father and mother were coming with him, to see him off.

I had no one there to see me off, but I did not care for that. I was sixteen years old, and felt quite like a man; whereas Rectus was only fourteen, and couldn't possibly feel like a man— unless his looks very much belied his feelings. My father and mother and sister lived in a small town some thirty miles from New York, and that was a very good reason for their not coming to the city just to see me sail away in a steam-ship. They took a good leave of me, though, before I left home.

I shall never forget how I first became acquainted with Rectus. About a couple of years before, he was a new boy in the academy at Willisville. One Saturday, a lot of us went down to the river to swim. Our favorite place was near an old wharf, which ran out into deep water, and a fellow could take a good dive there, when the tide was high. There were some of the smaller boys along that day, but they didn't dive any, and if they even swam, it was in shallow water near the shore, by the side of the wharf. But I think most of them spent their time wading about.

I was a good swimmer, and could dive very well. I was learning to swim under water, but had not done very much in that line at the time I speak of. We were nearly ready to come out, when I took a dive from a post on the end of the wharf, and then turned, under water, to swim in shore. I intended to try to keep under until I got into water shallow enough for me to touch bottom, and walk ashore. After half a dozen strokes, I felt for the bottom and my feet touched it. Then I raised my head, but I didn't raise it out of the water. It struck something hard.

In an instant I knew what had happened. There was a big mud-scow lying by the side of the wharf, and I had got under that! It was a great flat thing, ever so long and very wide. I knew I must get from under it as quickly as I could. Indeed, I could hardly hold my breath now. I waded along with my head bent down, but I didn't reach the side of it. Then I turned the other way, but my hands, which I held up, still touched nothing but the hard, slimy bottom of the scow. I must have been wading up and down the length of the thing. I was bewildered. I couldn't think which way to turn. I could only think of one thing. I would be drowned in less than a minute. Scott would be head of the class. My mother, and little Helen—but I can't tell what my thoughts were then. They were dreadful. But just as I was thinking of Helen and mother, I saw through the water some white things, not far from me. I knew by their looks that they were a boy's legs.

I staggered toward them, and in a moment my hands went out of water, just at the side of the scow. I stood up, and my head with half my body came up into the air.

What a breath I drew! But I felt so weak and shaky that I had to take hold of the side of the scow, and stand there for a while before I waded ashore. The boy who was standing by me was Rectus. He did not have that name then, and I didn't know him.

"It must be pretty hard to stay under water so long," he said.

"Hard!" I answered, as soon as I could get my breath; "I should think so. Why, I came near being drowned!"

"Is that so?" said he; "I didn't know that. I saw you go down, and have been watching for you to come up. But I didn't expect you to come from under the scow."

How glad I was that he had been standing there watching for me to come up! If he had not been there, or if his legs had been green or the color of water, I believe I should have drowned.

I always liked the boy after that, though, of course, there was no particular reason for it. He was a boarder. His parents lived in New York. Samuel Colbert was his real name, and the title of Rectus he obtained at school by being so good. He scarcely ever did anything wrong, which was rather surprising to the rest of us, because he was not sickly or anything of that kind. After a while, we got into the way of calling him Rectus, and as he didn't seem to mind it, the name stuck to him. The boys generally liked him, and he got on quite well in the school,—in every way except in his studies. He was not a smart boy, and did not pretend to be.

I went right through the academy, from the lowest to the highest class, and when I left, the professor, as we called our principal, said that I was ready to go to college, and urged me very much to do so. But I was not in any hurry, and my parents agreed with me that, after four years of school-life, I had better wait a while before beginning a new course. All this disturbed the professor very much, but he insisted on my keeping up my studies, so as not to get rusty, and he came up to our house very often, for the purpose of seeing what I was doing in the study line, and how I was doing it.

I thought over things a good deal for myself, and a few months after I left the academy I made up my mind to travel a little. I talked about it at home, and it was generally thought to be a good idea, although my sister was in favor of it only in case I took her with me. Otherwise she opposed it. But there were a great many reasons why I could not take her. She was only eleven.

I had some money of my own, which I thought I would rather spend in travel than in any other way, and, as it was not a large sum, and as my father could not afford to add anything to it, my journey could not be very extensive. Indeed, I only contemplated going to Florida and perhaps a few other Southern States, and then—if it could be done—a visit to some of the West India islands, and, as it was winter-time, that would be a very good trip. My father did not seem to be afraid to trust me to go alone. He and the professor talked it over, and they thought that I would take good enough care of myself. The professor would have much preferred to see me go to college, but, as I was not to do that, he thought travelling much better for me than staying at home, although I made no promise about taking my books along. But it was pretty well settled that I was to go to college in the fall, and this consoled him a little.

The person who first suggested this travelling plan was our old physician, Dr. Mathews. I don't know exactly what he said about it, but I knew he thought I had been studying too hard, and needed to "let up" for a while. And I'm sure, too, that he was quite positive that I would have no let up as long as I staid in the same town with the professor.

Nearly a year before this time, Rectus had left the academy. He had never reached the higher classes,—in fact, he didn't seem to get on well at all. He studied well enough, but he didn't take hold of things properly, and I believe he really did not care to go through the school. But he was such a quiet fellow that we could not make much out of him. His father was very rich, and we all thought that Rectus was taken away to be brought up as a partner in the firm. But we really knew nothing about it: for, as I found out afterward, Rectus spent all his time, after he left school, in studying music.

Soon after my trip was all agreed upon and settled, father had to go to New York, and there he saw Mr. Colbert, and of course told him of my plans. That afternoon, old Colbert came to my father's hotel, and proposed to him that I should take his son with me. He had always heard, he said, that I was a sensible fellow, and fit to be trusted, and he would be very glad to have his boy travel with me. And he furthermore said that if I had the care of Samuel—for of course he didn't call his son Rectus—he would pay me a salary. He had evidently read about young English fellows travelling on the continent with their tutors, and I suppose he wanted me to be his son's tutor, or something like it.

When father told me what Mr. Colbert had proposed, I agreed instantly. I liked Rectus, and the salary would help immensely. I wrote to New York that very night, accepting the proposition.

When my friends in the town, and those at the school, heard that Rectus and I were going off together, they thought it an uncommonly good joke, and they crowded up to our house to see me about it.

"Two such good young men as you and Rectus travelling together ought to have a beneficial influence upon whole communities," said Harry Alden; and Scott remarked that if there should be a bad storm at sea, he would advise us two to throw everybody else overboard to the whales, for the other people would be sure to be the wicked ones. I am happy to say that I got a twist on Scott's ear that made him howl, and then mother came in and invited them all to come and take supper with me, the Tuesday before I started. We invited Rectus to come up from the city, but he did not make his appearance. However, we got on first-rate without him, and had a splendid time. There was never a woman who knew just how to make boys have a good time, like my mother.

I had been a long while on the steamer waiting for Rectus. She was to sail at three o'clock, and it was then after two. The day was clear and fine, but so much sitting and standing about had made me cold, so that I was very glad to see a carriage drive up with Rectus and his father and mother. I went down to them. I was anxious to see Rectus, for it had been nearly a year since we had met. He seemed about the same as he used to be, and had certainly not grown much. He just shook hands with me and said, "How d' ye do, Gordon?" Mr. and Mrs. Colbert seemed ever so much more pleased to see me, and when we went on the upper deck, the old gentleman took me into the captain's room, the door of which stood open. The captain was not there, but I don't believe Mr. Colbert would have cared if he had been. All he seemed to want was to find a place where we could get away from the people on deck. When he had partly closed the door, he said:

"Have you got your ticket?"

"Oh, yes!" I answered; "I bought that ten days ago. I wrote for it."

"That's right," said he, "and here is Sammy's ticket. I was glad to see that you had spoken about the other berth in your state-room being reserved for Sammy."

I thought he needn't have asked me if I had my ticket when he knew that I had bought it. But perhaps he thought I had lost it by this time. He was a very particular little man.

"Where do you keep your money?" he asked me, and I told him that the greater part of it—all but some pocket-money—was stowed away in an inside pocket of my vest.

"Very good," said he; "that's better than a pocket-book or belt: but you must pin it in. Now, here is Sammy's money—for his travelling expenses and his other necessities; I have calculated that that will be enough for a four months' trip, and you wont want to stay longer than that. But if this runs out, you can write to me. If you were going to Europe, now, I'd get you a letter of credit, but for your sort of travelling, you'd better have the money with you. I did think of giving you a draft on Savannah, but you'd have to draw the money there—and you might as well have it here. You're big enough to know how to take care of it." And with this he handed me a lot of banknotes.

"And now, what about your salary? Would you like to have it now, or wait until you come back?"

This question made my heart jump, for I had thought a great deal about how I was to draw that salary. So, quick enough, I said that I'd like to have it now.

"I expected so," said he, "and here's the amount for four months. I brought a receipt. You can sign it with a lead-pencil. That will do. Now put all this money in your inside pockets. Some in your vest, and some in your under-coat. Don't bundle it up too much, and be sure and pin it in. Pin it from the inside, right through the money, if you can. Put your clothes under your pillow at night. Good-bye! I expect they'll be sounding the gong directly, for us to get ashore."

And so he hurried out. I followed him, very much surprised. He had spoken only of money, and had said nothing about his son,—what he wished me to do for him, what plans of travel or instruction he had decided upon, or anything, indeed, about the duties for which I was to be paid. I had expected that he would come down early to the steamer and have a long talk about these matters. There was no time to ask him any questions now, for he was with his wife, trying to get her to hurry ashore. He was dreadfully afraid that they would stay on board too long, and be carried to sea.

Mrs. Colbert, however, did not leave me in any doubt as to what she wanted me to do. She rushed up to me, and seized me by both hands.

"Now you will take the greatest and the best care of my boy, wont you? You'll cherish him as the apple of your eye? You'll keep him out of every kind of danger? Now do take good care of him,—especially in storms."

"SHE SEIZED ME BY BOTH HANDS."

I tried to assure Rectus's mother—she was a wide, good-humored lady—that I would do as much of all this as I could, and what I said seemed to satisfy her, for she wiped her eyes in a very comfortable sort of a way.

Mr. Colbert got his wife ashore as soon as he could, and Rectus and I stood on the upper deck and watched them get into the carriage and drive away. Rectus did not look as happy as I thought a fellow ought to look, when starting out on such a jolly trip as we expected this to be.

I proposed that we should go and look at our state-room, which was number twenty-two, and so we went below. The state-room hadn't much state about it. It was very small, with two shelves for us to sleep on. I let Rectus choose his shelf, and he took the lower one. This suited me very well, for I'd much rather climb over a boy than have one climb over me.

There wasn't anything else in the room to divide, and we were just about to come out and call the thing settled, when I heard a shout at the door. I turned around, and there stood Harry Alden, and Scott, and Tom Myers and his brother George!

I tell you, I was glad to see them. In spite of all my reasoning that it made no difference about anybody coming to see me off, it did make a good deal of difference. It was a lonely sort of business starting off in that way—especially after seeing Rectus's father and mother come down to the boat with him.

"We didn't think of this until this morning," cried Scott. "And then we voted it was too mean to let you go off without anybody to see you safely on board——"

"Oh, yes!" said I.

"And so our class appointed a committee," Scott went on, "to come down and attend to you, and we're the committee. It ought to have been fellows that had gone through the school, but there were none of them there."

"Irish!" said Harry.

"So we came," said Scott. "We raised all the spare cash there was in the class, and there was only enough to send four of us. We drew lots. If it hadn't been you, I don't believe the professor would have let us off. Any way, we missed the noon train, and were afraid, all the way here, that we'd be too late. Do you two fellows have to sleep in those 'cubby-holes'?"

"Certainly," said I; "they're big enough."

"Don't believe it," said Harry Alden; "they're too short."

"That's so," said Scott, who was rather tall for his age. "Let's try 'em."

This was agreed to on the spot, and all four of the boys took off their boots and got into the berths, while Rectus and I sat down on the little bench at the side of the room and laughed at them. Tom Myers and his brother George both climbed into the top berth at once, and as they found it was a pretty tight squeeze, they both tried to get out at once, and down they came on Scott, who was just turning out of the lower berth,—which was too long for him, in spite of all his talk,—and then there was a much bigger tussle, all around, than any six boys could make with comfort in a little room like that.

I hustled Tom Myers and his brother George out into the dining-room, and the other fellows followed.

"Is this where you eat?" asked Scott, looking up and down at the long tables, with the swinging shelves above them.

"No, this isn't where they eat," said Harry; "this is where they come to look at victuals, and get sick at the sight of them."

"Sick!" said I; "not much of it."

But the committee laughed, and didn't seem to agree with me.

"You'll be sick ten minutes after the boat starts," said Scott.

"We wont get into sea-sick water until we're out of the lower bay," I said. "And this isn't a boat—it's a ship. You fellows know lots!"

Tom Myers and his brother George were trying to find out why the tumblers and glasses were all stuck into holes in the shelves over the tables, when Harry Alden sung out:

"What's that swishing?"

"That what?" said I.

"There it goes again!" Harry cried. "Splashing!"

"It's the wheels!" exclaimed Rectus.

"That's so!" cried Scott. "The old thing's off! Rush up! Here! The hind-stairs! Quick!"

And upstairs to the deck we all went, one on top of another. The wheels were going around, and the steamer was off!

Already she was quite a distance from the wharf. I suppose the tide carried her out, as soon as the lines were cast off, for I'm sure the wheels had not been in motion half a minute before we heard them. But all that made no difference. We were off.

I never saw four such blank faces as the committee wore, when they saw the wide space of water between them and the wharf.

"Stop her!" cried Scott to me, as if I could do anything, and then he made a dive toward a party of men on the deck.

"They're passengers!" I cried. "We must find the captain."

"No, no!" said Harry. "Go for the steersman. Tell him to steer back! We mustn't be carried off!"

Tom Myers and his brother George had already started for the pilot-house, when Rectus shouted to them that he'd run down to the engineer and tell him to stop the engine. So they stopped, and Rectus was just going below when Scott called to him to hold up.

"You needn't be scared!" he said. (He had been just as much scared as anybody.) "That man over there says it will be all right. We can go back with the pilot. People often do that. It will be all the more fun. Don't bother the engineer. There's nothing I'd like better than a trip back with a pilot!"

"That's so," said Harry; "I never thought of the pilot."

"But are you sure he'll take you back?" asked Rectus, while Tom Myers and his brother George looked very pale and anxious.

"Take us? Of course he will," said Scott. "That's one of the things a pilot's for,—to take back passengers,—I mean people who are only going part way. Do you suppose the captain will want to take us all the way to Savannah for nothing?"

Rectus didn't suppose that, and neither did any of the rest of us, but I thought we ought to look up the captain and tell him.

"But, you see," said Scott, "it's just possible he might put back."

"Well, don't you want to go back?" I asked.

"Yes, of course, but I would like a sail back in a pilot-boat," said Scott, and Harry Alden agreed with him. Tom Myers and his brother George wanted to go back right away.

We talked the matter over a good deal. I didn't wish to appear as if I wanted to get rid of the fellows who had been kind enough to come all the way from Willisville to see me off, but I couldn't help thinking that it didn't look exactly fair and straightforward not to say that these boys were not passengers until the pilot was ready to go back. I determined to go and see about the matter, but I would wait a little while.

It was cool on deck, especially now that the vessel was moving along, but we all buttoned up our coats and walked up and down. The sun shone brightly, and the scene was so busy and lively with the tug-boats puffing about, and the vessels at anchor, and the ferry-boats, and a whole bay-full of sights curious to us country boys, that we all enjoyed ourselves very much—except Tom Myers and his brother George. They didn't look happy.

CHAPTER II.: GOING BACK WITH THE PILOT.

We were pretty near the Narrows when I thought it was about time to let the captain, or one of the officers, know that there were some people on board who didn't intend to take the whole trip. I had read in the newspapers that committees and friends who went part way with distinguished people generally left them in the lower bay.

But I was saved the trouble of looking for an officer, for one of them, the purser, came along, collecting tickets. I didn't give him a chance to ask Scott or any of the other fellows for something that they didn't have, but went right up to him and told him how the matter stood.

"I must see the captain about this," he said, and off he went.

"He didn't look very friendly," said Scott, and I had to admit that he didn't.

In a few moments the captain came walking rapidly up to us. He was a tall man, dressed in blue, with side-whiskers, and an oil-cloth cap. The purser came up behind him.

"What's all this?" said the captain. "Are you not passengers, you boys?" He did not look very friendly, either, as he asked this question.

THE VESSEL IS OFF.

"Two of us are," I said, "but four of us were carried off accidentally."

"Accident? Fiddlesticks!" exclaimed the captain. "Didn't you know the vessel was starting? Hadn't you time to get off? Didn't you hear the gong? Everybody else heard it. Are you all deaf?"

This was a good deal to answer at once, so I just said that I didn't remember hearing any gong. Tom Myers and his brother George, however, spoke up, and said that they had heard a gong, they thought, but did not know what it was for.

"Why didn't you ask, then?" said the captain, who was getting worse in his humor. I had a good mind to tell him that it would take up a good deal of the crew's time if Tom Myers and his brother George asked about everything they didn't understand on board this ship, but I thought I had better not. I have no doubt the gong sounded when we were having our row in the state-room, and were not likely to pay attention to it even if we did hear it.

"And why, in the name of common sense," the captain went on, "didn't you come and report, the instant you found the vessel had started? Did you think we were fast to the pier all this time?"

Then Scott thought he might as well come out square with the truth; and he told how they made up their minds, after they found that the steamer had really started, with them on board, not to make any fuss about it, nor give anybody any trouble to stop the ship, or to put back, but just to stay quietly on board, and go back with the pilot. They thought that would be most convenient, all around.

"Go back with the pilot!" the captain cried. "Why, you young idiot, there is no pilot! Coastwise steamers don't carry pilots. I am my own pilot. There is no pilot going back!"

You ought to have seen Scott's face!

SCOTT AND THE CAPTAIN.

Nobody said anything. We all just stood and looked at the captain. Tears began to come into the eyes of Tom Myers and his brother George.

"What are they to do?" asked the purser of the captain. "Buy tickets for Savannah?"

"We can't do that," said Scott, quickly. "We haven't any money."

"I don't know what they're to do," replied the captain. "I'd like to chuck 'em overboard." And with this agreeable little speech he walked away.

The purser now took the two tickets for Rectus and myself, and saying: "We'll see what's to be done with the rest of you fellows," he walked away, too.

Then we all looked at one another. We were a pretty pale lot, and I believe that Rectus and I, who were all right, felt almost as badly as the four other boys, who were all wrong.

"We can't go to Savannah!" said Harry Alden. "What right have they to take us to Savannah?"

"Well, then, you'd better get out and go home," said Scott. "I don't so much mind their taking us to Savannah, for they can't make us pay if we haven't any money. But how are we going to get back? That's the question. And what'll the professor think? He'll write home that we've run away. And what'll we do in Savannah without any money?"

"You'd better have thought of some of these things before you got us into waiting to go back with the pilot," said Harry.

As for Tom Myers and his brother George, they just sat down and put their arms on the railing, and clapped their faces down on their arms. They cried all over their coat-sleeves, but kept as quiet as they could about it. Whenever these two boys had to cry before any of the rest of the school-fellows, they had learned to keep very quiet about it.

While the rest of us were talking away, and Scott and Harry finding fault with each other, the captain came back. He looked in a little better humor.

"The only thing that can be done with you boys," he said, "is to put you on some tug or small craft that's going back to New York. If we meet one, I'll lie to and let you off. But it will put me to a great deal of trouble, and we may meet with nothing that will take you aboard. You have acted very badly. If you had come right to me, or to any of the officers, the moment you found we had started, I could have easily put you on shore. There are lots of small boats about the piers that would have come out after you, or I might even have put back. But I can do nothing now but look out for some craft bound for New York that will take you aboard. If we don't meet one, you'll have to go on to Savannah."

This made us feel a little better. We were now in the lower bay, and there would certainly be some sort of a vessel that would stop for the boys. We all went to the forward deck and looked out. It was pretty cold there, and we soon began to shiver in the wind, but still we stuck it out.

There were a good many vessels, but most of them were big ones. We could hardly have the impudence to ask a great three-masted ship, under full sail, to stop and give us a lift to New York. At any rate, we had nothing to do with the asking. The captain would attend to that. But every time we came near a vessel going the other way, we looked about to see if we could see anything of an officer with a trumpet, standing all ready to sing out, "Sail ho!"

But, after a while, we felt so cold that we couldn't stand it any longer, and we went below. We might have gone and stood by the smoke-stack and warmed ourselves, but we didn't know enough about ships to think of this.

We hadn't been standing around the stove in the dining-room more than ten minutes, before the purser came hurrying toward us.

"Come, now," he said, "tumble forward! The captain's hailed a pilot-boat."

"Hurrah!" said Scott; "we're going back in a pilot-boat, after all!" and we all ran after the purser to the lower forward deck. Our engines had stopped, and not far from us was a rough-looking little schooner with a big "17" painted in black on her mainsail. She was "putting about," the purser said, and her sails were flapping in the wind.

There was a great change in the countenances of Tom Myers and his brother George. They looked like a couple of new boys.

"Isn't this capital?" said Scott. "Everything's turned out all right."

But all of a sudden he changed his tune.

"Look here!" said he to me, pulling me on one side; "wont that pilot want to be paid something? He wont stop his vessel and take us back for nothing, will he?"

I couldn't say anything about this, but I asked the purser, who still stood by us.

"I don't suppose he'll make any regular charge," said he; "but he'll expect you to give him something,—whatever you please."

"But we haven't anything," said Scott to me. "We have our return tickets to Willisville, and that's about all."

"Perhaps we can't go back, after all," said Harry, glumly, while Tom Myers and his brother George began to drop their lower jaws again.

I did not believe that the pilot-boat people would ask to see the boys' money before they took them on board; but I couldn't help feeling that it would be pretty hard for them to go ashore at the city and give nothing for their passages but promises, and so I called Rectus on one side, and proposed to lend the fellows some money. He agreed, and I unpinned a banknote and gave it to Scott. He was mightily tickled to get it, and vowed he'd send it back to me in the first letter he wrote (and he did it, too).

The pilot-schooner did not come very near us, but she lowered a boat with two men in it, and they rowed up to the steamer. Some of our sailors let down a pair of stairs, and one of the men in the boat came up to see what was wanted. The purser was telling him, when the captain, who was standing on the upper deck, by the pilot-house, sung out:

"Hurry up there, now, and don't keep this vessel here any longer. Get 'em out as quick as you can, Mr. Brown."

The boys didn't stop to have this kind invitation repeated, and Scott scuffled down the stairs into the boat as fast as he could, followed closely by Harry Alden. Tom Myers and his brother George stopped long enough to bid each of us good-bye, and shake hands with us, and then they went down the stairs. They had to climb over the railing to the platform in front of the wheel-house to get to the stairs, and as the steamer rolled a little, and the stairs shook, they went down very slowly, backward, and when they got to the bottom were afraid to step into the boat, which looked pretty unsteady as it wobbled about under them.

"Come, there! Be lively!" shouted the captain.

Just then, Rectus made a step forward. He had been looking very anxiously at the boys as they got into the boat, but he hadn't said anything.

"Where are you going?" said I; for, as quick as a flash, the thought came into my mind that Rectus's heart had failed him, and that he would like to back out.

"I think I'll go back with the boys," he said, making another step toward the top of the stairs, down which the man from the pilot-boat was hurrying.

"Just you try it!" said I, and I put out my arm in front of him.

He didn't try it, and I'm glad he didn't, for I should have been sorry enough to have had the boys go back and say that when they last saw Rectus and I we were having a big fight on the deck of the steamer.

The vessel now started off, and Rectus and I went to the upper deck and stood and watched the little boat, as it slowly approached the schooner. We were rapidly leaving them, but we saw the boys climb on board, and one of them—it must have been Scott—waved his handkerchief to us. I waved mine in return, but Rectus kept his in his pocket. I don't think he felt in a wavy mood.

While we were standing looking at the distant pilot-boat, I began to consider a few matters; and the principal thing was this: How were Rectus and I to stand toward each other? Should we travel like a couple of school-friends, or should I make him understand that he was under my charge and control, and must behave himself accordingly? I had no idea what he thought of the matter, and by the way he addressed me when we met, I supposed that it was possible that he looked upon me very much as he used to when we went to school together. If he had said Mr. Gordon, it would have been more appropriate, I thought, and would have encouraged me, too, in taking position as his supervisor. As far as my own feelings were concerned, I think I would have preferred to travel about on a level with Rectus, and to have a good time with him, as two old school-fellows might easily have, even if one did happen to be two years older than the other. But that would not be earning my salary. After a good deal of thought, I came to the conclusion that I would let things go on as they would, for a while, giving Rectus a good deal of rope; but the moment he began to show signs of insubordination, I would march right on him, and quell him with an iron hand. After that, all would be plain sailing, and we could have as much fun as we pleased, for Rectus would know exactly how far he could go.

There were but few passengers on deck, for it was quite cold, and it now began to grow dark, and we went below. Pretty soon the dinner-bell rang, and I was glad to hear it, for I had the appetite of a horse. There was a first-rate dinner, ever so many different kinds of dishes, all up and down the table, which had ridges running lengthwise, under the table-cloth, to keep the plates from sliding off, if a storm should come up. Before we were done with dinner the shelves above the table began to swing a good deal,—or rather the vessel rolled and the shelves kept their places,—so I knew we must be pretty well out to sea, but I had not expected it would be so rough, for the day had been fine and clear. When we left the table, it was about as much as we could do to keep our feet, and in less than a quarter of an hour I began to feel dreadfully. I stuck it out as long as I could, and then I went to bed. The old ship rolled, and she pitched, and she heaved, and she butted, right and left, against the waves, and made herself just as uncomfortable for human beings as she could, but, for all that, I went to sleep after a while.

I don't know how long I slept, but when I woke up, there was Rectus, sitting on a little bench by the state-room wall, with his feet braced against the berth. He was hard at work sucking a lemon. I turned over and looked down at him. He didn't look a bit sick. I hated to see him eating lemons.

"Don't you feel badly, Rectus?" said I.

"Oh no!" said he; "I'm all right. You ought to suck a lemon. Have one?"

I declined his offer. The idea of eating or drinking anything was intensely disagreeable to me. I wished that Rectus would put down that lemon. He did throw it away after a while, but he immediately began to cut another one.

RECTUS AND THE LEMONS.

"Rectus," said I, "you'll make yourself sick. You'd better go to bed."

"It's just the thing to stop me from being sick," said he, and at that minute the vessel gave her stern a great toss over sideways, which sent Rectus off his seat, head foremost into the wash-stand. I was glad to see it. I would have been glad of almost anything that stopped that lemon business.

But it didn't stop it; and he only picked himself up, and sat down again, his lemon at his mouth.

"Rectus!" I cried, leaning out of my berth. "Put down that lemon and go to bed!"

He put down the lemon without a word, and went to bed. I turned over with a sense of relief. Rectus was subordinate!

CHAPTER III.: RECTUS OPENS HIS EYES.

I was all right the next day, and we staid on deck most of the time, standing around the smoke-stack when our noses got a little blue with the cold. There were not many other people on deck. I was expecting young Rectus to have his turn at sea-sickness, but he disappointed me. He spent a good deal of his time calculating our position on a little folding-map he had. He inquired how fast we were going, and then he worked the whole thing out, from Sandy Hook to Savannah, marking on the map the hours at which he ought to be at such and such a place. He tried his best to get his map of the course all right, and made a good many alterations, so that we were off Cape Charles several times in the course of the day. Rectus had never been very good at calculations, and I was glad to see that he was beginning to take an interest in such things.

The next morning, just after day-break, we were awakened by a good deal of tramping about on deck, over our heads, and we turned out, sharp, to see what the matter was. Rectus wanted me to wait, after we were dressed, until he could get out his map and calculate where we were, but I couldn't stop for such nonsense, for I knew that his kind of navigation didn't amount to much, and so we scrambled up on deck. The ship was pitching and tossing worse than she had done yet. We had been practising the "sea-leg" business the day before, and managed to walk along pretty well; but this morning our sea-legs didn't work at all, and we couldn't take a step without hanging on to something. When we got on deck, we found that the first officer, or mate,—his name was Randall,—with three or four sailors, was throwing the lead to see how deep the water was. We hung on to a couple of stays and watched them. It was a rousing big lead, a foot long, and the line ran out over a pulley at the stern. A sailor took the lead a good way forward before he threw it, so as to give it a chance to get to the bottom before the steamer passed over it and began to tow it. When they pulled it in, we were surprised to see that it took three men to do it. Then Mr. Randall scooped out a piece of tallow that was in a hollow in the bottom of the lead, and took it to show to the captain, whose room was on deck. I knew this was one way they had of finding out where they were, for they examined the sand or mud on the tallow, and so knew what sort of a bottom they were going over; and all the different kinds of bottom were marked out on their charts.

As Mr. Randall passed us, Rectus sung out to him, and asked him where we were now.

"Off Hatteras," said he, quite shortly.

I didn't think Rectus should have bothered Mr. Randall with questions when he was so busy; but after he went into the captain's room, the men did not seem to have much to do, and I asked one of them how deep it was.

"About seventeen fathoms," said he.

"Can we see Cape Hatteras?" I said, trying to get a good look landward as the vessel rolled over that way.

"No," said the man. "We could see the light just before day-break, but the weather's gettin' thick now, and we're keepin' out."

It was pretty thick to the west, that was true. All that I could see in the distance was a very mixed-up picture of wave-tops and mist. I knew that Cape Hatteras was one of the most dangerous points on the coast, and that sailors were always glad when they had safely rounded it, and so I began to take a good deal of interest in what was going on. There was a pretty strong wind from the south-east, and we had no sail set at all. Every now and then the steamer would get herself up on top of a big wave, and then drop down, sideways, as if she were sliding off the top of a house. The mate and the captain soon came out on deck together, and the captain went forward to the pilot-house, while Mr. Randall came over to his men, and they got ready to throw the lead again. It didn't seem to me that the line ran out as far as it did the last time, and I think I heard Mr. Randall say, "Fourteen." At any rate, a man was sent forward to the pilot-house, and directly we heard the rudder-chains creaking, and the big iron arms of the rudder, which were on deck, moved over toward the landward side of the vessel, and I knew by that that the captain was putting her head out to sea. Mr. Randall took out the tallow from the lead and laid it in an empty bucket that was lashed to the deck. He seemed to be more anxious now about the depth of water than about the kind of bottom we were passing over. The lead was just about to be thrown again, when Rectus, who had taken the tallow out of the bucket, which stood near us, and had examined it pretty closely, started off to speak to Mr. Randall, with the tallow in his hand.

"'HOLD YOUR TONGUE!' ROARED MR. RANDALL."

"Look here!" said Rectus, holding on to the railing. "I'll tell you what would be a sight better than tallow for your leads. Just you get some fine, white Castile-soap, and——"

"Confound you!" roared Mr. Randall, turning savagely on him. "Hold your tongue! For three cents I'd tie you to this line and drag the bottom with you!"

Rectus made no answer. He didn't offer him the three cents, but came away promptly, and put the piece of tallow back in the bucket. He didn't get any comfort from me.

"Haven't you got any better sense," I said to him, "than to go, with your nonsense, to the first officer at such a time as this? I never saw such a boy!"

"But the soap is better than the tallow," said Rectus. "It's finer and whiter, and would take up the sand better."

"No, it wouldn't," I growled at him; "the water would wash it out in half a minute. You needn't be trying to tell anybody on this ship what they ought to do."

"But supposing——" said he.

"No," I exclaimed, in a way that made him jump, "there's no supposing about it. If you know their business better than they do, why, just let it stand that way. It wont hurt you."

I was pretty mad, I must say, for I didn't want to see a fellow like Rectus trying to run the ship. But you couldn't stay mad with Rectus long. He didn't mean any wrong, and he gave no words back, and so, as you might expect, we were all right again by breakfast-time.

The next morning we were surprised to feel how warm it was on deck. We didn't need our overcoats. The sea was ever so much smoother, too. There were two or three ladies on deck, who could walk pretty well.

About noon, I was standing on the upper deck, when I saw Rectus coming toward me, looking very pale. He was generally a dark sort of a boy, and it made a good deal of difference in him to look pale. I was sure he was going to be sick, at last,—although it was rather queer for him to knock under when the voyage was pretty nearly over,—and I began to laugh, when he said to me, in a nervous sort of way:

"I tell you what it is, I believe that we've gone past the mouth of the Savannah River. According to my calculations," said he, pointing to a spot on his map, which he held in his hand, "we must be down about here, off the Georgia coast."

I have said that I began to laugh, and now I kept on. I just sat down and roared, so that the people looked at me.

"You needn't laugh," said Rectus. "I believe it's so."

"All right, my boy," said I; "but we wont tell the captain. Just let's wait and have the fun of seeing him turn around and go back."

Rectus didn't say anything to this, but walked off with his map.

"RECTUS SHOWED ME THE MAP."

Now, that boy was no fool. I believe that he was beginning to feel like doing something, and, as he had never done anything before, he didn't know how.

About twelve o'clock we reached the mouth of the Savannah (without turning back), and sailed twenty miles up the river to the city.

We were the first two persons off that vessel, and we took a hack to the hotel that the purser had recommended to us, and had the satisfaction of reaching it about ten minutes ahead of the people who came in the omnibus; although I don't know that that was of much use to us, as the clerk gave us top rooms, any way.

We went pretty nearly all over Savannah that afternoon and the next day. It's a beautiful city. There is a little public square at nearly every corner, and one of the wide streets has a double row of big trees running right down the middle of it, with grass under them, and, what seemed stranger yet, the trees were all in leaf, little children were playing on the grass, and the weather was warm and splendid. The gardens in front of the houses were full of roses and all sorts of flowers in blossom, and Rectus wanted to buy a straw hat and get his linen trousers out of his trunk.

"No, sir," said I; "I'm not going around with a fellow wearing a straw hat and linen breeches in January. You don't see anybody else wearing them."

"No," said he; "but it's warm enough."

"You may think so," I answered; "but I guess they know their own business best. This is their coldest season, and if they wore straw hats and linen clothes now, what would they put on when the scorching hot weather comes?"

Rectus didn't know, and that matter was dropped. There is a pretty park at the back of the town, and we walked about it, and sat under the trees, and looked at the flowers, and the fountain playing, and enjoyed it ever so much. If it had been summer, and we had been at home, we shouldn't have cared so much for these things; but sitting under trees, and lounging about over the green grass, while our folks at home were up to their eyes, or thereabouts, in snow and ice, delighted both of us, especially Rectus. I never heard him talk so much.

We reached Savannah on Tuesday, and were to leave in the steamer for St. Augustine Thursday afternoon. Thursday morning we went out to the cemetery of Bonaventure, one of the loveliest places in the whole world, where there are long avenues of live-oaks that stretch from one side of the road to the other, like great covered arbors, and from every limb of every tree hang great streamers of gray moss, four and five feet long. It was just wonderful to look at. The whole place seemed dripping with waving fringe. Rectus said it looked to him as if this was a graveyard for old men, and that every old fellow had had to hang his beard on a tree before he went down into his grave.

This was a curious idea for Rectus to have, and the colored man who was driving us—we went out in style, in a barouche, but I wouldn't do that kind of thing again without making a bargain beforehand—turned around to look at him as if he thought he was a little crazy. Rectus was certainly in high spirits. There was a sort of change coming over him. His eyes had a sparkle in them that I never saw before. No one could say that he didn't take interest in things now. I think the warm weather had something to do with it.

"I tell you what it is, Gordon," said he,—he still called me Gordon, and I didn't insist on "Mr.," because I thought that, on the whole, perhaps it wouldn't do,—"I'm waking up. I feel as if I had been asleep all my life, and was just beginning to open my eyes."

A graveyard seemed a queer place to start out fresh in this way, but it wasn't long before I found that, if Rectus hadn't really wakened up, he could kick pretty hard in his sleep.

Nothing much happened on the trip down to St. Augustine, for we travelled nearly all the way by night. Early the next morning we were lying off that old half Spanish town, wishing the tide would rise so that we could go in. There is a bar between two islands that lie in front of the town, and you have to go over that to get into the harbor. We were on the "Tigris," the Bahama steamer that touched at St. Augustine on her way to Nassau, and she couldn't get over that bar until high tide. We were dreadfully impatient, for we could see the old town, with its trees, all green and bright, and its low, wide houses, and a great light-house, marked like a barber's pole or a stick of old-fashioned mint-candy, and, what was best of all, a splendid old castle, or fort, built by the Spaniards three hundred years ago! We declared we would go there the moment we set foot on shore. In fact, we soon had about a dozen plans for seeing the town.

If we had been the pilots, we would have bumped that old steamer over the bar, somehow or other, long before the real pilot started her in; but we had to wait. When we did go in, and steamed along in front of the old fort, we could see that it was gray and crumbling, and moss-covered in places, and it was just like an oil-painting. The whole town, in fact, was like an oil-painting to us.

The moment the stairs were put down, we scuffled ashore, and left the steamer to go on to the Bahamas whenever she felt like it. We gave our valises and trunk-checks to a negro man with a wagon, and told him to take the baggage to a hotel that we could see from the wharf, and then we started off for the fort. But on my way along the wharf I made up my mind that, as the fort had been there for three hundred years, it would probably stand a while longer, and that we had better go along with our baggage, and see about getting a place to live in, for we were not going to be in any hurry to leave St. Augustine.

We didn't go to any hotel at all. I had a letter of introduction to a Mr. Cholott, and on our way up from the wharf, I heard some one call out that name to a gentleman. So I remembered my letter, and went up and gave it to him. He was a first-rate man, and when we told him where we were going, we had quite a talk, and he said he would advise us to go to a boarding-house. It would be cheaper, and if we were like most boys that he knew, we'd like it better. He said that board could be had with several families that he knew, and that some of the Minorcans took boarders in the winter.

Of course, Rectus wanted to know, right away, what a Minorcan was. I didn't think it was exactly the place to ask questions which probably had long answers, but Mr. Cholott didn't seem to be in a hurry, and he just started off and told us about the Minorcans. A chap called Turnbull, more than a hundred years ago, brought over to Florida a lot of the natives of the island of Minorca, in the Mediterranean, and began a colony. But he was a mean sort of chap; he didn't care for anything but making money out of the Minorcans, and it wasn't long before they found it out, for he was really making slaves of them. So they just rose up and rebelled, and left old Turnbull to run his colony by himself. Served him right, too. They started off on their own accounts, and most of them came to this town, where they settled, and have had a good time ever since. There are a great many of them here now, descendants of the original Minorcans, and they keep pretty much together and keep their old name, too. They look a good deal like Spaniards, Mr. Cholott said, and many of them are very excellent people.

Rectus took the greatest interest in these Minorcans, but we didn't take board with any of them. We went to the house of a lady who was a friend of Mr. Cholott, and she gave us a splendid room, that looked right out over the harbor. We could see the islands, and the light-house, and the bar with the surf outside, and even get a glimpse of the ocean. We saw the "Tigris" going out over the bar. The captain wanted to get out on the same tide he came in on, and he did not lose any time. As soon as she got fairly out to sea, we hurried down, to go to the fort. But first, Rectus said, we ought to go and buy straw hats. There were lots of men with straw hats in St. Augustine. This was true, for it was just as warm here as we have it in June, and we started off to look for a straw-hat store.

We found that we were in one of the queerest towns in the world. Rectus said it was all back-streets, and it looked something that way. The streets were very narrow, and none of them had any pavement but sand and powdered shell, and very few had any sidewalks. But they didn't seem to be needed. Many of the houses had balconies on the second story, which reached toward each other from both sides of the street, and this gave the town a sociable appearance. There were lots of shops, and most of them sold sea-beans. There were other things, like alligators' teeth, and shells, and curiosities, but the great trade of the town seemed to be in sea-beans. Rectus and I each bought one for our watch-chains.

I think we tried on every straw hat in town, and we bought a couple in a little house, where two or three young women were making them. Rectus asked me, in a low voice, if I didn't think one of the young women was a Mohican. I hushed him up, for it was none of his business if she was.

I had a good deal of trouble in making Rectus say "Minorcan." Whenever we had met a dark-haired person, he had said to me: "Do you think that is a Mohican?" It was a part of his old school disposition to get things wrong in this way. But he never got angry when I corrected him. His temper was perfect.

I bought a common-sized hat, but Rectus bought one that spread out far and wide. It made him look like a Japanese umbrella. We stuffed our felt hats into our pockets, and started for the fort. But I looked at my watch and found it was supper-time. I had suspected it when I came out of the hat-shop. The sea-trip and fine air here had given us tremendous appetites, which our walk had sharpened.

So we turned back at once and hurried home, agreeing to begin square on the fort the next day.

CHAPTER IV.: TO THE RESCUE.

The next morning, I was awakened by Rectus coming into the room.

"Hello!" said I; "where have you been? I didn't hear you get up."

"I called you once or twice," said Rectus, "but you were sleeping so soundly I thought I'd let you alone. I knew you'd lost some sleep by being sick on the steamer."

"That was only the first night," I exclaimed. "I've made up that long ago. But what got you up so early?"

"I went out to take a warm salt-water bath before breakfast," answered Rectus. "There's an eight-cornered bath-house right out here, almost under the window, where you can have your sea-water warm if you like it."

"Do they pump it from the tropics?" I asked, as I got up and began to dress.

"No; they heat it in the bath-house. I had a first-rate bath, and I saw a Minorcan."

"You don't say so!" I cried. "What was he like? Had he horns? And how did you know what he was?"

"I asked him," said Rectus.

"Asked him!" I exclaimed. "You don't mean to say that you got up early and went around asking people if they were Mohicans!"

"Minorcans, I said."

"Well, it's bad enough, even if you got the name right. Did you ask the man plump to his face?"

"Yes. But he first asked me what I was. He was an oldish man, and I met him just as I was coming out of the bath-house. He had a basket of clams on his arm, and I asked him where he caught them. That made him laugh, and he said he dug them out of the sand under the wharf. Then he asked me if my name was Cisneros, and when I told him it was not, he said that I looked like a Spaniard, and he thought that that might be my name. And so, as he had asked me about myself, I asked him if he was a Minorcan, and he said 'yes.'"

"And what then?" I asked.

"Nothing," said Rectus. "He went on with his clams, and I came home."

"You didn't seem to make much out of him, after all," said I. "I don't wonder he thought you were a Spaniard, with that hat. I told you you'd make a show of yourself. But what are you going to do with your Minorcans, Rectus, when you catch them?"

He laughed, but didn't mention his plans.

"I didn't know how you got clams," he said. "I thought you caught them some way. It would never have entered my head to dig for them."

"There's lots to learn in this town about fish, and ever so many other things besides; and I tell you what it is, Rectus, as soon as we get through with the fort,—and I don't know how long that will take us, for I heard on the steamer that it had underground dungeons,—we'll go off on a first-class exploring expedition."

That suited Rectus exactly.

After breakfast we started for the fort. It is just outside of the town, and you can walk all the way on the sea-wall, which is about a yard wide on top,—just a little too wide for one fellow, but not quite wide enough for two.

The United States government holds the fort now, of course, and calls it Fort Marion, but the old Spanish name was San Marco, and we disdained to call it anything else. When we went over the drawbridge, and across the moat, we saw the arms of Spain on a shield over the great gate of the fort. We walked right in, into a wide hall, with dark door-ways on each side, and then out into a great inclosed space, like a parade-ground, in the centre of the fort, and here we saw a whole crowd of Indians. We didn't expect to find Indians here, and we were very much surprised. They did not wear Indian clothes, but were dressed in United States military uniform. They didn't look like anything but Indians, though, for all that. I asked one of them if he belonged here, and he smiled and said "How?" and held out his hand. We both shook it, but could make nothing out of him. A good many of them now came up and said "How?" to us, and shook hands, and we soon found that this meant "How d' ye do?" and was about all they knew of English.

"HOW?"

We were lucky enough, before we got through shaking hands with our new friends, to see Mr. Cholott coming toward us, and he immediately took us in charge, and seemed to be glad to have a job of the kind. There was nothing about the fort that he didn't know. He told us that the Indians were prisoners, taken in the far West by United States troops, and that some of them were the worst Indians in the whole country. They were safe enough now, though, and were held here as hostages. Some were chiefs, and they were all noted men,—some as murderers, and others in less important ways. They had been here for some years, and a few of them could speak a little English.

He then took us all over the fort,—up an inclined plane to the top of the ramparts, and into the Indian barracks on one of the wide walls, where we saw a lot of Cheyennes and Kiowas, and Indians from other tribes, sitting around and making bows and arrows, and polishing sea-beans to sell to visitors. At each corner of the fort was a "lookout tower,"—a little box of a place, stuck out from the top of the wall, with loopholes and a long, narrow passage leading to it, with a high wall on each side to protect from bullets and arrows the man who went to look out. One of the towers had been knocked off, probably by a cannon-ball. These towers and slim little passages took our fancy greatly. Then Mr. Cholott took us downstairs to see the dungeons. He got the key and gave it to a big old Indian, named Red Horse, who went ahead with a lighted kerosene-lamp.

We first saw the dungeon where the Indian chief, Osceola, was shut up during the Seminole war. It was a dreary place. There was another chief, Wild Cat, who was imprisoned with Osceola, and one night Osceola "boosted" him to a high window, where he squeezed through the bars and got away. If Osceola had had any one to give him a lift, I suppose he would have been off, too. Rectus and I wondered how the two Indians managed this little question of who should be hoisted. Perhaps they tossed up, or perhaps Wild Cat was the lighter of the two. The worst dungeon, though, was a place that was discovered by accident about thirty years ago. There was nothing there when we went in; but, when it was first found, a chained skeleton was lying on the floor. Through a hole in the wall we crept into another dungeon, worse yet, in which two iron cages were found hung to the wall, with skeletons in them. It seemed like being in some other country to stand in this dark little dungeon, and hear these dreadful stories, while a big Indian stood grinning by, holding a kerosene-lamp.

Mr. Cholott told us that one of the cages and the bones could now be seen in Washington.

After Mr. Cholott went home, we tramped all over the fort again by ourselves, and that afternoon we sat on the outer wall that runs along the harbor-front of the fort, and watched the sail-boats and the fishermen in their "dug-outs." There were a couple of sharks swimming up and down in front of the town, and every now and then they would come up and show themselves. They were the first sharks we had ever seen.

Rectus was worked up about the Indians. We had been told that, while a great many of the chiefs and braves imprisoned here were men known to have committed crimes, still there were others who had done nothing wrong, and had been captured and brought here as prisoners, simply because, in this way, the government would have a good hold on their tribes.

Rectus thought this was the worst kind of injustice, and I agreed with him, although I didn't see what we were going to do about it.

On our way home we met Rectus's Minorcan; he was a queer old fellow.

"Hello!" said he, when he saw Rectus. "Have you been out catching clams?"

We stopped and talked a little while about the sharks, and then the old man asked Rectus why he wanted to know, that morning, whether he was a Minorcan or not.

"I just wanted to see one," said Rectus, as if he had been talking of kangaroos or giraffes. "I've been thinking a good deal about them, and their bold escape from slavery, and their——"

"Slavery!" sung out the old man. "We were never slaves! What do you mean by that? Do you take us for niggers?"

He was pretty mad, and I don't wonder, if that was the way he understood Rectus, for he was just as much a white man as either of us.

"Oh no!" said Rectus. "But I've heard all about you, and that tyrant Turnbull, and the way you cast off his yoke. I mean your fathers, of course."

"I reckon you've heard a little too much, young man," said the Minorcan. "Somebody's been stuffin' you. You'd better get a hook and line, and go out to catch clams."

"Why, you don't understand me!" cried Rectus. "I honor you for it."

The old man looked at him and then at me, and then he laughed. "All right, bub," said he. "If ever you want to hire a boat, I've got one. My name is Menendez. Just ask for my boat at the club-house wharf." And then he went on.

"That's all you get for your sympathy with oppressed people," said Rectus. "They call you bub."

"Well, that old fellow isn't oppressed," I said; "and if any of his ancestors were, I don't suppose he cares about remembering it. We ought to hire his boat some time."

That evening we took a walk along the sea-wall. It was a beautiful starlight night, and a great many people were walking about. When we got down near the fort,—which looked bigger and grayer than ever by the starlight,—Rectus said he would like to get inside of it by night, and I agreed that it would be a good thing to do. So we went over the drawbridge (this place has a drawbridge, and portcullises, and barbicans, and demi-lunes, and a moat, just as if it were a castle or a fort of some old country in Europe),—but the big gate was shut. We didn't care to knock, for all was dark, and we came away. Rectus proposed that we should reconnoitre the place, and I agreed, although, in reality, there wasn't anything to reconnoitre. We went down into the moat, which was perfectly dry, and very wide, and walked all around the fort.

We examined the walls, which were pretty jagged and rough in some places, and we both agreed that if we had to do it, we believed we could climb to the top.

As we walked home, Rectus proposed that we should try to climb in some night.

"What's the good?" I asked.

"Why, it would be a splendid thing," said he, "to scale the walls of an old Middle-Age fort, like that. Let's try it, anyway."

I couldn't help thinking that it would be rather a fine thing to do, but it did seem rather foolish to risk our necks to get over the walls at night, when we could walk in, whenever we pleased, all day.

But it was of no use to say anything like that to Rectus. He was full of the idea of scaling the walls, and I found that, when the boy did get worked up to anything, he could talk first-rate, and before we went to sleep I got the notion of it, too, and we made up our minds that we would try it.

The next day we walked around the walls two or three times, and found a place where we thought we could get up, if we had a rope fastened to the top of the wall. When General Oglethorpe bombarded the fort,—at the time the Spaniards held it,—he made a good many dents in the wall, and these would help us. I did climb up a few feet, but we saw that it would never do to try to get all the way up without a rope.

How to fasten the rope on the top of the wall was the next question. We went in the fort, and found that if we could get a stout grapnel over the wall, it would probably catch on the inside of the coping, and give us a good enough hold. There is a wide walk on top, with a low wall on the outside, just high enough to shelter cannon, and to enable the garrison to dodge musketry and arrows.

We had a good deal of trouble finding a rope, but we bought one, at last, which was stout enough,—the man asked us if we were going to fish for sharks, and didn't seem to believe us when we said no,—and we took it to our room, and made knots in it about a foot apart. The fort walls are about twenty feet high, and we made the rope plenty long enough, with something to spare. We didn't have much trouble to find a grapnel. We bought a small one, but it was strong enough. We talked the matter over a great deal, and went to the fort several times, making examinations, and measuring the height of the wall, from the top, with a spool of cotton.

It was two or three days before we got everything ready, and in our trips to the fort we saw a good deal of the Indians. We often met them in the town, too, for they were frequently allowed to go out and walk about by themselves. There was no danger, I suppose, of their trying to run away, for they were several thousand miles from their homes, and they probably would not care to run to any other place with no larger stock of the English language than one word, "How?" Some of them, however, could talk a little English. There was one big fellow—he was probably the largest of them all—who was called "Maiden's Heart." I couldn't see how his name fitted, for he looked like an out-and-out savage, and generally wore a grin that seemed wicked enough to frighten settlers out of his part of the country. But he may have had a tender spot, somewhere, which entitled him to his name, and he was certainly very willing to talk to us, to the extent of his ability, which was not very great. We managed, however, to have some interesting, though rather choppy, conversations.

There was another fellow, a young chief, called Crowded Owl, that we liked better than any of the others, although we couldn't talk to him at all. He was not much older than I was, and so seemed to take to us. He would walk all around with us, and point out things. We had bought some sea-beans of him, and it may be that he hoped to sell us some more. At any rate, he was very friendly.

We met Mr. Cholott several times, and he told us of some good places to go to, and said he'd take us out fishing before long. But we were in no hurry for any expedition until we had carried out our little plan of surprising the fort. I gave the greater part of our money, however, to Mr. Cholott to lock up in his safe. I didn't like old Mr. Colbert's plan of going about with your capital pinned to your pockets. It might do while we were travelling, but I would rather have had it in drafts or something else not easily lost.

We had a good many discussions about our grapnel. We did not know whether there was a sentinel on duty in the fort at night or not, but supposed there was, and, if so, he would be likely to hear the grapnel when we threw it up and it hit the stones. We thought we could get over this difficulty by wrapping the grapnel in cotton wool. This would deaden the sound when it struck, but would not prevent the points of the hooks from holding to the inner edge of the wall. Everything now seemed all right, except that we had no object in view after we got over the wall. I always like to have some reason for doing a thing, especially when it's pretty hard to do. I said this to Rectus, and he agreed with me.

"What I would like to do," said he, "would be to benefit the innocent Indian prisoners."

"I don't know what we can do for them," said I. "We can't let them out, and they'd all go back again if we did."

"No, we can't do that," said he; "but we ought to do something. I've been around looking at them all carefully, and I feel sure that there are at least forty men among those Indians who haven't done a thing to warrant shutting them up."

"Why, how do you know?" I exclaimed.

"I judge from their faces," said Rectus.

Of course this made me laugh, but he didn't care.

"I'll tell you what we could do," said he; "we could enter a protest that might be heard of, and do some good. We could take a pot of black paint and a brush with us, and paint on one of the doors that open into the inner square,—where everybody could see it,—something like this: 'Let the righteous Indian go free.' That would create talk, and something might be done."

"Who'd do it?" said I. "The captain in command couldn't. He has no power to let any of them go free."

"Well, we might address the notice to the President of the United States—in big black letters. They could not conceal such a thing."

"Well, now, look here, Rectus," said I; "this thing is going to cost too much money. That rope was expensive, and the grapnel cost a good deal more than we thought it would; and now you want a big pot of black paint. We mustn't spend our money too fast, and if we've got to economize, let's begin on black paint. You can write your proclamation on paper, and stick it on the door with tacks. They could send that easier to the President than they could send a whole door."

"You may make as much fun as you please," said Rectus, "but I'm going to write it out now." And so he did, in big letters, on half a sheet of foolscap.

CHAPTER V.: STORMING SAN MARCO.

We started out on our storming expedition on a Tuesday night, about nine o'clock; we had a latch-key, so we could come home when we pleased. Rectus carried the rope, and I had the grapnel, wrapped in its cotton wool. We put newspapers around these things, and made pretty respectable packages of them. We did not go down the sea-wall, but walked around through some of the inner streets. It seemed to us like a curious expedition. We were not going to do anything wrong, but we had no idea what the United States government would think about it. We came down to the fort on its landward side, but our attack was to be made upon the waterfront, and so we went around that way, on the side farthest from the town. There were several people about yet, and we had to wait. We dropped our packages into the moat, and walked about on the water-battery, which is between the harbor and the moat, and is used as a sort of pleasure-ground by the people of the town. It was a pretty dark night, although the stars were out, and the last of the promenaders soon went home; and then, after giving them about ten minutes to get entirely out of sight and hearing, we jumped down into the moat, which is only five or six feet below the water-battery, and, taking our packages, went over to that part of the wall which we had fixed upon for our assault.

We fastened the rope to the grapnel, and then Rectus stood back while I made ready for the throw. It was a pretty big throw, almost straight up in the air, but I was strong, and was used to pitching, and all that sort of thing. I coiled the rope on the ground, took the loose end of it firmly in my left hand, and then, letting the grapnel hang from my right hand until it nearly touched the ground, I swung it round and round, perpendicularly, and when it had gone round three or four times, I gave it a tremendous hurl upward.

It rose beautifully, like a rocket, and fell inside of the ramparts, making only a little thud of a sound.

"First-rate!" said Rectus, softly; and I felt pretty proud myself.

I pulled on the rope, and found the grapnel had caught. I hung with my whole weight on it, but it held splendidly.

"Now, then," said I to Rectus, "you can climb up. Go slowly, and be very careful. There's no hurry. And mind you take a good hold when you get to the top."

We had arranged that Rectus was to go first. This did not look very brave on my part, but I felt that I wanted to be under him, while he was climbing, so that I could break his fall if he should slip down. It would not be exactly a perpendicular fall, for the wall slanted a little, but it would be bad enough. However, I had climbed up worse places than that, and Rectus was very nimble; so I felt there was no great danger.

Up he went, hand over hand, and putting his toes into nicks every now and then, thereby helping himself very much. He took it slowly and easily, and I felt sure he would be all right. As I looked at him, climbing up there in the darkness, while I was standing below, holding the rope so that it should not swing, I could not help thinking that I was a pretty curious kind of a tutor for a boy. However, I was taking all the care of him that I could, and if he came down he'd probably hurt me worse than he would hurt himself. Besides, I had no reason to suppose that old Mr. Colbert objected to a little fun. Then I began to think of Mrs. Colbert, and while I was thinking of her, and looking up at Rectus, I was amazed to see him going up quite rapidly, while the end of the rope slipped through my fingers. Up he went, and when I ran back, I could see a dark figure on the wall, above him. Somebody was pulling him up.

In a very few moments he disappeared over the top, rope and all!

Now, I was truly frightened. What might happen to the boy?

I was about to shout, but, on second thoughts, decided to keep quiet; yet I instantly made up my mind that, if I didn't see or hear from him pretty soon, I would run around to the gate and bang up the people inside. However, it was not necessary for me to trouble myself, for, in a minute, the rope came down again, and I took hold of it. I pulled on it and found it all firm, and then I went up. I climbed up pretty fast, and two or three times I felt a tug, as if somebody above was trying to pull me up. But it was of no use, for I was a great deal stouter and heavier than Rectus, who was a light, slim boy. But as I neared the top, a hand came down and clutched me by the collar, and some one, with a powerful arm and grip, helped me over the top of the wall. There stood Rectus, all right, and the fellow who had helped us up was the big Indian, "Maiden's Heart."

I looked at Rectus, and he whispered:

"He says there's a sentinel down there in the square."

At this, Maiden's Heart bobbed his head two or three times, and, motioning to us to crouch down, he crept quietly over to the inner wall of the ramparts and looked down.

"What shall we say we came for?" I whispered, quickly.

"I don't know," said Rectus.

"Well, we must think of something," I said, "or we shall look like fools."

But before he had time to think, Maiden's Heart crept back. He put his finger on his lips, and, beckoning us to follow him, he led the way to a corner of the fort near one of the lookout towers. We followed as quietly as we could, and then we all three slipped into the narrow entrance to the tower, the Indian motioning us to go first. When we two stood inside of the little round tower, old Maiden's Heart planted himself before us in the passage, and waited to hear what we had to say.

But we couldn't think of anything to say. Directly, however, I thought I must do something, so I whispered to the Indian:

"Does the sentry ever come up here?"

He seemed to catch my meaning.

"I go watch," he said. "Come back. Tell you." And off he stole, making no more noise than a cat.

"Bother on him!" said Rectus. "If I'd known he was up here, I would never have come."

"I reckon not," said I. "But now that we have come, what are we going to do or say? That fellow evidently thinks we have some big project on hand, and he's ready to help us; we must be careful, or he'll rush down and murder the sentinel."

"I'm sure I don't know what to say to him," said Rectus. "We ought to have thought of this before. I suppose it would be of no use to mention my poster to him."

"No, indeed," said I; "he'd never understand that. And, besides, there's a man down there. Let's peep out and see what he's doing."

So we crept to the entrance of the passage, and saw Maiden's Heart, crouched near the top of the inclined plane which serves as a stairway from the square to the ramparts, and looking over the low wall, evidently watching the sentry.

"I'll tell you what let's do," said Rectus. "Let's make a rush for our rope, and get out of this."

"No, sir!" said I. "We'd break our necks if we tried to hurry down that rope. Don't think of anything of that kind. And, besides, we couldn't both get down before he'd see us."

In a few minutes, Maiden's Heart crept quickly back to us, and seemed surprised that we had left our hiding-place. He motioned us farther back into the passage, and slipped in himself.

We did not have time to ask any questions before we heard the sentry coming up the stairway, which was near our corner. When he reached the top, he walked away from us over toward the Indian barracks, which were on the ramparts, at the other end of the fort. As soon as he reached the barracks, Maiden's Heart took me by the arm and Rectus by the collar, and hurried us to the stairway, and then down as fast as we could go. He made no noise himself, but Rectus and I clumped a good deal. We had to wear our shoes, for the place was paved with rough concrete and oyster-shells.

The sentry evidently heard the clumping, for he came running down after us, and caught up to us almost as soon as we reached the square.

"Eugh!" said he, for he was an Indian; and he ran in front of us, and held his musket horizontally before us. Of course we stopped. And then, as there was nothing else that seemed proper to do, we held out our hands and said "How?" The sentinel took his gun in his left hand, and shook hands with us. Then Maiden's Heart, who probably remembered that he had omitted this ceremony, also shook hands with us and said "How?"

The two Indians now began to jabber to each other, in a low voice; but we could not, of course, make out what they said, and I don't think they were able to imagine what we intended to do. We were standing near the inner door of the great entrance-way, and into this they now marched us. There was a lamp burning on a table.

Said Rectus: "I guess they're going to put us out of the front door;" but he was mistaken. They walked us into a dark room, on one side of the hall, and Maiden's Heart said to us: "Stay here. Him mad. I come back. Keep still," and then he went out, probably to discuss with the sentinel the nature of our conspiracy. It was very dark in this room, and, at first, we couldn't see anything at all; but we soon found, from the smell of the bread, that we were in the kitchen or bakery. We had been here before, and had seen the head-cook, a ferocious Indian squaw, who had been taken in the act of butchering a poor emigrant woman on the plains. She always seemed sullen and savage, and never said a word to anybody. We hoped she wasn't in here now.

"I didn't know they had Indian sentinels," said Rectus. "That seems a little curious to me. I suppose they set the innocent ones to watch the guilty."

"I don't believe that would work," said I, "for the innocent chaps would want to get away, just as much as the others. I guess they make 'em take turns to stand guard. There has to be a sentinel in a fort, you know, and I suppose these fellows are learning the business."

We didn't settle this question, nor the more important one of our reason for this visit; for, at this moment, Maiden's Heart came back, carrying the lamp. He looked at us in a curious way, and then he said:

"What you want?"

I couldn't think of any good answer to this question, but Rectus whispered to me:

"Got any money with you?"

"Yes," said I.

"Let's buy some sea-beans," said Rectus.

"All right," I answered.

"Sea-beans?" said Maiden's Heart, who had caught the word; "you want sea-beans?"

"Yes," said Rectus, "if you have any good ones."

At this, the Indian conducted us into the hall, put the lamp on the table, and took three or four sea-beans from his pocket. They were very nice ones, and beautifully polished.

"Good," said I; "we'll take these. How much, Maiden's Heart?"

"Fifty cents," said the Indian.

"For all?" I asked.

"No. No. For one. Four bean two dollar."

We both exclaimed at this, for it was double the regular price of the beans.

"All right," said Maiden's Heart. "Twenty-five cents, daytime. Fifty cents, night."

We looked at each other, and concluded to pay the price and depart. I gave him two dollars, and asked him to open the gate and let us out.

"ANOTHER BEAN."

He grinned.

"No. No. We got no key. Captain got key. Come up wall. Go down wall."

At this, we walked out into the square, and were about to ascend the inclined plane when the sentinel came up and stopped us. Thereupon a low conversation ensued between him and Maiden's Heart, at the end of which the sentry put his hand into his pocket and pulled out three beans, which he held out to us. I did not hesitate, but gave him a dollar and a half for them. He took the money and let us pass on,—Maiden's Heart at my side.

"You want more bean?" said he.

"Oh, no!" I answered. "No, indeed," said Rectus.

When we reached the place where we had left our apparatus, I swung the rope over the wall, and, hooking the grapnel firmly on the inside, prepared to go down, for, as before, I wished to be under Rectus, if he should slip. But Maiden's Heart put his hand on my shoulder.

"Hold up!" he said. "I got 'nother bean. Buy this."

"Don't want it," said I.

"Yes. Yes," said Maiden's Heart, and he coolly unhooked the grapnel from the wall.

I saw that it was of no use to contend with a big fellow like that, as strong as two common men, and I bought the bean.

I took the grapnel from Maiden's Heart, who seemed to give it up reluctantly, and as I hooked it on the wall, I felt a hand upon my shoulder. I looked around, and saw the sentinel. He held out to me another bean. It was too dark to see the quality of it, but I thought it was very small. However, I bought it. One of these fellows must be treated as well as the other.

Maiden's Heart and the sentry were now feeling nervously in their pockets.

I shook my head vigorously, and saying, "No more! no more!" threw myself over the wall, and seized the rope, Rectus holding the grapnel in its place as I did so. As I let myself down from knot to knot, a thought crossed my mind: "How are we going to get that grapnel after we both are down?"

It was a frightening thought. If the two Indians should choose, they could keep the rope and grapnel, and, before morning, the whole posse of red-skins might be off and away! I did not think about their being so far from home, and all that. I only thought that they'd be glad to get out, and that they would all come down our rope.

These reflections, which ran through my mind in no time at all, were interrupted by Rectus, who called down from the top of the wall, in a voice that was a little too loud to be prudent:

"Hurry! I think he's found another bean!"

I was on the ground in a few moments, and then Rectus came down. I called to him to come slowly and be very careful, but I can't tell how relieved I was when I saw him fairly over the wall and on his way down.

When we both stood on the ground, I took hold of the rope and shook it. I am not generally nervous, but I was a little nervous then. I did not shake the grapnel loose. Then I let the rope go slack, for a foot or two, and gave it a big sweep to one side. To my great delight, over came the grapnel, nearly falling on our heads. I think I saw Maiden's Heart make a grab at it as it came over, but I am not sure. However, he poked his head over the wall and said:

"Good-bye! Come again."

We answered, "Good-bye," but didn't say anything about coming again.

As we hurried along homeward, Rectus said:

"If one of those Indians had kept us up there, while the other one ran into the barracks and got a fresh stock of sea-beans, they would have just bankrupted us."

"No, they wouldn't," I said. "For I hadn't much more change with me. And if I had had it, I wouldn't have given them any more. I'd have called up the captain first. The thing was getting too expensive."

"Well, I'm glad I'm out of it," said Rectus. "And I don't believe much in any of those Indians being very innocent. I thought Maiden's Heart was one of the best of them, but he's a regular rascal. He knew we wanted to back out of that affair, and he just fleeced us."

"I believe he would rather have had our scalps than our money, if he had had us out in his country," I said.

"That's so," said Rectus. "A funny kind of a maiden's heart he's got."

We were both out of conceit with the noble red man. Rectus took his proclamation out of his pocket as we walked along the sea-wall, and, tearing it into little pieces, threw it into the water. When we reached the steam-ship wharf, we walked out to the end of it, to get rid of the rope and grapnel. I whirled the grapnel round and round, and let the whole thing fly far out into the harbor. It was a sheer waste of a good strong rope, but we should have had a dreary time getting the knots out of it.

After we got home I settled up our accounts, and charged half the sea-beans to Rectus, and half to myself.

CHAPTER VI.: THE GIRL ON THE BEACH.

I was not very well satisfied with our trip over the walls of San Marco. In the first place, when the sea-beans, the rope and the grapnel were all considered, it was a little too costly. In the second place, I was not sure that I had been carrying out my contract with Mr. Colbert in exactly the right spirit; for although he had said nothing about my duties, I knew that he expected me to take care of his son, and paid me for that. And I felt pretty sure that helping a fellow climb up a knotted rope into an old fort by night was not the best way of taking care of him. The third thing that troubled me in regard to this matter was the feeling I had that Rectus had led me into it; that he had been the leader and not I. Now, I did not intend that anything of that kind should happen again. I did not come out on this expedition to follow Rectus around; indeed, it was to be quite the other way. But, to tell the truth, I had not imagined that he would ever try to make people follow him. He never showed at school that such a thing was in him. So, for these three reasons, I determined that there were to be no more scrapes of that sort, which generally came to nothing, after all.

For the next two or three days we roved around the old town, and into two or three orange-groves, and went out sailing with Mr. Cholott, who owned a nice little yacht, or sail-boat, as we should call it up north.

The sailing here is just splendid, and, one morning, we thought we'd hire a boat for ourselves and go out fishing somewhere. So we went down to the yacht-club wharf to see about the boat that belonged to old Menendez—Rectus's Minorcan. There were lots of sail-boats there as well as row-boats, but we hunted up the craft we were after, and, by good luck, found Menendez in her, bailing her out.

So we engaged her, and he said he'd take us over to the North Beach to fish for bass. That suited us,—any beach and any kind of fish,—provided he'd hurry up and get his boat ready. While he was scooping away, and we were standing on the wharf watching him, along came Crowded Owl, the young Indian we had always liked—that is, ever since we had known any of them. He came up, said "How?" and shook hands, and then pulled out some sea-beans. The sight of these things seemed to make me sick, and as for Rectus, he sung out:

"Do' wan' 'em!" so suddenly that it seemed like one word, and a pretty savage one at that.

Crowded Owl looked at me, but I shook my head, and said, "No, no, no!" Then he drew himself up and just stood there. He seemed struck dumb; but that didn't matter, as he couldn't talk to us, anyway. But he didn't go away. When we walked farther up the wharf, he followed us, and again offered us some beans. I began to get angry, and said "No!" pretty violently. At this, he left us, but as we turned at the end of the wharf, we saw him near the club-house, standing and talking with Maiden's Heart.

"I think it's a shame to let those Indians wander about here in that way," said Rectus. "They ought to be kept within bounds."

I couldn't help laughing at this change of tune, but said that I supposed only a few of them got leave of absence at a time.

"Well," said Rectus, "there are some of them that ought never to come out."

"Hello!" said old Menendez, sticking his head up above the edge of the wharf. "We're ready now. Git aboard."

And so we scrambled down into the sail-boat, and Menendez pushed off, while the two Indians stood and watched us as we slowly moved away.

When we got fairly out, our sail filled, and we went scudding away on a good wind. Then said old Menendez, as he sat at the tiller:

"What were you hollerin' at them Injuns about?"

"I didn't know that we were hollerin'," said I, "but they were bothering us to buy their sea-beans."

"That's curious," he said. "They aint much given to that sort of thing. But there's no tellin' nothin' about an Injun. If I had my way, I'd hang every one of 'em."

"Rather a blood-thirsty sentiment," said I. "Perhaps some of them don't deserve hanging."

"Well, I've never seen one o' that kind," said he, "and I've seen lots of Injuns. I was in the Seminole war, in this State, and was fightin' Injuns from the beginnin' to the end of it. And I know all about how to treat the rascals. You must hang 'em, or shoot 'em, as soon as you get hold of 'em."

This aroused all the old sympathy for the oppressed red man that dwelt in the heart of young Rectus, and he exclaimed:

"That would be murder! There are always two kinds of every sort of people—all are not bad. It is wrong to condemn a whole division of the human race that way."

"You're right about there bein' two kinds of Injuns," said the old fellow. "There's bad ones and there's wuss ones. I know what I've seen for myself. I'd hang 'em all."

We debated this matter some time longer, but we could make no impression on the old Minorcan. For some reason or other, probably on account of his sufferings or hardships in the war, he was extremely bitter against all Indians. "You can't tell me," he replied to all of our arguments, and I think he completely destroyed all the sympathy which Rectus had had for the once down-trodden and deceived Minorcans, by this animosity toward members of another race who were yet in captivity and bondage. To be sure, there was a good deal of difference in the two cases, but Rectus wasn't in the habit of turning up every question to look at the bottom of it.

The North Beach is the seaward side of one of the islands that enclose the harbor, or the Matanzas River, as it is called. We landed on the inland side, and then walked over to the beach, which is very wide and smooth. Here we set to work to fish. Old Menendez baited our lines, and told us what to do. It was new sport to us.

First, we took off our shoes and stockings, and rolled up our trousers, so as to wade out in the shallow water. We each had a long line, one end of which we tied around our waists. Menendez had his tied to a button-hole of his coat, but he thought he had better make our lines very safe, as they belonged to him. There was a big hook and a heavy lead to the other end of the line, with a piece of fish for bait, and we swung the lead around our heads, and threw it out into the surf as far as we could. I thought I was pretty good on the throw, but I couldn't begin to send my line out as far as Menendez threw his. As for Rectus, he didn't pretend to do much in the throwing business. He whirled his line around in such a curious way that I was very much afraid he would hook himself in the ear. But Menendez put his line out for him. He didn't want me to do it.

Then we stood there in the sand, with the water nearly up to our knees every time the waves came in, and waited for a bite. There wasn't much biting. Menendez said that the tide was too low, but I've noticed that something is always too something, every time any one takes me out fishing, so I didn't mind that.

Menendez did hook one fellow, I think, for he gave a tremendous jerk at his line, and began to skip inshore as if he were but ten years old; but it was of no use. The fish changed his mind.

Then we stood and waited a while longer, until, all of a sudden, Rectus made a skip. But he went the wrong way. Instead of skipping out of the water, he skipped in. He went in so far that he got his trousers dripping wet.

"Hello!" I shouted. "What's up?"

He didn't say anything, but began to pull back, and dig his heels into the sand. Old Menendez and I saw, at the same moment, what was the matter, and we made a rush for him. I was nearest, and got there first. I seized Rectus by the shoulder, and pulled him back a little.

"Whew-w!" said he; "how this twine cuts!"

Then I took hold of the line in front of him, and there was no mistaking the fact—he had a big fish on the other end of it.

"Run out!" cried Menendez, who thought there was no good of three fellows hauling on the line; and out we ran.

When we had gone up the beach a good way, I looked back and saw a rousing big fish flopping about furiously in the shallow water.

"Go on!" shouted Menendez; and we ran on until we had pulled it high and dry up on the sand.

Then Menendez fell afoul of it to take out the hook, and we hurried back to see it. It was a whopping big bass, and by the powerful way it threw itself around on the sand, I didn't wonder that Rectus ran into the water when he got the first jerk.

Now, this was something like sport, and we all felt encouraged, and went to work again with a will, only Menendez untied the line from Rectus's waist and fastened it to his button-hole.

"It may pull out," he said; "but, on the whole, it's better to lose a fishin'-line than a boy."

We fished quietly and steadily for some time, but got no more bites, when suddenly I heard some one say, behind me:

"They don't ever pull in!"

I turned around, and it was a girl. She was standing there with a gentleman,—her father, I soon found out,—and I don't know how long they had been watching us. She was about thirteen years old, and came over with her father in a sail-boat. I remembered seeing them cruising around as we were sailing over.

"They haven't got bites," said her father; "that's the reason they don't pull in."

It was very disagreeable to me, and I know it was even more so to Rectus, to stand here and have those strangers watch us fishing. If we had not been barefooted and bare-legged, we should not have minded it so much. As for the old Minorcan, I don't suppose he cared at all. I began to think it was time to stop.

"As the tide's getting lower and lower," I said to Menendez, "I suppose our chances are getting less and less."

"Yes," said he; "I reckon we'd better shut up shop before long."

"Oh!" cried out the girl, "just look at that fish! Father! Father! Just look at it. Did any of you catch it? I didn't see it till this minute. I thought you hadn't caught any. If I only had a fishing-line now, I would like to catch just one fish. Oh, father! why didn't you bring a fishing-line?"

"I didn't think of it, my dear," said he. "Indeed, I didn't know there were any fish here."

Old Menendez turned around and grinned at this, and I thought there was a good chance to stop fishing; so I offered to let the girl try my line for a while, if she wanted to.

It was certain enough that she wanted to, for she was going to run right into the water to get it. But I came out, and as her father said she might fish if she didn't have to walk into the water, old Menendez took a spare piece of line from his pocket and tied it on to the end of mine, and he put on some fresh bait and gave it a tremendous send out into the surf. Then he put the other end around the girl and tied it. I suppose he thought that it didn't matter if a girl should be lost, but he may have considered that her father was there to seize her if she got jerked in.

She took hold of the line and stood on the edge of the dry sand, ready to pull in the biggest kind of a fish that might come along. I put on my shoes and stockings, and Rectus his; he'd had enough glory for one day. Old Menendez wound up his line, too, but that girl saw nothing of all this. She just kept her eyes and her whole mind centred on her line. At first, she talked right straight ahead, asking what she should do when it bit; how big we thought it would be; why we didn't have a cork, and fifty other things, but all without turning her head to the right or the left. Then said her father:

"My dear, you mustn't talk; you will frighten the fish. When persons fish, they always keep perfectly quiet. You never heard me talking while I was fishing. I fish a good deal when I am at home," said he, turning to us, "and I always remain perfectly quiet."

Menendez laughed a little at this, and said that he didn't believe the fish out there in the surf would mind a little quiet chat; but the gentleman said that he had always found it best to be just as still as possible. The girl now shut her mouth tight, and held herself more ready, if possible, than ever, and I believe that if she had got a bite she would have jerked the fish's head off. We all stood around her, and her father watched her as earnestly as if she was about to graduate at a normal school.

We stood and waited and waited, and she didn't move, and neither did the line. Menendez now said he thought she might as well give it up. The tide was too low, and it was pretty near dinner-time, and, besides this, there was a shower coming on.

"Oh, no!" said she; "not just yet. I feel sure I'll get a bite in a minute or two now. Just wait a little longer."

And so it went on, every few minutes, until we had waited about half an hour, and then Menendez said he must go, but if the gentleman wanted to buy the line, and stay there until the tide came in again, he'd sell it to him. At this, the girl's father told her that she must stop, and so she very dolefully let Menendez untie the line.

"It's too bad!" she said, almost with tears in her eyes. "If they had only waited a few minutes longer!" And then she ran up to Rectus and me, and said:

"When are you coming out here again? Do you think you will come to-morrow, or next day?"

"I don't know," said I. "We haven't settled our plans for to-morrow."

"Oh, father! father!" she cried, "perhaps they will come out here to-morrow, and you must get me a fishing-line, and we will come and fish all day."

We didn't stay to hear what her father said, but posted off to our boat, for we were all beginning to feel pretty hungry. We took Rectus's fish along, to give to our landlady. The gentleman and the girl came close after us, as if they were afraid to be left alone on the island. Their boat was hauled up near ours, and we set off at pretty much the same time.

We went ahead a little, and Menendez turned around and called out to the gentleman that he'd better follow us, for there were some bad shoals in this part of the harbor, and the tide was pretty low.

"All right, my hearty!" called out the gentleman. "This isn't the first time I've sailed in this harbor. I guess I know where the shoals are," and just at that minute he ran his boat hard and fast on one of them.

He jumped up, and took an oar and pushed and pushed: but it was of no good—he was stuck fast. By this time we had left him pretty far behind; but we all had been watching, and Rectus asked if we couldn't go back and help him.

"Well, I s'pose so," said Menendez; "but it's a shame to keep three decent people out of their dinner for the sake of a man like that, who hasn't got sense enough to take good advice when it's give to him."

"We'd better go," said I, and Menendez, in no good humor, put his boat about. We found the other boat aground, in the very worst way. The old Minorcan said that he could see that sand-bar through the water, and that they might as well have run up on dry land. Better, for that matter, because then we could have pushed her off.

"There aint nuthin' to be done," he said, after we had worked at the thing for a while, "but to jist wait here till the tide turns. It's pretty near dead low now, an' you'll float off in an hour or two."

This was cold comfort for the gentleman, especially as it was beginning to rain; but he didn't seem a bit cast down. He laughed, and said:

"Well, I suppose it can't be helped: but I am used to being out in all weathers. I can wait, just as well as not. But I don't want my daughter here to get wet, and she has no umbrella. Would you mind taking her on your boat? When you get to the town, she can run up to our hotel by herself. She knows the way."

Of course we had no objection to this, and the girl was helped aboard. Then we sailed off, and the gentleman waved his hat to us. If I had been in his place, I don't think I should have felt much like waving my hat.

"THE GENTLEMAN WAVED HIS HAT TO US."

Menendez now said that he had an oil-skin coat stowed away forward, and I got it and put it around the girl. She snuggled herself up in it as comfortably as she could, and began to talk.

"The way of it was this," she said. "Father, he said we'd go out sailing, and mother and I went with him, and when we got down to the wharf, there were a lot of boats, but they all had men to them, and so father, he said he wanted to sail the boat himself, and mother, she said that if he did she wouldn't go; but he said pooh! he could do it as well as anybody, and wasn't going to have any man. So he got a boat without a man, and mother, she didn't want me to go; but I went, and he stuck fast coming back, because he never will listen to anything anybody tells him, as mother and I found out long ago. And here we are, almost at the wharf! I didn't think we were anywhere near it."

"Well, you see, sis, sich a steady gale o' talkin', right behind the sail, is bound to hurry the boat along. And now, s'pose you tell us your name," said Menendez.

"My name's Cornelia; but father, he calls me Corny, which mother hates to hear the very sound of," said she; "and the rest of it is Mary Chipperton. Father, he came down here because he had a weak lung, and I'm sure I don't see what good it's going to do him to sit out there in the rain. We'll take a man next time. And father and I'll be sure to be here early to-morrow to go out fishing with you. Good-bye!"

And with this, having mounted the steps to the pier, off ran Miss Corny.

"I wouldn't like to be the ole man o' that family," said Mr. Menendez.

That night, after we had gone to bed, Rectus began to talk. We generally went to sleep in pretty short order; but the moon did not shine in our windows now until quite late, and so we noticed for the first time the curious way in which the light-house—which stood almost opposite on Anastasia Island—brightened up the room, every minute or two. It is a revolving light, and when the light got on the landward side it gave us a flash, which produced a very queer effect on the furniture, and on Rectus's broad hat, which hung on the wall right opposite the window. It seemed exactly as if this hat was a sort of portable sun of a very mild power, which warmed up, every now and then, and lighted the room.

But Rectus did not talk long about this.

"I think," said he, "that we have had about enough of St. Augustine. There are too many Indians and girls here."

"And sea-beans, too, perhaps," said I. "But I don't think there's any reason for going so soon. I'm going to settle those Indians, and you've only seen one girl, and perhaps we'll never see her again."

"Don't you believe that," said Rectus, very solemnly, and he turned over, either to ponder on the matter, or to go to sleep. His remarks made me imagine that perhaps he was one of those fellows who soon get tired of a place and want to be moving on. But that wasn't my way, and I didn't intend to let him hurry me. I think the Indians worried him a good deal. He was afraid they would keep on troubling us. But, as I had said, I had made up my mind to settle the Indians. As for Corny, I know he hated her. I don't believe he spoke a word to her all the time we were with her.

The next morning, we talked over the Indian question, and then went down to the fort. We hadn't been there for three or four days, but now we had decided not to stand nagging by a couple of red-skinned savages, but to go and see the captain and tell him all about it. All except the proclamation—Rectus wouldn't agree to have that brought in at all. Mr. Cholott had introduced us to the captain, and he was a first-rate fellow, and when we told him how we had stormed his old fort, he laughed and said he wondered we didn't break our necks, and that the next time we did it he'd put us in the guard-house, sure.

"That would be cheaper for you than buying so many beans," he said.

As to the two Indians, he told us he would see to it that they let us alone. He didn't think that Maiden's Heart would ever harm us, for he was more of a blower than anything else; but he said that Crowded Owl was really one of the worst-tempered Indians in the fort, and he advised us to have nothing more to do with him, in any way.

All of this was very good of the captain, and we were very glad we had gone to see him.

"I tell you what it is," said Rectus, as we were coming away, "I don't believe that any of these Indians are as innocent as they try to make out. Did you ever see such a rascally set of faces?"

Somehow or other, I seldom felt sorry when Rectus changed his mind. I thought, indeed, that he ought to change it as much as he could. And yet, as I have said, he was a thoroughly good fellow. The trouble with him was that he wasn't used to making up his mind about things, and didn't make a very good beginning at it.

The next day, we set out to explore Anastasia Island, right opposite the town. It is a big island, but we took our lunch and determined to do what we could. We hired a boat and rowed over to the mouth of a creek in the island. We went up this creek quite a long way, and landed at a little pier, where we made the boat fast. The man who owned the boat told us just how to go. We first made a flying call at the coquina quarries, where they dig the curious stuff of which the town is built. This is formed of small shells, all conglomerated into one solid mass that becomes as hard as stone after it is exposed to the air. It must have taken thousands of years for so many little shell-fish to pile themselves up into a quarrying-ground. We now went over to the light-house, and climbed to the top of it, where we had a view that made Rectus feel even better than he felt in the cemetery at Savannah.

When we came down, we started for the beach and stopped a little while at the old Spanish light-house, which looked more like a cracker-bakery than anything else, but I suppose it was good enough for all the ships the Spaniards had to light up. We would have cared more for the old light-house if it had not had an inscription on it that said it had been destroyed, and rebuilt by some American. After that, we considered it merely in the light of a chromo.

We had a good time on the island, and stayed nearly all day. Toward the end of the afternoon, we started back for the creek and our boat. We had a long walk, for we had been exploring the island pretty well, and when, at last, we reached the creek, we saw that our boat was gone!

This was astounding. We could not make out how the thing could have happened. The boatman, from whom we had hired it, had said that it would be perfectly safe for us to leave the boat at the landing if we tied her up well and hid the oars. I had tied her up very well and we had hidden the oars so carefully, under some bushes, that we found them there when we went to look for them.

"Could the old thing have floated off of itself?" said Rectus.

"That couldn't have happened," I said. "I tied her hard and fast."

"But how could any one have taken her away without oars?" asked Rectus.

"Rectus," said I, "don't let us have any more riddles. Some one may have cut a pole and poled her away, up or down the creek, or———"

"I'll tell you," interrupted Rectus. "Crowded Owl!"

I didn't feel much like laughing, but I did laugh a little.

"Yes," I said. "He probably swam over with a pair of oars on purpose to steal our boat. But, whether he did it or not, it's very certain that somebody has taken the boat, and there isn't any way, that I see, of getting off this place to-night. There'll be nobody going over so late in the afternoon—except, to be sure, those men we saw at the other end of the island with a flat-boat."

"But that's away over at the upper end of the island," said Rectus.

"That's not so very far," said I. "I wonder if they have gone back yet? If one of us could run over there and ask them to send a boatman from the town after us, we might get back by supper-time."

"Why not both of us?" asked Rectus.

"One of us should stay here to see if our boat does come back. It must have been some one from the island who took it, because any one from the mainland would have brought his own boat."

"Very well," said Rectus. "Let's toss up to see who goes. The winner stays."

I pitched up a cent.

"Heads," said Rectus.

"Tails," said I.

Tails it was, and Rectus started off like a good fellow.

I sat down and waited. I waited a long, long time, and then I got up and walked up and down. In about an hour I began to get anxious. It was more than time for Rectus to return. The walk to the end of the island and back was not much over a mile—at least, I supposed it was not. Could anything have happened to the boy? It was not yet sunset, and I couldn't imagine what there was to happen.

After waiting about half an hour longer, I heard a distant sound of oars. I ran to the landing and looked down the creek. A boat with a man in it was approaching. When it came nearer, I saw plainly that it was our boat. When it had almost reached the landing, the man turned around, and I was very much surprised, indeed, to see that he was Mr. Chipperton.

CHAPTER VII.: MR. CHIPPERTON.

"WHY, HOW DO YOU DO?"

I took hold of the boat, and pulled the bow up on the beach. Mr. Chipperton looked around at me.

"Why, how do you do?" said he.

For an instant I could not answer him, I was so angry, and then I said:

"What did you——? How did you come to take our boat away?"

"Your boat!" he exclaimed. "Is this your boat? I didn't know that. But where is my boat? Did you see a sail-boat leave here? It is very strange—remarkably strange! I don't know what to make of it."

"I know nothing about a sail-boat," said I. "If we had seen one leave here, we should have gone home in her. Why did you take our boat?"

Mr. Chipperton had now landed.

"I came over here," he said, "with my wife and daughter. We were in a sail-boat, with a man to manage it. My wife would not come otherwise. We came to see the light-house, but I do not care for light-houses,—I have seen a great many of them. I am passionately fond of the water. Seeing a small boat here which no one was using, I let the man conduct my wife and Corny—my daughter—up to the light-house, while I took a little row. I know the man. He is very trustworthy. He would let no harm come to them. There was a pair of oars in the sail-boat, and I took them, and rowed down the creek, and then went along the river, below the town; and, I assure you, sir, I went a great deal farther than I intended, for the tide was with me. But it wasn't with me coming back, of course, and I had a very hard time of it. I thought I never should get back. This boat of yours, sir, seems to be an uncommonly hard boat to row."

"Against a strong tide, I suppose it is," said I; "but I wish you hadn't taken it. Here I have been waiting ever so long, and my friend——"

"Oh! I'm sorry, too," interrupted Mr. Chipperton, who had been looking about, as if he expected to see his sail-boat somewhere under the trees. "I can't imagine what could have become of my boat, my wife, and my child. If I had staid here, they could not have sailed away without my knowing it. It would even have been better to go with them, although, as I said before, I don't care for light-houses."

"Well," said I, not quite as civilly as I generally speak to people older than myself, "your boat has gone, that is plain enough. I suppose, when your family came from the light-house, they thought you had gone home, and so went themselves."

"That's very likely," said he,—"very likely indeed. Or, it may be that Corny wouldn't wait. She is not good at waiting. She persuaded her mother to sail away, no doubt. But now I suppose you will take me home in your boat, and the sooner we get off the better, for it is growing late."

"You needn't be in a hurry," said I, "for I am not going off until my friend comes back. You gave him a good long walk to the other end of the island."

"Indeed!" said Mr. Chipperton. "How was that?"

Then I told him all about it.

"Do you think that the flat-boat is likely to be there yet?" he asked.

"It's gone, long ago," said I; "and I'm afraid Rectus has lost his way, either going there or coming back."

I said this as much to myself as to my companion, for I had walked back a little to look up the path. I could not see far, for it was growing dark. I was terribly worried about Rectus, and would have gone to look for him, but I was afraid that if I left Mr. Chipperton he would go off with the boat.

Directly Mr. Chipperton set up a yell.

"Hi! hi! hi!" he cried.

I ran down to the pier, and saw a row-boat approaching.

"Hi!" cried Mr. Chipperton. "Come this way! Come here! Boat ahoy!"

"We're coming!" shouted a man from the boat. "Ye needn't holler for us."

And in a few more strokes the boat touched land. There were two men in it.

"Did you come for me?" cried Mr. Chipperton.

"No," said the man who had spoken. "We came for this other party, but I reckon you can come along."

"For me?" said I. "Who sent you?"

"Your pardner," said the man. "He came over in a flat-boat, and he said you was stuck here, for somebody had stole your boat, and so he sent us for you."

"And he's over there, is he?" said I.

"Yes, he's all right, eatin' his supper, I reckon. But isn't this here your boat?"

"Yes, it is," I said, "and I'm going home in it. You can take the other man."

And, without saying another word, I picked up my oars, which I had brought from the bushes, jumped into my boat, and pushed off.

"I reckon you're a little riled, aint ye?" said the man; but I made him no answer, and left him to explain to Mr. Chipperton his remark about stealing the boat. They set off soon after me, and we had a race down the creek. I was "a little riled," and I pulled so hard that the other boat did not catch up to me until we got out into the river. Then it passed me, but it didn't get to town much before I did.

The first person I met on the pier was Rectus. He had had his supper, and had come down to watch for me. I was so angry that I would not speak to him. He kept by my side, though, as I walked up to the house, excusing himself for going off and leaving me.

"You see, it wasn't any use for me to take that long walk back there to the creek. I told the men of the fix we were in, and they said they'd send somebody for us, but they thought I'd better come along with them, as I was there."

I had a great mind to say something here, but I didn't.

"It wouldn't have done you any good for me to come back through the woods in the dark. The boat wouldn't get over to you any faster. You see, if there'd been any good at all in it, I would have come back—but there wasn't."

All this might have been very true, but I remembered how I had sat and walked and thought and worried about Rectus, and his explanation did me no good.

When I reached the house, I found that our landlady, who was one of the very best women in all Florida, had saved me a splendid supper—hot and smoking. I was hungry enough, and I enjoyed this meal until there didn't seem to be a thing left. I felt in a better humor then, and I hunted up Rectus, and we talked along as if nothing had happened. It wasn't easy to keep mad with Rectus, because he didn't get mad himself. And, besides, he had a good deal of reason on his side.

It was a lovely evening, and pretty nearly all the people of the town were out-of-doors. Rectus and I took a walk around the "Plaza,"—a public square planted thick with live-oak and pride-of-India trees, and with a monument in the centre with a Spanish inscription on it, stating how the king of Spain once gave a very satisfactory charter to the town. Rectus and I agreed, however, that we would rather have a pride-of-India tree than a charter, as far as we were concerned. These trees have on them long bunches of blossoms, which smell deliciously.

"Now, then," said I, "I think it's about time for us to be moving along. I'm beginning to feel about that Corny family as you do."

"Oh, I only objected to the girl," said Rectus, in an off-hand way.

"Well, I object to the father," said I. "I think we've had enough, anyway, of fathers and daughters. I hope the next couple we fall in with will be a mother and a son."

"What's the next place on the bill?" asked Rectus.

"Well," said I, "we ought to take a trip up the Oclawaha River. That's one of the things to do. It will take us two or three days, and we can leave our baggage here and come back again. Then, if we want to stay, we can, and if we don't, we needn't."

"All right," said Rectus. "Let's be off to-morrow."

The next morning, I went to buy the Oclawaha tickets, while Rectus staid home to pack up our handbags, and, I believe, to sew some buttons on his clothes. He could sew buttons on so strongly that they would never come off again without bringing the piece out with them.

The ticket-office was in a small store, where you could get any kind of alligator or sea-bean combination that the mind could dream of. We had been in there before to look at the things. I found I was in luck, for the storekeeper told me that it was not often that people could get berths on the little Oclawaha steam-boats without engaging them some days ahead; but he had a couple of state-rooms left, for the boat that left Pilatka the next day. I took one room as quick as lightning, and I had just paid for the tickets when Mr. Chipperton and Corny walked in.

"How d' ye do?" said he, as cheerfully as if he had never gone off with another fellow's boat. "Buying tickets for the Oclawaha?"

I had to say yes, and then he wanted to know when we were going. I wasn't very quick to answer; but the storekeeper said:

"He's just taken the last room but one in the boat that leaves Pilatka to-morrow morning."

"And when do you leave here to catch that boat?" said Mr. Chipperton.

"This afternoon,—and stay all night at Pilatka."

"Oh, father! father!" cried Corny, who had been standing with her eyes and ears wide open, all this time, "let's go! let's go!"

"I believe I will," said Mr. Chipperton,—"I believe I will. You say you have one more room. All right. I'll take it. This will be very pleasant, indeed," said he, turning to me. "It will be quite a party. It's ever so much better to go to such places in a party. We've been thinking of going for some time, and I'm so glad I happened in here now. Good-bye. We'll see you this afternoon at the dépôt."

I didn't say anything about being particularly glad, but just as I left the door Corny ran out after me.

"Do you think it would be any good to take a fishing-line?" she cried.

"Guess you'd better," I shouted back, and then I ran home, laughing.

"Here are the tickets!" I cried out to Rectus, "and we've got to be at the station by four o'clock this afternoon. There's no backing out now."

"Who wants to back out?" said Rectus, looking up from his trunk, into which he had been diving.

"Can't say," I answered. "But I know one person who wont back out."

"Who's that?"

"Corny," said I.

Rectus stood up.

"Cor——!" he exclaimed.

"Ny," said I, "and father and mother. They took the only room left,—engaged it while I was there."

"Can't we sell our tickets?" asked Rectus.

"Don't know," said I. "But what's the good? Who's going to be afraid of a girl,—or a whole family, for that matter? We're in for it now."

Rectus didn't say anything, but his expression saddened.

We had studied out this trip the night before, and knew just what we had to do. We first went from St. Augustine, on the sea-coast, to Tocoi, on the St. John's River, by a railroad fifteen miles long. Then we took a steam-boat up the St. John's to Pilatka, and the next morning left for the Oclawaha, which runs into the St. John's about twenty-five miles above, on the other side of the river.

We found the Corny family at the station, all right, and Corny immediately informed me that she had a fishing-line, but didn't bring a pole, because her father said he could cut her one, if it was needed. He didn't know whether it was "throw-out" fishing or not, on that river.

There used to be a wooden railroad here, and the cars were pulled by mules. It was probably more fun to travel that way, but it took longer. Now they have steel rails and everything that a regular grown-up railroad has. We knew the engineer, for Mr. Cholott had introduced us to him one day, on the club-house wharf. He was a first-rate fellow, and let us ride on the engine. I didn't believe, at first, that Rectus would do this; but there was only one passenger car, and after the Corny family got into that, he didn't hesitate a minute about the engine.

We had a splendid ride. We went slashing along through the woods the whole way, and as neither of us had ever ridden on an engine before, we made the best of our time. We found out what every crank and handle was for, and kept a sharp look-out ahead, through the little windows in the cab. If we had caught an alligator on the cow-catcher, the thing would have been complete. The engineer said there used to be alligators along by the road, in the swampy places, but he guessed the engine had frightened most of them away.

The trip didn't take forty minutes, so we had scarcely time to learn the whole art of engine-driving, but we were very glad to have had the ride.

We found the steam-boat waiting for us at Tocoi, which is such a little place that I don't believe either of us noticed it, as we hurried aboard. The St. John's is a splendid river, as wide as a young lake; but we did not have much time to see it, as it grew dark pretty soon, and the supper-bell rang.

We reached Pilatka pretty early in the evening, and there we had to stay all night. Mr. Chipperton told me, confidentially, that he thought this whole arrangement was a scheme to make money out of travellers. The boat we were in ought to have kept on and taken us up the Oclawaha; "but," said he, "I suppose that wouldn't suit the hotel-keepers. I expect they divide the profits with the boats."

By good luck, I thought, the Corny family and ourselves went to different hotels to spend the night. When I congratulated Rectus on this fact, he only said:

"It don't matter for one night. We'll catch 'em all bad enough to-morrow."

And he was right. When we went down to the wharf the next morning, to find the Oclawaha boat, the first persons we saw were Mr. Chipperton, with his wife and daughter. They were standing, gazing at the steam-boat which was to take us on our trip.

"Isn't this a funny boat?" said Corny, as soon as she saw us. It was a very funny boat. It was not much longer than an ordinary tug, and quite narrow, but was built up as high as a two-story house, and the wheel was in the stern. Rectus compared her to a river wheelbarrow.

Soon after we were on board she started off, and then we had a good chance to see the St. John's. We had been down to look at the river before, for we got up very early and walked about the town. It is a pretty sort of a new place, with wide streets and some handsome houses. The people have orange-groves in their gardens, instead of potato-patches, as we have up north. Before we started, we hired a rifle. We had been told that there was plenty of game on the river, and that most gentlemen who took the trip carried guns. Rectus wanted to get two rifles, but I thought one was enough. We could take turns, and I knew I'd feel safer if I had nothing to do but to keep my eye on Rectus while he had the gun.

There were not many passengers on board, and, indeed, there was not room for more than twenty-five or thirty. Most of them who could find places sat out on a little upper deck, in front of the main cabin, which was in the top story. Mrs. Chipperton, however, staid in the saloon, or dining-room, and looked out of the windows. She was a quiet woman, and had an air as if she had to act as shaft-horse for the team, and was pretty well used to holding back. And I reckon she had a good deal of it to do.

One party attracted our attention as soon as we went aboard. It was made up of a lady and two gentlemen-hunters. The lady wasn't a hunter, but she was dressed in a suitable costume to go about with fellows who had on hunting-clothes. The men wore long yellow boots that came ever so far up their legs, and they had on all the belts and hunting-fixings that the law allows. The lady wore yellow gloves, to match the men's boots. As we were going up the St. John's, the two men strode about, in an easy kind of a way, as if they wanted us to understand that this sort of thing was nothing to them. They were used to it, and could wear that style of boots every day if they wanted to. Rectus called them "the yellow-legged party," which wasn't a bad name.

After steaming about twenty-five miles up the St. John's River, we went in close to the western shore, and then made a sharp turn into a narrow opening between the tall trees, and sailed right into the forest.

CHAPTER VIII.: THE STEAM-BOAT IN THE FOREST.

We were in a narrow river, where the tall trees met overhead, while the lower branches and the smaller trees brushed against the little boat as it steamed along. This was the Oclawaha River, and Rectus and I thought it was as good as fairy-land. We stood on the bow of the boat, which wasn't two feet above the water, and took in everything there was to see.

The river wound around in among the great trees, so that we seldom could see more than a few hundred yards ahead, and every turn we made showed us some new picture of green trees and hanging moss and glimpses into the heart of the forest, while everything was reflected in the river, which was as quiet as a looking-glass.

"Talk of theatres!" said Rectus.

"No, don't," said I.

At this moment we both gave a little jump, for a gun went off just behind us. We turned around quickly, and saw that the tall yellow-legs had just fired at a big bird. He didn't hit it.

"Hello!" said Rectus; "we'd better get our gun. The game is beginning to show itself." And off he ran for the rifle.

I didn't know that Rectus had such a bloodthirsty style of mind; but there were a good many things about him that I didn't know. When he came back, he loaded the rifle, which was a little breech-loader, and began eagerly looking about for game.

Corny had been on the upper deck; but in a minute or two she came running out to us.

"Oh! do you know," she called out, "that there are alligators in this river? Do you think they could crawl up into the boat? We go awfully near shore sometimes. They sleep on shore. I do hope I'll see one soon."

"Well, keep a sharp look-out, and perhaps you may," said I.

She sat down on a box near the edge of the deck, and peered into the water and along the shore as if she had been sent there to watch for breakers ahead. Every now and then she screamed out:

"There's one! There! There! There!"

But it was generally a log, or a reflection, or something else that was not an alligator.

Of course we were very near both shores at all times, for the river is so narrow that a small boy could throw a ball over it; but occasionally the deeper part of the channel flowed so near one shore that we ran right up close to the trees, and the branches flapped up against the people on the little forward deck, making the ladies, especially the lady belonging to the yellow-legged party, crouch and scream as if some wood-demon had stuck a hand into the boat and made a grab for their bonnets.

This commotion every now and then, and the almost continual reports from the guns on board, and Corny's screams when she thought she saw an alligator, made the scene quite lively.

Rectus and I took a turn every half-hour at the rifle. It was really a great deal more agreeable to look out at the beautiful pictures that came up before us every few minutes; but, as we had the gun, we couldn't help keeping up a watch for game, besides.

"There!" I whispered to Rectus; "see that big bird! On that limb! Take a crack at him!"

It was a water-turkey, and he sat placidly on a limb close to the water's edge, and about a boat's length ahead of us.

Rectus took a good aim. He slowly turned as the boat approached the bird, keeping his aim upon him, and then he fired.

The water-turkey stuck out his long, snake-like neck, and said:

"Quee! Quee! Quee!"

And then he ran along the limb quite gayly.

"Bang! bang!" went the guns of the yellow-legs, and the turkey actually stopped and looked back. Then he said:

"Quee! Quee!" again, and ran in among the thick leaves.

I believe I could have hit him with a stone.

"It don't seem to be any use," said Mr. Chipperton, who was standing behind us, "to fire at the birds along this river. They know just what to do. I'm almost sure I saw that bird wink. It wouldn't surprise me if the fellows that own the rifles are in conspiracy with these birds. They let out rifles that wont hit, and the birds know it, and sit there and laugh at the passengers. Why, I tell you, sir, if the people who travel up and down this river were all regular shooters, there wouldn't be a bird left in six months."

At this moment Corny saw an alligator,—a real one. It was lying on a log, near shore, and just ahead of the boat. She set up such a yell that it made every one of us jump, and her mother came rushing out of the saloon to see if she was dead. The alligator, who was a good-sized fellow, was so scared that he just slid off his log without taking time to get decently awake, and before any one but Rectus and myself had a chance to see him. The ladies were very much annoyed at this, and urged Corny to scream softly the next time she saw one. Alligators were pretty scarce this trip, for some reason or other. For one thing, the weather was not very warm, and they don't care to come out in the open air unless they can give their cold bodies a good warming up.

Corny now went up on the upper deck, because she thought that she might see alligators farther ahead if she got up higher. In five minutes, she had her hat taken off by a branch of a tree, which swept upon her, as she was leaning over the rail. She called to the pilot to stop the boat and go back for her hat, but the captain, who was up in the pilot-house, stuck out his head and said he reckoned she'd have to wait until they came back. The hat would hang there for a day or two. Corny made no answer to this, but disappeared into the saloon.

In a little while, she came out on the lower deck, wearing a seal-skin hat. She brought a stool with her, and put it near the bow of the boat, a little in front and on one side of the box on which Rectus and I were sitting. Then she sat quietly down and gazed out ahead. The seal-skin cap was rather too warm for the day, perhaps, but she looked very pretty in it.

Directly she looked around at us.

"Where do you shoot alligators?" said she.

"Anywhere, where you may happen to see them," said I, laughing. "On the land, in the water, or wherever they may be."

"I mean in what part of their bodies?" said she.

"Oh! in the eye," I answered.

"Either eye?" she asked.

"Yes; it don't matter which. But how are you going to hit them?"

"I've got a revolver," said she.

And she turned around, like the turret of an iron-clad, until the muzzle of a big seven-shooter pointed right at us.

"My conscience!" I exclaimed; "where did you get that? Don't point it this way!"

"Oh! it's father's. He let me have it. I am going to shoot the first alligator I see. You needn't be afraid of my screaming this time," and she revolved back to her former position.

"One good thing," said Rectus to me, in a low voice; "her pistol isn't cocked."

I had noticed this, and I hoped also that it wasn't loaded.

"Which eye do you shut?" said Corny, turning suddenly upon us.

"Both!" said Rectus.

She did not answer, but looked at me, and I told her to shut her left eye, but to be very particular not to turn around again without lowering her pistol.

She resumed her former position, and we breathed a little easier, although I thought that it might be well for us to go to some other part of the boat until she had finished her sport.

I was about to suggest this to Rectus, when suddenly Corny sprang to her feet, and began blazing away at something ahead. Bang! bang! bang! she went, seven times.

"Why, she didn't stop once to cock it!" cried Rectus, and I was amazed to see how she had fired so rapidly. But as soon as I had counted seven, I stepped up to her and took her pistol. She explained to me how it worked. It was one of those pistols in which the same pull of the trigger jerks up the hammer and lets it down,—the most unsafe things that any one can carry.

"Too bad!" she exclaimed. "I believe it was only a log! But wont you please load it up again for me? Here are some cartridges."

"Corny," said I, "how would you like to have our rifle? It will be better than a pistol for you."

She agreed, instantly, to this exchange, and I showed her how to hold and manage the gun. I didn't think it was a very good thing for a girl to have, but it was a great deal safer than the pistol for the people on board. The latter I put in my pocket.

Corny made one shot, but did no execution. The other gunners on board had been firing away, for some time, at two little birds that kept ahead of us, skimming along over the water, just out of reach of the shot that was sent scattering after them.

"I think it's a shame," said Corny, "to shoot such little birds as that. They can't eat 'em."

"No," said I; "and they can't hit 'em, either, which is a great deal better."

But very soon after this, the shorter yellow-legged man did hit a bird. It was a water-turkey, that had been sitting on a tree, just as we turned a corner. The big bird spread out its wings, made a doleful flutter, and fell into the underbrush by the shore.

"Wont they stop to get him?" asked Corny, with her eyes open as wide as they would go.

One of the hands was standing by, and he laughed.

"Stop the boat when a man shoots a bird? I reckon not. And there isn't anybody that would go into all that underbrush and water only for a bird like that, anyway."

"Well, I think it's murder!" cried Corny. "I thought they ate 'em. Here! Take your gun. I'm much obliged; but I don't want to kill things just to see them fall down and die."

I took the gun very willingly,—although I did not think that Corny would injure any birds with it,—but I asked her what she thought about alligators. She certainly had not supposed that they were killed for food.

"Alligators are wild beasts," she said. "Give me my pistol. I am going to take it back to father."

And away she went. Rectus and I did not keep up our rifle practice much longer. We couldn't hit anything, and the thought that, if we should wound or kill a bird, it would be of no earthly good to us or anybody else, made us follow Corny's example, and we put away our gun. But the other gunners did not stop. As long as daylight lasted a ceaseless banging was kept up.

We were sitting on the forward deck, looking out at the beautiful scenes through which we were passing, and occasionally turning back to see that none of the gunners posted themselves where they might make our positions uncomfortable, when Corny came back to us.

"Can either of you speak French?" she asked.

Rectus couldn't; but I told her that I understood the language tolerably well, and asked her why she wished to know.

"It's just this," she said. "You see those two men with yellow boots, and the lady with them? She's one of their wives."

"How many wives have they got?" interrupted Rectus, speaking to Corny almost for the first time.

"I mean she is the wife of one of them, of course," she answered, a little sharply; and then she turned herself somewhat more toward me. "And the whole set try to make out they're French, for they talk it nearly all the time. But they're not French, for I heard them talk a good deal better English than they can talk French; and every time a branch nearly hits her, that lady sings out in regular English. And, besides, I know that their French isn't French French, because I can understand a great deal of it, and if it was I couldn't do it. I can talk French a good deal better than I can understand it, anyway. The French people jumble everything up so that I can't make head or tail of it. Father says he don't wonder they have had so many revolutions, when they can't speak their own language more distinctly. He tried to learn it, but didn't keep it up long, and so I took lessons. For, when we go to France, one of us ought to know how to talk, or we shall be cheated dreadfully. Well, you see, over on the little deck, up there, is that gentleman with his wife and a young lady, and they're all travelling together, and these make-believe French people have been jabbering about them ever so long, thinking that nobody else on board understands French. But I listened to them. I couldn't make out all they said, but I could tell that they were saying all sorts of things about those other people, and trying to settle which lady the gentleman was married to, and they made a big mistake, too, for they said the small lady was the one."

"How do you know they were wrong?" I said.

"Why, I went to the gentleman and asked him. I guess he ought to know. And now, if you'll come up there, I'd just like to show those people that they can't talk out loud about the other passengers and have nobody know what they're saying."

"You want to go there and talk French, so as to show them that you understand it?" said I.

"Yes," answered Corny, "that's just it."

"All right; come along," said I. "They may be glad to find out that you know what they're talking about."

And so we all went to the upper deck, Rectus as willing as anybody to see the fun.

Corny seated herself on a little stool near the yellow-legged party, the men of which had put down their guns for a time. Rectus and I sat on the forward railing, near her. Directly she cleared her throat, and then, after looking about her on each side, said to me, in very distinct tones:

"Voy-ezz vows cett hommy ett ses ducks femmys seelah?"

I came near roaring out laughing, but I managed to keep my face straight, and said: "Oui."

"Well, then,—I mean Bean donk lah peetit femmy nest pah lah femmy due hommy. Lah oter femmy este sah femmy."

"VOY-EZZ VOWS CETT HOMMY ETT SES DUCKS FEMMYS SEELAH?"

At this, there was no holding in any longer. I burst out laughing, so that I came near falling off the railing; Rectus laughed because I did; the gentleman with the wife and the young lady laughed madly, and Mr. Chipperton, who came out of the saloon on hearing the uproar, laughed quite cheerfully, and asked what it was all about. But Corny didn't laugh. She turned around short to see what effect her speech had had on the yellow-legged party. It had a good deal of effect. They reddened and looked at us. Then they drew their chairs closer together, and turned their backs to us. What they thought, we never knew; but Corny declared to me afterward that they talked no more French,—at least when she was about.

The gentleman who had been the subject of Corny's French discourse called her over to him, and the four had a gay talk together. I heard Corny tell them that she never could pronounce French in the French way. She pronounced it just as it was spelt, and her father said that ought to be the rule with every language. She had never had a regular teacher; but if people laughed so much at the way she talked, perhaps her father ought to get her one.

I liked Corny better the more I knew of her. It was easy to see that she had taught herself all that she knew. Her mother held her back a good deal, no doubt; but her father seemed more like a boy-companion than anything else, and if Corny hadn't been a very smart girl, she would have been a pretty bad kind of a girl by this time. But she wasn't anything of the sort, although she did do and say everything that came into her head to say or do. Rectus did not agree with me about Corny. He didn't like her.

When it grew dark, I thought we should stop somewhere for the night, for it was hard enough for the boat to twist and squeeze herself along the river in broad daylight. She bumped against big trees that stood on the edge of the stream, and swashed through bushes that stuck out too far from the banks; but she was built for bumping and scratching, and didn't mind it. Sometimes she would turn around a corner and make a short cut through a whole plantation of lily-pads and spatterdocks,—or things like them,—and she would scrape over a sunken log as easily as a wagon-wheel rolls over a stone. She drew only two feet of water, and was flat-bottomed. When she made a very short turn, the men had to push her stern around with poles. Indeed, there was a man with a pole at the bow a good deal of the time, and sometimes he had more pushing off to do than he could manage by himself.

When Mr. Chipperton saw what tight places we had to squeeze through, he admitted that it was quite proper not to try to bring the big steam-boats up here.

But the boat didn't stop. She kept right on. She had to go a hundred and forty miles up that narrow river, and if she made the whole trip from Pilatka and back in two days, she had no time to lose. So, when it was dark, a big iron box was set up on top of the pilot-house, and a fire was built in it of pine-knots and bits of fat pine. This blazed finely, and lighted up the river and the trees on each side, and sometimes threw out such a light that we could see quite a distance ahead. Everybody came out to see the wonderful sight. It was more like fairy-land than ever. When the fire died down a little, the distant scenery seemed to fade away and become indistinct and shadowy, and the great trees stood up like their own ghosts all around us; and then, when fresh knots were thrown in, the fire would blaze up, and the whole scene would be lighted up again, and every tree and bush, and almost every leaf, along the water's edge would be tipped with light, while everything was reflected in the smooth, glittering water.

Rectus and I could hardly go in to supper, and we got through the meal in short order. We staid out on deck until after eleven o'clock, and Corny staid with us a good part of the time. At last, her father came down after her, for they were all going to bed.

"This is a grand sight," said Mr. Chipperton. "I never saw anything to equal it in any transformation scene at a theatre. Some of our theatre people ought to come down here and study it up, so as to get up something of the kind for exhibition in the cities."

Just before we went into bed, our steam-whistle began to sound, and away off in the depths of the forest we could hear every now and then another whistle. The captain told us that there was a boat coming down the river, and that she would soon pass us. The river did not look wide enough for two boats; but when the other whistle sounded as if it were quite near, we ran our boat close into shore among the spatterdocks, in a little cove, and waited there, leaving the channel for the other boat.

Directly, it came around a curve just ahead of us, and truly it was a splendid sight. The lower part of the boat was all lighted up, and the fire was blazing away grandly in its iron box, high up in the air.

To see such a glowing, sparkling apparition as this come sailing out of the depths of the dark forest, was grand! Rectus said he felt like bursting into poetry; but he didn't. He wasn't much on rhymes. He had opportunity enough, though, to get up a pretty good-sized poem, for we were kept awake a long time after we went to bed by the boughs of the trees on shore scratching and tapping against the outside of our state-room.

When we went out on deck the next morning, the first person we saw was Corny, holding on to the flag-staff at the bow and looking over the edge of the deck into the water.

"What are you looking at?" said I, as we went up to her.

"See there!" she cried. "See that turtle! And those two fishes! Look! look!"

We didn't need to be told twice to look. The water was just as clear as crystal, and you could see the bottom everywhere, even in the deepest places, with the great rocks covered with some glittering green substance that looked like emerald slabs, and the fish and turtles swimming about as if they thought there was no one looking at them.

I couldn't understand how the water had become so clear; but I was told that we had left the river proper and were now in a stream that flowed from Silver Spring, which was the end of our voyage into the cypress woods. The water in the spring and in this stream was almost transparent,—very different from the regular water of the river.

About ten o'clock, we reached Silver Spring, which is like a little lake, with some houses on the bank. We made fast at a wharf, and, as we were to stop here some hours, everybody got ready to go ashore.

Corny was the first one ready. Her mother thought she ought not to go, but her father said there was no harm in it.

"If she does," said Mrs. Chipperton, "she'll get herself into some sort of a predicament before she comes back."

I found that in such a case as this Mrs. Chipperton was generally right.

CHAPTER IX.: THE THREE GRAY BEANS.

Corny went ashore, but she did not stay there three minutes. From the edge of the wharf we could see that Silver Spring was better worth looking at than anything we should be likely to see on shore. The little lake seemed deeper than a three-story house, and yet, even from where we stood, we could see down to the very bottom.

There were two boys with row-boats at the wharf. We hired one of the boats right off, and Corny gave me such a look, that I told her to get in. After she was in the boat, she asked her mother, who was standing on the deck of the steam-boat, if she might go. Mrs. Chipperton said she supposed so, and away we went. When we had rowed out to the middle of the spring, I stopped rowing, and we looked down into the depths. It was almost the same as looking into air. Far down at the bottom we could see the glittering sand and the green rocks, and sometimes a fish, as long as my arm, would slowly rise and fall, and paddle away beneath us. We dropped nickels and copper cents down to the bottom, and we could plainly see them lying there. In some parts of the bottom there were "wells," or holes, about two feet in diameter, which seemed to go down indefinitely. These, we were told, were the places where the water came up from below into the spring. We could see the weeds and grasses that grew on the edges of these wells, although we could not see very far down into them.

"If I had only known," said Rectus, "what sort of a place we were coming to, I should have brought something to lower down into these wells. I tell you what would have been splendid!—a heavy bottle filled with sweet oil and some phosphorus, and a long cord. If we shook up the bottle it would shine, so that, when we lowered it into the wells, we could see it go down to the very bottom, that is, if the cord should be long enough."

At this instant, Corny went overboard! Rectus made a grab at her, but it was too late. He sprang to his feet, and I thought he was going over after her, but I seized him.

"Sit down!" said I. "Watch her! She'll come up again. Lean over and be ready for her!"

We both leaned over the bow as far as was safe. With one hand I gently paddled the boat, this way and that, so as to keep ourselves directly over Corny. It would have been of no use to jump in. We could see her as plainly as anything.

She was going down, all in a bunch, when I first saw her, and the next instant she touched the bottom. Her feet were under now, and I saw her make a little spring. She just pushed out her feet.

Then she began to come right up. We saw her slowly rising beneath us. Her face was turned upward, and her eyes were wide open. It was a wonderful sight. I trembled from head to foot. It seemed as if we were floating in the air, and Corny was coming up to us from the earth.

Before she quite reached the surface, I caught her, and had her head out of water in an instant. Rectus then took hold, and with a mighty jerk, we pulled her into the boat.

Corny sat down hard and opened her mouth.

"There!" she said; "I didn't breathe an inch!"

And then she puffed for about two minutes, while the water ran off her into the bottom of the boat. I seized the oars to row to shore.

"How did you fall over?" said Rectus, who still shook as if he had had a chill.

"Don't know," answered Corny. "I was leaning far over, when my hand must have slipped, and the first thing I knew I was into it. It's good I didn't shut my eyes. If you get into water, with your eyes shut, you can't open them again." She still puffed a little. "Coming up was the best. It's the first time I ever saw the bottom of a boat."

"Weren't you frightened?" I asked.

"Hadn't time at first. And when I was coming up, I saw you reaching out for me."

"WE SAW HER SLOWLY RISING BENEATH US."

"Did you think we'd get you?" said Rectus, his face flushing.

"Yes," said Corny, "but if you'd missed me that time, I'd never have trusted you again."

The gentleman-with-a-wife-and-a-young-lady was in another boat, not very far off, but it was nearer the upper end of the little lake, and none of the party knew of our accident until we were pulling Corny out of the water. Then they rowed toward us as fast as they could, but they did not reach us until we were at the wharf. No one on shore, or on the steam-boat, seemed to have noticed Corny's dive. Indeed, the whole thing was done so quietly, and was so soon over, that there was not as much of a show as the occasion demanded.

"I never before was in deep water that seemed so little like real water," said Corny, just before we reached the wharf. "This was cold, and that was the only thing natural about it."

"Then this is not the first time you've been in deep water?" I asked.

"No," said Corny, "not the very first time;" and she scrambled up on the wharf, where her mother was standing, talking to some ladies.

"Why, Cornelia!" exclaimed Mrs. Chipperton, as soon as she saw the dripping girl, "have you been in the water again?"

"Yes, ma'am," said Corny, drawing her shoulders up to her ears, "and I must be rubbed down and have dry clothes as quick as lightning."

And with this, she and her mother hurried on board the steam-boat.

Rectus and I went back on the lake, for we had not gone half over it when Corny went into it. We had rowed about for half an hour or so, and were just coming in, when Corny appeared on the deck of the steam-boat, with a handkerchief tied around her head.

"Are you going to take a walk on shore?" she called out.

"Yes!" we shouted.

"All right," said she; "if you'll let me, I'll go with you, for mother says I must take a good run in the sun. I look funny, don't I? but I haven't any more hats."

We gave her a good run, although it was not altogether in the sun. The country hereabout was pretty well wooded, but there were roads cut through the woods, and there were some open places, and everywhere, underfoot, the sand was about six inches deep. Rectus took Corny by one hand, and I took her by the other, and we made her trot through that sand, in sunshine and shade, until she declared she was warm enough to last for a week. The yellow-legged party and some of the other passengers were wandering about, gathering the long gray moss,—from limbs where they could reach it,—and cutting great palmetto leaves which grew on low bushes all through the woods, and carrying them about as fans or parasols; but although Corny wanted to join in this fun, we would not stop. We just trotted her until she was tired, and then we ran her on board the boat, where her mother was waiting for her.

"Now, then," said Mrs. Chipperton, "immediately to bed."

The two disappeared, and we saw no more of Corny until supper-time. Her mother was certainly good at cure, if she didn't have much of a knack at prevention.

Just as the boat was about to start off on her return trip, and after she had blown her whistle two or three times, Mr. Chipperton appeared, carrying an immense arm-load of gray moss. He puffed and blew as he threw it down on deck. When his wife came out and told him of Corny's disaster, he stopped dusting his clothes, and looked up for an instant.

"I declare," said he, "Corny must keep out of the water. It seems to me that I can never leave her but she gets into some scrape. But I'm sure our friends here have proved themselves good fellows, indeed," and he shook hands with both of us.

"Now then, my dear," said he to his wife, "I've enough moss here for the parlor and sitting-room, and the little back-room, upstairs. I didn't get any for the dining-room, because it might blow about and get into the food."

"Do you mean to take that moss all the way home?" asked Mrs. Chipperton, in surprise. "Why, how will you ever carry it?"

"Of course I mean to take it home," said he. "I gathered this with my own hands from the top of one of the tallest trees on the banks of this famous Silver Spring."

"Mr. Chipperton!" exclaimed his wife.

"To be sure, the tree was cut down, but that makes no difference in the fact. It is both an ornament and a trophy of travel. If necessary, I'll buy a trunk for it. What did you do with Corny after they got her out?"

Our journey home was very much like our trip up the river, but there were a few exceptions. There was not so much firing, for I think the ammunition got pretty low; we saw more alligators, and the yellow-legged party, which had joined us at Pilatka, went all the way to St. Augustine with us. There was still another difference, and that was in Rectus. He was a good deal livelier,—more in the spirit that had hatched out in him in the cemetery at Savannah. He seemed to be all right with Corny now, and we had a good time together. I was going to say to him, once, that he had changed his mind about girls, but I thought I wouldn't. It would be better to let well enough alone, and he was a ticklish customer.

The day after we returned to St. Augustine, we were walking on the sea-wall, when we met Corny. She said she had been looking for us. Her father had gone out fishing with some gentlemen, and her mother would not walk in the sun, and, besides, she had something to say to us.

So we all walked to the fort and sat down on the wide wall of the water-battery. Rectus bestrode one of the cannon that stood pointing out to sea, but Corny told him she wanted him to get down and sit by her, so that she wouldn't have to shout.

"Now then," said she, after pausing a little, as if she wanted to be sure and get it right, "you two saved my life, and I want to give you something to remember me by."

We both exclaimed against this.

"You needn't do that," said I, "for I'm sure that no one who saw you coming up from the bottom, like the fairy-women float up on wires at the theatre, could ever forget you. We'll remember you, Corny, without your giving us anything."

"But that wont do," said she. "The only other time that I was ever really saved was by a ferryman, and father gave him some money, which was all right for him, but wouldn't do for you two, you know; and another time there wasn't really any danger, and I'm sorry the man got anything; but he did.

"We brought scarcely anything with us, because we didn't expect to need things in this way; but this is my own, and I want to give it to you both. One of you can't use it by himself, and so it will be more like a present for both of you together, than most things would be." And she handed me a box of dominoes.

"I give it to you because you're the oldest, but, remember, it's for both of you."

Of course we took it, and Corny was much pleased. She was a good little girl and, somehow or other, she seemed to be older and more sensible when she was with us than when she was bouncing around in the bosom of her family.

We had a good deal of talk together, and, after a while, she asked how long we were going to stay in St. Augustine.

"Until next Tuesday," I said, "and then we shall start for Nassau in the 'Tigris.'"

"Nassau!" she exclaimed, "where's that?"

"Right down there," I said, pointing out to sea with a crook of my finger, to the south. "It's on one of the Bahamas, and they lie off the lower end of Florida, you know."

"No," said she; "I don't remember where they are. I always get the Bahamas mixed up with the Bermudas, anyway. So does father. We talked of going to one of those places, when we first thought of travelling for his lung, but then they thought Florida would be better. What is there good about Nassau? Is it any better than this place?"

"Well," said I, "it's in the West Indies, and it's semi-tropical, and they have cocoa-nuts and pineapples and bananas there; and there are lots of darkeys, and the weather is always just what you want———"

"I guess that's a little stretched," said Corny, and Rectus agreed with her.

"And it's a new kind of a place," I continued; "an English colony, such as our ancestors lived in before the Revolution, and we ought to see what sort of a thing an English colony is, so as to know whether Washington and the rest of them should have kicked against it."

"Oh, they were all right!" said Corny, in a tone which settled that little matter.

"And so, you see," I went on, "Rectus and I thought we should like to go out of the country for a while, and see how it would feel to live under a queen and a cocoa-nut tree."

"Good!" cried Corny. "We'll go."

"Who?" I asked.

"Father and mother and I," said Corny, rising. "I'll tell them all about it; and I'd better be going back to the hotel, for if the steamer leaves on Tuesday, we'll have lots to do."

As we were walking homeward on the sea-wall, Rectus looked back and suddenly exclaimed:

"There! Do you see that Crowded Owl following us? He's been hanging round us all the afternoon. He's up to something. Don't you remember the captain told us he was a bad-tempered fellow?"

"What did he do?" asked Corny, looking back at the Indian, who now stood in the road, a short distance from the wall, regarding us very earnestly.

"Well, he never did anything, much," I said. "He seemed to be angry, once, because we would not buy some of his things, and the captain said he'd have him told not to worry us. That may have made him madder yet."

"He don't look mad," said Corny.

"Don't you trust him," said Rectus.

"I believe all these Indians are perfectly gentle, now," said Corny, "and father thinks so, too. He's been over here a good deal, and talked to some of them. Let's go ask him what he wants. Perhaps he's only sorry."

"If he is, we'll never find it out," I remarked, "for he can only speak one word of English."

I beckoned to Crowded Owl, and he immediately ran up to the wall, and said "How?" in an uncertain tone, as if he was not sure how we should take it. However, Corny offered him her hand, and Rectus and I followed suit. After this, he put his hand into his pocket, and pulled out three sea-beans.

"There!" said Rectus. "At it again. Disobeying military orders."

"But they're pretty ones," said Corny, taking one of the beans in her hand.

They were pretty. They were not very large, but were beautifully polished, and of a delicate gray color, the first we had seen of the kind.

"These must be a rare kind," said Rectus. "They are almost always brown. Let's forgive him this once, and buy them."

"Perhaps he wants to make up with you," said Corny, "and has brought these as a present."

"I can soon settle that question," said I, and I took the three beans, and pulled from my pocket three quarter-dollars, which I offered to the Indian.

Crowded Owl took the money, grinned, gave a bob of his head, and went home happy.

If he had had any wish to "make up" with us, he had shown it by giving us a chance at a choice lot of goods.

"Now," said I, reaching out my hand to Corny, "here's one for each of us. Take your choice."

"For me?" said Corny. "No, I oughtn't to. Yes, I will, too. I am ever so much obliged. We have lots of sea-beans, but none like this. I'll have a ring fastened to it, and wear it, somehow."

"That'll do to remember us by," said I.

"Yes," said Rectus, "and whenever you're in danger, just hold up that bean, and we'll come to you."

"I'll do it," said Corny. "But how about you? What can I do?"

"Oh, I don't suppose we shall want you to help us much," I said.

"Well, hold up your beans, and we'll see," said Corny.

CHAPTER X.: THE QUEEN ON THE DOOR-STEP.

We found that Corny had not been mistaken about her influence over her family, for the next morning, before we were done breakfast, Mr. Chipperton came around to see us. He was full of Nassau, and had made up his mind to go with us on Tuesday. He asked us lots of questions, but he really knew as much about the place as we did, although he had been so much in the habit of mixing his Bahamas and his Bermudas.

"My wife is very much pleased at the idea of having you two with us on the trip over," said he; "although, to be sure, we may have a very smooth and comfortable voyage."

I believe that, since the Silver Spring affair, he regarded Rectus and me as something in the nature of patent girl-catchers, to be hung over the side of the vessel in bad weather.

We were sorry to leave St. Augustine, but we had thoroughly done up the old place, and had seen everything, I think, except the Spring of Ponce de Leon, on the other side of the St. Sebastian River. We didn't care about renewing our youth,—indeed, we should have objected very much to anything of the kind,—and so we felt no interest in old Ponce's spring.

On Tuesday morning, the "Tigris" made her appearance on time, and Mr. Cholott and our good landlady came down to see us off. The yellow-legged party also came down, but not to see us off. They, too, were going to Nassau.

Rectus had gone on board, and I was just about to follow him, when our old Minorcan stepped up to me.

"Goin' away?" said he.

"Yes," said I, "we're off at last."

"Other feller goin'?"

"Oh, yes," I answered, "we keep together."

"Well now, look here," said he, drawing me a little on one side. "What made him take sich stock in us Minorcans? Why, he thought we used to be slaves; what put that in his head, I'd like to know? Did he reely think we ever was niggers?"

"Oh, no!" I exclaimed. "He had merely heard the early history of the Minorcans in this country, their troubles and all that, and he——"

"But what difference did it make to him?" interrupted the old man.

I couldn't just then explain the peculiarities of Rectus's disposition to Mr. Menendez, and so I answered that I supposed it was a sort of sympathy.

"I can't see, for the life of me," said the old man, reflectively, "what difference it made to him."

And he shook hands with me, and bade me good-bye. I don't believe he has ever found anybody who could give him the answer to this puzzle.

The trip over to Nassau was a very different thing from our voyage down the coast from New York to Savannah. The sea was comparatively smooth, and, although the vessel rolled a good deal in the great swells, we did not mind it much. The air was delightful, and after we had gone down the Florida coast, and had turned to cross the Gulf Stream to our islands, the weather became positively warm, even out here on the sea, and we were on deck nearly all the time.

Mr. Chipperton was in high spirits. He enjoyed the deep blue color of the sea; he went into ecstasies over the beautiful little nautiluses that sailed along by the ship; he watched with wild delight the porpoises that followed close by our side, and fairly shouted when a big fellow would spring into the air, or shoot along just under the surface, as if he had a steam-engine in his tail. But when he saw a school of flying-fish rise up out of the sea, just a little ahead of us, and go skimming along like birds, and then drop again into the water, he was so surprised and delighted that he scarcely knew how to express his feelings.

Of course, we younger people enjoyed all these things, but I was surprised to see that Corny was more quiet than usual, and spent a good deal of her time in reading, although she would spring up and run to the railing whenever her father announced some wonderful discovery. Mr. Chipperton would have been a splendid man for Columbus to have taken along with him on his first trip to these islands. He would have kept up the spirits of the sailors.

I asked Corny what she was reading, and she showed me her book. It was a big, fat pamphlet about the Bahamas, and she was studying up for her stay there. She was a queer girl. She had not been to school very much, her mother said, for they had been travelling about a good deal of late years; but she liked to study up special things, in which she took an interest. Sometimes she was her own teacher, and sometimes, if they staid in any one place long enough, she took regular lessons.

"I teach her as much as I can," said her mother, "although I would much rather have her go regularly to school. But her father is so fond of her that he will not have her away from him, and as Mr. Chipperton's lung requires him to be moving from place to place, we have to go, too. But I am determined that she shall go to a school next fall."

"What is the matter with Mr. Chipperton's lung?" I asked.

"I wish we knew," said Mrs. Chipperton, earnestly. "The doctors don't seem to be able to find out the exact trouble, and besides, it isn't certain which lung it is. But the only thing that can be done for it is to travel."

"He looks very well," said I.

"Oh, yes!" said she. "But"—and she looked around to see where he was—"he doesn't like people to tell him so."

After a while, Rectus got interested in Corny's book, and the two read a good deal together. I did not interrupt them, for I felt quite sure that neither of them knew too much.

The captain and all the officers on the steamer were good, sociable men, and made the passengers feel at home. I had got somewhat acquainted with them on our trip from Savannah to St. Augustine, and now the captain let me come into his room and showed me the ship's course, marked out on a chart, and pointed out just where we were, besides telling me a good many things about the islands and these waters.

I mentioned to Corny and Rectus, when I went aft again,—this was the second day out,—that we should see one end of the Great Bahama early in the afternoon.

"I'm glad of that," said Corny; "but I suppose we sha'n't go near enough for us to see its calcareous formation."

"Its what?" I exclaimed.

"Its cal-car-e-ous formation," repeated Corny, and she went on with her reading.

"Oh!" said I, laughing, "I guess the calcareous part is all covered up with grass and plants,—at least it ought to be in a semi-tropical country. But when we get to Nassau you can dig down and see what it's like."

"Semi-tropical!" exclaimed Mr. Chipperton, who just came up; "there is something about that word that puts me all in a glow," and he rubbed his hands as if he smelt dinner.

Each of us wore a gray bean. Rectus and I had ours fastened to our watch-guards, and Corny's hung to a string of beads she generally wore. We formed ourselves into a society—Corny suggested it—which we called the "Association of the Three Gray Beans," the object of which was to save each other from drowning, and to perform similar serviceable acts, if circumstances should call for them. We agreed to be very faithful, and, if Corny had tumbled overboard, I am sure that Rectus and I would have jumped in after her; but I am happy to say that she did nothing of the kind on this trip.

Early the next morning, we reached Nassau, the largest town in the Bahamas, on one of the smallest islands, and found it semi-tropical enough to suit even Mr. Chipperton.

Before we landed, we could see the white, shining streets and houses,—just as calcareous as they could be; the black negroes; the pea-green water in the harbor; the tall cocoa-nut trees, and about five million conch-shells, lying at the edges of the docks. The colored people here live pretty much on the conch-fish, and when we heard that, it accounted for the shells. The poorer people on these islands often go by the name of "conchs."

As we went up through the town we found that the darkeys were nearly as thick as the conch-shells, but they were much more lively. I never saw such jolly, dont-care-y people as the colored folks that were scattered about everywhere. Some of the young ones, as joyful skippers, could have tired out a shrimp.

There is one big hotel in the town, and pretty nearly all our passengers went there. The house is calcareous, and as solid as a rock. Rectus and I liked it very much, because it reminded us of pictures we had seen of Algiers, or Portugal, or some country where they have arches instead of doors; but Mr. Chipperton wasn't at all satisfied when he found that there was not a fireplace in the whole house.

"This is coming the semi-tropical a little too strong," he said to me; but he soon found, I think, that gathering around the hearth-stone could never become a popular amusement in this warm little town.

Every day, for a week, Mr. Chipperton hired a one-horse barouche, and he and his wife and daughter rode over the island. Rectus and I walked, and we saw a good deal more than they did. Corny told us this, the first walk she took with us. We went down a long, smooth, white road that led between the queer little cottages of the negroes, where the cocoa-nut and orange trees and the bananas and sappadilloes, and lots of other trees and bushes stood up around the houses just as proudly as if they were growing on ten-thousand-dollar lots. Some of these trees had the most calcareous foundations anybody ever saw. They grew almost out of the solid rock. This is probably one of the most economical places in the world for garden mould. You couldn't sweep up more than a bucketful out of a whole garden, and yet the things grow splendidly. Rectus said he supposed the air was earthy.

Corny enjoyed this walk, because we went right into the houses and talked to the people, and bought cocoa-nuts off the trees, and ate the inside custard with a spoon, and made the little codgers race for pennies, and tried all the different kinds of fruits. She said she would like to walk out with us always, but her mother said she must not be going about too much with boys.

"But there are no girls on the island," said she; "at least, no white ones,—as far as I have seen."

I suppose there were white children around, but they escaped notice in the vast majority of little nigs.

The day after this walk, the shorter "yellow-legs" asked me to go out fishing with him. He couldn't find anybody else, I suppose, for his friend didn't like fishing. Neither did Rectus; and so we went off together in a fishing-smack, with a fisherman to sail the boat and hammer conch for bait. We went outside of Hog Island,—which lies off Nassau, very much as Anastasia Island lies off St. Augustine, only it isn't a quarter as big,—and fished in the open sea. We caught a lot of curious fish, and the yellow-legs, whose name was Burgan, turned out to be a very good sort of a fellow. I shouldn't have supposed this of a man who had made such a guy of himself; but there are a great many different kinds of outsides to people.

When we got back to the hotel, along came Rectus and Corny. They had been out walking together, and looked hot.

"Oh," cried Corny, as soon as she saw me. "We have something to talk to you about! Let's go and sit down. I wish there was some kind of an umbrella or straw hat that people could wear under their chins to keep the glare of these white roads out of their eyes. Let's go up into the silk-cotton tree."

I proposed that I should go to my room and clean up a little first, but Corny couldn't wait. As her father had said, she wasn't good at waiting; and so we all went up into the silk-cotton tree. This was an enormous tree, with roots like the partitions between horse-stalls; it stood at the bottom of the hotel grounds, and had a large platform built up among the branches, with a flight of steps leading to it. There were seats up here, and room enough for a dozen people.

"Well," said I, when we were seated, "what have you to tell? Anything wonderful? If it isn't, you'd better let me tell you about my fish."

"Fish!" exclaimed Rectus, not very respectfully.

"Fish, indeed!" said Corny. "We have seen a queen!"

"Queen of what?" said I.

"Queen of Africa," replied Corny. "At least a part of it,—she would be, I mean, if she had stayed there. We went over that way, out to the very edge of the town, and there we found a whole colony of real native Africans,—just the kind Livingstone and Stanley discovered,—only they wear clothes like us."

"Oh, my!" exclaimed Rectus.

"I don't mean exactly that," said Corny; "but coats and trousers and frocks, awfully old and patched. And nearly all the grown-up people there were born in Africa, and rescued by an English man-of-war from a slave-ship that was taking them into slavery, and were brought here and set free. And here they are, and they talk their own language,—only some of them know English, for they've been here over thirty years,—and they all keep together, and have a governor of their own, with a flag-pole before his house, and among them is a real queen, of royal blood!"

"How did you find out that?" I asked.

"Oh, we heard about the African settlement this morning, at the hotel, and we went down there, right after dinner. We went into two or three of the houses and talked to the people, and they all told us the same thing, and one woman took us to see the queen."

"In her palace?" said I.

"No," said Corny, "she don't live in a palace. She lives in one of the funniest little huts you ever saw, with only two rooms. And it's too bad; they all know she's a queen, and yet they don't pay her one bit of honor. The African governor knows it, but he lives in his house with his flag-pole in front of it, and rules her people, while she sits on a stone in front of her door and sells red peppers and bits of sugar-cane."

"Shameful!" said I; "you don't mean that?"

"Yes, she does," put in Rectus. "We saw her, and bought some sugar-cane. She didn't think we knew her rank, for she put her things away when the women told her, in African, why we came to see her."

"What did she say to you?" I asked, beginning to be a good deal interested in this royal colored person.

"Nothing at all," said Corny; "she can't talk a word of English. If she could, she might get along better. I suppose her people want somebody over them who can talk English. And so they've just left her to sell peppers, and get along as well as she can."

"It's a good deal of a come-down, I must say," said I. "I wonder how she likes it?"

"Judging from her looks," said Rectus, "I don't believe she likes it at all."

"No, indeed!" added Corny. "She looks woe-begone, and I don't see why she shouldn't. To be taken captive with her people—may be she was trying to save them—and then to have them almost cut her acquaintance after they all get rescued and settled down!"

"Perhaps," said I, "as they are all living under Queen Victoria, they don't want any other queen."

"That's nothing," said Corny, quickly. "There's a governor of this whole island, and what do they want with another governor? If Queen Victoria and the governor of this island were Africans, of course they wouldn't want anybody else. But as it is, they do, don't you see?"

"They don't appear to want another queen," I said, "for they wont take one that is right under their noses."

Corny looked provoked, and Rectus asked me how I knew that.

"I tell you," said Corny, "it don't make any difference whether they want her or not, they haven't any right to make a born queen sit on a stone and sell red-peppers. Do you know what Rectus and I have made up our minds to do?"

"What is it?" I asked.

Corny looked around to see that no one was standing or walking near the tree, and then she leaned toward me and said:

"We are going to seat her on her throne!"

"You?" I exclaimed, and began to laugh.

"Yes, we are," said Rectus; "at least, we're going to try to."

"You needn't laugh," said Corny. "You're to join."

"In an insurrection,—a conspiracy," said I. "I can't go into that business."

"You must!" cried Corny and Rectus, almost in a breath.

"You've made a promise," said Corny.

"And are bound to stick to it," said Rectus, looking at Corny.

Then, both together, as if they had settled it all beforehand, they held up their gray sea-beans, and said, in vigorous tones:

"Obey the bean!"

I didn't hesitate a moment. I held up my bean, and we clicked beans all around.

I became a conspirator!

CHAPTER XI.: REGAL PROJECTS.

The next morning, we all went around to see the queen, and on the way we tried to arrange our affair. I was only sorry that my old school-fellows were not there, to go into the thing with us. There couldn't have been better fun for our boys, than to get up a revolution and set up a dethroned queen. But they were not there, and I determined to act as their representative as well as I could.

We three—Corny, Rectus and I—were agreed that the re-enthronement—we could think of no better word for the business—should be done as quietly and peacefully as possible. It was of no use, we thought, to make a great fuss about what we were going to do. We would see that this African ex-sovereigness was placed in a suitable regal station, and then we would call upon her countrymen to acknowledge her rank.

"It isn't really necessary for her to do any governing," said Rectus. "Queens do very little of that. Look at Queen Victoria! Her Prime Minister and Parliament run the country. If the African governor here is a good man, the queen can take him for a Prime Minister. Then he can just go along and do what he always did. If she is acknowledged to be the queen, that's all she need want."

"That's so," said Corny. "And, above all, there must be no blood shed."

"None of yours, any way," said I; and Rectus tapped his bean, significantly.

Rectus had been chosen captain of this revolutionary coalition, because Corny, who held the controlling vote, said that she was afraid I had not gone into the undertaking heart and soul, as Rectus had. Otherwise, she would have voted for me, as the oldest of the party. I did not make any objections, and was elected Treasurer. Corny said that the only office she had ever held was that of Librarian, in a girls' society, but as we did not expect to need a Librarian in this undertaking, we made her Secretary and Manager of Restoration, which, we thought, would give her all the work that she could stand under.

I suggested that there was one sub-officer, or employé, that we should be sure to need, and who should be appointed before we commenced operations. This was an emissary. Proper communications between ourselves and the populace would be difficult, unless we obtained the service of some intelligent and whole-souled darkey. My fellow-revolutionists agreed with me, and, after a moment of reflection, Corny shouted that she had thought of the very person.

"It's a girl!" she cried. "And it's Priscilla!"

We all knew Priscilla. It would have been impossible to be at the hotel for a week and not know her. After breakfast, and after dinner, there was always a regular market at the entrance of the hotel, under the great arched porch, where the boarders sat and made themselves comfortable after meals. The dealers were negroes of every age,—men, women, boys, and girls, and they brought everything they could scrape up, that they thought visitors might buy,—fruit, shells, sponges, flowers, straw hats, canes, and more traps than I can remember. Some of them had very nice things, and others would have closed out their stock for seven cents. The liveliest and brightest of all these was a tall, slim, black, elastic, smooth-tongued young girl, named Priscilla.

She nearly always wore shoes, which distinguished her from her fellow-countrywomen. Her eyes sparkled like a fire-cracker of a dark night, and she had a mind as sharp as a fish-hook. The moment Corny mentioned her she was elected emissary.

We determined, however, to be very cautious in disclosing our plans to her. We would sound her, first, and make a regular engagement with her.

"It will be a first-rate thing for me," said Corny, "to have a girl to go about with me, for mother said, yesterday, that it wouldn't do for me to be so much with boys. It looked tomboyish, she said, though she thought you two were very good for boys."

"Are you going to tell your father and mother about this?" asked Rectus.

"I think I'll tell mother," said Corny, "because I ought to, and I don't believe she'll object, if I have a girl along with me. But I don't think I'll say anything to father just yet. I'm afraid he'd join."

Rectus and I agreed that it might be better to postpone saying anything to Mr. Chipperton.

It was very true that the queen did not live in a palace. Her house was nearly large enough to hold an old-fashioned four-posted bedstead, such as they have at my Aunt Sarah's. The little room that was cut off from the main apartment was really too small to count. The queen was hard at work, sitting on her door-stone by the side of her bits of sugar-cane and pepper-pods. There were no customers. She was a good-looking old body, about sixty, perhaps, but tall and straight enough for all queenly purposes.

She arose and shook hands with us, and then stepped into her door-way and courtesied. The effect was very fine.

"This is dreadful!" said Corny. "She ought to give up this pepper-pod business right away. If I could only talk to her, I'd make her understand. But I must go get somebody for an interpreter."

And she ran off to one of the neighboring huts.

"If this thing works," said Rectus, "we ought to hire a regular interpreter."

"It wont do to have too many paid officials," said I, "but we'll see about that."

Corny soon returned with a pleasant-faced woman, who undertook to superintend our conversation with the queen.

"What's her name—to begin with?" asked Corny, of the woman.

"Her African name is Poqua-dilla, but here they call her Jane Henderson, when they talk of her. She knows that name, too. We all has to have English names."

"Well, we don't want any Jane Henderson," said Corny. "Poqua-dilla! that's a good name for a queen. But what we first want is to have her stop selling things at the front door. We'll do better for her than that."

"Is you goin' to sen' her to the 'sylum?" asked the woman.

"The asylum!" exclaimed Corny. "No, indeed! You'll see. She's to live here, but she's not to sell pepper-pods, or anything else."

"Well, young missy," said the woman, "you better buy 'em of her. I reckon she'll sell out for 'bout fourpence."

This was a sensible proposition, and, as treasurer, I bought the stock, the queen having signified her willingness to the treaty by a dignified nod and a courtesy. She was very much given to style, which encouraged us a good deal.

"Now, then," said Rectus, who thought it was about time that the captain should have something to say, "you must tell her that she isn't to lay in any more stock. This is to be the end of her mercantile life."

I don't believe the woman translated all of this speech, but the queen gave another nod and courtesy, and I pocketed the peppers to keep as trophies. The other things we kept, to give to the children and make ourselves popular.

"How much do you think it would cost," asked Corny of me, "to make this place a little more like a palace?"

I made a rough sort of a calculation, and came to the conclusion that the room could be made a little more like a palace for about eight dollars.

"That's cheap enough," said Rectus to me. "You and I will each give four dollars."

"No, indeed!" said Corny. "I'm going to give some. How much is three into eight?"

"Two and two-thirds," said I, "or, in this case, two dollars, sixty-six cents and some sixes over."

"All right!" said Corny; "I'll ask father for three dollars. There ought to be something for extras. I'll tell mother what I want it for, and that will satisfy him. He can know afterward. I don't think he ought to worry his lung with anything like this."

"She wont want a throne," said Rectus, turning the conversation from Mr. Chipperton, "for she has a very good rocking-chair, which could be fixed up."

"Yes," said I, "it could be cushioned. She might do it herself."

At this, the colored woman made a remark to the queen, but what it was we did not know.

"Of course she could," said Corny. "Queens work. Queen Victoria etches on steel."

"I don't believe Porker-miller can do that," said Rectus, "but I guess she can pad her chair."

"Do thrones rock?" asked Corny.

"Some of 'em do," I said. "There was the throne of France, you know."

"Well, then, that will be all right," said Corny; "and how about a crown and sceptre?"

"Oh, we wont want a sceptre," I said; "that sort of thing's pretty old-fashioned. But we ought to have a crown, so as to make a difference between her and the other people."

"How much are crowns?" asked Corny, in a thoughtful tone.

"Various prices," I answered; "but I think we can make one, that will do very well, for about fifty cents. I'll undertake to make the brass part, if you'll cushion it."

"Brass!" exclaimed Corny, in astonishment.

"You don't suppose we can get gold, do you?" I asked, laughing.

"Well, no," she said, but not quite satisfied.

"And there must be a flag and a flag-pole," said Rectus. "But what sort of a flag are we going to have?"

"The African flag," said Corny, confidently.

None of us knew what the African flag was, although Corny suggested that it was probably black. But I told her that if we raised a black flag before the queen's palace, we should bring down the authorities on us, sure. They'd think we had started a retail piratical establishment.

We now took leave of the queen, and enjoined her neighbor to impress on her mind the necessity of not using her capital to lay in a new stock of goods. Leaving a quarter of a dollar with her, for contingent expenses during the day, we started for home.

"I'll tell you what it is," said I, "we must settle this matter of revenue pretty soon. If she don't sell peppers and sugar-cane, she'll have to be supported in some way, and I'm sure we can't do it."

"Her subjects ought to attend to that," said Rectus.

"But she hasn't got any yet," I answered.

"That's a fact," said Corny. "We must get her a few, to start with."

"Hire 'em, do you mean?" asked Rectus.

"No; call upon them in the name of their country and their queen," she replied.

"I think it would be better, at first," said I, "to call upon them in the name of about twopence a head. Then, when we get a nice little body of adherents to begin with, the other subjects will fall in, of their own accord, if we manage the thing right."

"There's where the emissary will come in," said Rectus. "She can collect adherents."

"We must engage her this very day," said Corny. "And now, what about the flag? We haven't settled that yet."

"I think," said I, "that we'd better invent a flag. When we get back to the hotel, we can each draw some designs, and the one we choose can easily be made up. We can buy the stuff anywhere."

"I'll sew it," said Corny.

"Do you think," said Rectus, who had been reflecting, "that the authorities of this place will object to our setting up a queen?"

"Can't tell," I said. "But I hardly think they will. They don't object to the black governor, and our queen wont interfere with them in any way that I can see. She will have nothing to do with anybody but those native Africans, who keep to themselves, anyway."

"If anybody should trouble us, who would it be? Soldiers or the policemen? How many soldiers have they here?" asked Corny.

"There's only one company now in the barracks," said Rectus. "I was down there. There are two men-of-war in the harbor, but one of them's a Spanish vessel, and I'm pretty sure she wouldn't bother us."

"Is that all?" said Corny, in a tone of relief.

I didn't want to dash her spirits, but I remarked that there were a good many policemen in the town.

"And they're all colored men," said Corny. "I'd hate to have any of them coming after us."

"The governor of the colony is at the head of the army, police and all, isn't he?" said Rectus.

"Yes," I answered.

"And I know where he lives," put in Corny. "Let's go and see him, sometime, and ask him about it."

This was thought to be a good idea, and we agreed to consider it at our next meeting.

"As to revenue," said Rectus, just before we reached the hotel, "I don't believe these people have much money to give for the support of a queen, and so I think they ought to bring in provisions. The whole thing might be portioned out. She ought to have so many conchs a week, so many sticks of sugar-cane, and so many yams and other stuff. This might be fixed so that it wouldn't come hard on anybody."

Corny said she guessed she'd have to get a little book to put these things down, so that we could consider them in order.

I could not help noticing that there was a good deal of difference between Corny and Rectus, although they were much alike, too. Corny had never learned much, but she had a good brain in her head, and she could reason out things pretty well, when she had anything in the way of a solid fact to start with. Rectus was better on things he'd heard reasoned out. He seemed to know a good thing when it came before him, and he remembered it, and often brought it in very well. But he hadn't had much experience in reasoning on his own account, although he was getting more in practice every day.

Corny was just as much in earnest as she was the first day we saw her, but she seemed to have grown more thoughtful. Perhaps this was on account of her having important business on hand. Her thoughtfulness, however, did not prevent her from saying some very funny things. She spoke first and did her thinking afterward. But she was a good girl, and I often wished my sister knew her. Helen was older, to be sure, but she could have learned a great deal from Corny.

That afternoon, we had a meeting up in the silk-cotton tree, and Priscilla, who had sold out her small stock of flowers in the hotel-door market, was requested to be present. A variety-show, consisting of about a dozen young darkeys with their baskets and strings of sponges, accompanied her up the steps; but she was ordered to rout them, and she did it in short order. When we were alone, Rectus, as captain, began to state to her what we desired of her; but he was soon interrupted by Corny, who could do a great deal more talking in a given time than he could, and who always felt that she ought to begin early, in order to get through in good season.

"Now, Priscilla," said Corny, "in the first place, you must promise never to tell what we are going to say to you."

Priscilla promised in a flash.

"We want you, then," continued Corny, "to act as our emissary, or general agent, or errand-girl, if you don't know what the other two things mean."

"I'll do dat, missy," said Priscilla. "Whar you want me to go?"

"Nowhere just now," said Corny. "We want to engage you by the day, to do whatever we tell you."

"Cahn't do dat, missy. Got to sell flowers and roses. Sell 'em for de fam'ly, missy."

"But in the afternoon you can come," said Corny. "There isn't any selling done then. We'll pay you."

"How much?" asked Priscilla.

This question was referred to me, and I offered sixpence a day.

The money in this place is English, of course, as it is an English colony; but there are so many visitors from the United States, that American currency is as much in use, for large sums, as the pounds-shillings-and-pence arrangement. But all sums under a quarter are reckoned in English money,—pennies, half-pennies, four, six and eight-pences, and that sort of thing. One of our quarters passes for a shilling, but a silver dime wont pass in the shops. The darkeys will take them—or almost anything else—as a gift. I didn't have to get our money changed into gold. I got a draft on a Nassau house, and generally drew greenbacks. But I saw, pretty plainly, that I couldn't draw very much for this new monarchical undertaking, and stay in Nassau as long as we had planned.

"A whole afternoon," exclaimed Priscilla, "for sixpence!"

"Why not?" I asked. "That's more than you generally make all day."

"Only sixpence!" said Priscilla, looking as if her tender spirit had been wounded. Corny glanced at me with an air that suggested that I ought to make a rise in the price, but I had dealt with these darkeys before.

"That's all," I said.

"All right, then, boss," said Priscilla. "I'll do it. What you want me to do?"

The colored people generally gave the name "boss" to all white men, and I was pleased to see that Priscilla said boss to me much more frequently than to Rectus.

We had a talk with her about her duties, and each of us had a good deal to say. We made her understand—at least we hoped so—that she was to be on hand, every afternoon, to go with Corny, if necessary, whenever we went out on our trips to the African settlement; and, after giving her an idea of what we intended doing with the queen,—which interested her very much indeed, and seemed to set her on pins and needles to see the glories of the new reign,—we commissioned her to bring together about twenty sensible and intelligent Africans, so that we could talk to them, and engage them as subjects for the re-enthroned queen.

"What's ole Goliah Brown goin' to say 'bout dat?" said Priscilla.

"Who's he?" we asked.

"He's de Afrikin gubner. He rule 'em all."

"Oh!" said Rectus, "he's all right. We're going to make him prime minister."

I was not at all sure that he was all right, and proposed that Rectus and I should go to his house in the evening, when he was at home, and talk to him about it.

"Yes, and we'll all go and see the head governor to-morrow morning," said Corny.

We had our hands completely full of diplomatic business.

The meeting of the adherents was appointed for the next afternoon. We decided to have it on the Queen's Stair-way, which is a long flight of steps, cut in the solid limestone, and leading up out of a deep and shadowy ravine, where the people of the town many years ago cut out the calcareous material for their houses. There has been no stone cut here for a long time, and the walls of the ravine, which stand up as straight as the wall of a house, are darkened by age and a good deal covered up by vines. At the bottom, on each side of the pathway which runs through the ravine to the town, bushes and plants of various semi-tropical kinds grow thick and close. At the top of the flight of stairs are open fields and an old fort. Altogether, this was considered a quiet and suitable place for a meeting of a band of revolutionists. We could not have met in the silk-cotton tree, for we should have attracted too much attention, and, besides, the hotel-clerk would have routed us out.

CHAPTER XII.: RECTUS LOSES RANK.

After supper, Rectus and I went to see the African governor, Goliah Brown. He was a good-natured old colored man, who lived in a house a trifle better than most of those inhabited by his fellow-countrymen. The main room was of a fair size, and there was a centre-table, with some books on it.

When we saw this, we hesitated. Could we ask a man who owned books, and could probably read, to play second fiddle to a woman who could not speak the English language, and who for years, perhaps, had devoted the energies of her soul to the sale of pepper-pods?

However, the office of prime minister was no trifle, and many more distinguished and more learned men than Goliah Brown have been glad to get it. Besides this, we considered that blood is blood, and, in monarchical countries, a queen is a queen. This was a colony of a monarchy, and we would push forward the claims of Poqua-dilla the First. We called her "The First," because, although she may have had a good many ancestors of her name in Africa, she certainly started the line in the Bahamas.

Goliah proved himself a steady-going talker. He seemed pleased to have us call on him, and told us the whole story of the capture of himself and the rest of the Africans. We had heard pretty much all of it before, but, of course, we had to politely listen to it again.

When he finished, we asked a few questions about the queen, and finding that Goliah admitted her claims to royal blood, we told him what we proposed to do, and boldly asked him to take the position of prime minister in the African community.

At first, he did not understand, and we had to go over the thing two or three times before he saw into it. Then, it was evident that he could not see what business this was of ours, and we had to explain our motives, which was some trouble, because we had not quite straightened them out in our own minds.

Then he wanted to know which was the head person, a queen or a prime minister. We set forth the strict truth to him in this matter. We told him that although a queen in a well-regulated monarchy actually occupies the highest place, that the prime minister is the fellow who does the real governing. He thought this might all be so, but he did not like the idea of having any one, especially Jane Henderson, as he called her, in a position higher than his own. We did not say anything to him, then, about giving the queen her English name, because we supposed that he had been used to speak of her in that way, to white people, but we determined to refer to this when matters should be settled.

He was so set in his own opinion on this point of position, that we were afraid we should be obliged to give the thing up. He used very good arguments, too. He said that he had been elected to his present office by his fellow Africans; that he had held it a long time; that he didn't think the rest of his people wanted him to give it up, and he didn't think he wanted to give it up himself. A prime minister might be all very well, but he didn't know anything about it. He knew what it was to be governor, and was very well satisfied to leave things as they were.

This was dampening. Just as the old fellow thought he had settled the matter, a happy thought struck me: we might make the monarchy an independent arrangement. Perhaps Goliah would have no objection to that, provided we did not interfere with his governorship. If Poqua-dilla should be recognized as a queen, and crowned, and provided with an income sufficient to keep her out of any retail business, it was about all she could expect, at her time of life. She certainly would not care to do any governing. The few subjects that we should enlist would be more like courtiers than anything else.

I called Rectus to the door, and suggested this arrangement to him. He thought it would be better than nothing, and that it would be well to mention it.

We did this, and Goliah thought a while.

"Ef I lets her be call' queen," he said, "an' she jist stay at home an' min' her own business, an' don' run herse'f agin me, no way, how much you s'pose she able to gib fur dat?"

"'ALL RIGHT,' SAID GOLIAH, WITH A SMILE."

Rectus and I went again to the front door to consult, and when we came back, we said we thought she would be able to give a dollar.

"All right," said Goliah, with a smile. "She kin jist go ahead, and be queen. Only don' let her run herse'f ag'in me."

This suited us, and we paid the dollar, and came away.

"More cash!" said Rectus, as we walked home.

"Yes," said I, "but what troubles me is that queen's income. I don't see now where it's to come from, for old Goliah wont allow his people to be taxed for her, that's certain."

Rectus agreed that things looked a little bluish, but he thought we might pay the income ourselves, until after the coronation, and then we could see what else could be done. This wasn't much of a plan, but I couldn't think of anything better.

The next day, about noon, we all went to see the real governor of the colony. Rectus and I didn't care much about doing this, but Corny insisted on it. She was afraid of the police,—and probably of the army and navy, although she made light of them,—and so she thought it would be a good thing to see whether or not we should have to combat with all these forces, if we should carry out our plans. We took Priscilla along with us on Corny's account. It would look respectable for her to have an attendant. This being an extra job, Priscilla earned two sixpences that day.

The governor lived in a fine house, on the hill back of the town, and although we all knew where it was, Priscilla was of great use to us here, for she took us in at a side gate, where we could walk right up to the door of the governor's office, without going to the grand entrance, at the front of the house, where the English flag was flying. There was a red-coated soldier standing just in the door-way, and when we saw him, we put ourselves on our stiffest behavior. We told Priscilla to wait outside, in the path, and try and behave so that people would think there was a pretty high-toned party inside. We then went up to the red-coat, and asked to see the governor. The soldier looked at us a little queerly, and went back into the house.

He staid a good while, but when he came out he told us to follow him, and took us through a hall into a room where two gentlemen were sitting at desks. One of these jumped up and came to meet us.

"There is the secretary," said the soldier, in a low voice to me, and then he left us.

We now had to ask the secretary if we could see the governor. He inquired our business, but we didn't seem anxious to tell him.

"Anything private?" he said, with a smile.

"Well, sir," said I, "it's not exactly private, but it's not a very easy thing to put straight before anybody, and if it don't make any difference, we'd rather not have to tell it twice."

He hesitated for a minute, and then he said he'd see, and went into another room.

"Now, look here," I whispered to Rectus, "if you're captain, you've got to step up and do the talking. It isn't my place."

The secretary now returned, and said the governor could give us a few minutes. I think the probability was that he was curious to know what two boys and a girl could want with him.

The governor's office, into which we now were shown, was a large room, with plenty of book-cases and shelves against the walls, and in the middle of the floor a big table, which was covered with papers, packages of manuscript tied up with tape, and every kind of thing necessary to make matters look as if business was brisk in these islands. The governor himself was a tall, handsome gentleman, not old a bit, as Corny put it afterward, and dressed all in white linen, which gave him an air of coolness and cleanness that was quite agreeable to us after our walk in the sun. He was sitting at one end of the long table, and he politely motioned us to seats at one side of him. I expect the secretary arranged the chairs before we came in. We made our manners and sat down.

"Well," said he, "what can I do for you?"

If Corny hadn't been along, I don't believe he would have seen us at all. There can be nothing attractive to a governor about two boys. But almost any one would take an interest in a girl like Corny. The secretary was very polite to her.

Rectus now gave his throat a clearing, and pushed off.

"Our business with you, sir, is to see about doing something for a poor queen, a very good and honest woman——"

"A poor but honest queen!" interrupted the governor, with a smile.

"Oh, he don't mean a common queen," said Corny, quickly. "He means a black queen,—an African,—born royal, but taken prisoner when young, and brought here, and she lives over there in the African settlements, and sells peppers, but is just as much a queen as ever, you know, sir, for selling things on a door-step can't take the royal blood out of a person."

"Oh no, indeed!" said the governor, and he looked very much tickled.

"And this poor woman is old, now, and has no revenue, and has to get along as well as she can, which is pretty poorly, I know, and nobody ever treats her any better than if she had been born a common person, and we want to give her a chance of having as many of her rights as she can before she dies."

"At any rate," said Rectus, who had been waiting for a chance to make a fresh start, "if we can't give her all her royal rights, we want to let her know how it feels to be a queen, and to give her a little show among her people."

"You are talking of an old native African woman?" said the governor, looking at Corny. "I have heard of her. It seems to be generally agreed that she belonged to a royal family in one of the African tribes. And you want to restore her to her regal station?"

"We can't do that, of course," said Corny; "but we do think she's been shamefully used, and all we want to do is to have her acknowledged by her people. She needn't do any ruling. We'll fix her up so that she'll look enough like a queen for those dreadfully poor people."

"Yes," put in Rectus, who had been getting warm on the subject, "they are dreadfully poor, but she's the poorest of the lot, and it's a shame to see how she, a regular queen, has to live, while a governor, who wasn't anybody before he got his place, lives in the best house, with tables and books, and everything he wants, for all I know, and a big flag in front of his door, as if he was somebody great, and———"

"What?" said the governor, pretty quick and sharp, and turning around square on Rectus.

"Oh, he don't mean you!" said Corny. "He's talking about the black governor, Goliah Brown."

"Ah, indeed!" said he, turning away from Rectus as if he didn't like his looks. "And what does Brown think of all this?"

I thought I'd better say a word or two now, because I didn't know where Rectus would fetch us up next, if we should give him another chance, and so I said to the governor that I knew Goliah Brown would make no objections to the plan, because we had talked it over with him, and he had agreed to it.

"Well, then, what do you want that I should do for you?" said the governor to Corny.

"Oh, nothing sir," said she, "but just to make it all safe for us. We didn't know exactly what the rules were on this island, and so we thought we'd come and see you about it. We don't want the policemen, or the soldiers or sailors, or anybody, to get after us."

"There is no rule here against giving a queen her rights," said the governor, who seemed to be in a good humor as long as he talked to Corny, "and no one shall interfere with you, provided you do not commit any disorder, and I'm sure you will not do that."

"Oh, no!" said Corny; "we just intend to have a little coronation, and to ask the people to remember that she's a queen and not a pepper-pod woman; and if you could just give us a paper commission, and sign it, we should—at least I should—feel a good deal easier."

"You shall have it," said the governor, and he took some paper and a pen.

"It seems a little curious," said he to Corny, as he dipped his pen in the ink, "that I should serve a queen, and have a queen under me at the same time, doesn't it?"

"Kind o' sandwiched," remarked Rectus, who had a face like frozen brass.

The governor went on writing, and Corny and I looked at Rectus as if we would singe his hair.

"You are all from the States, I suppose," said the governor.

I said we were.

"What are your names?" he asked, looking at Corny first.

"Cornelia V. Chipperton," said Corny, and he wrote that down. Then he looked at me.

"William Taylor Gordon," said I. When the governor had put that on his paper, he just gave his head a little wag toward Rectus. He didn't look at him.

"My name is Samuel Colbert," said Rectus.

Corny turned short on him, with eyes wide open.

"Samuel!" she said, in a sort of theatre-whisper.

"Now, then," said the governor, "this paper will show that you have full permission to carry out your little plans, provided that you do nothing that may create any disorder. If the woman—your queen, I mean—has been in the habit of earning her own livelihood, don't make a pauper of her." And he gave us a general look as if the time had come to say good-bye. So we got up and thanked him, and he shook hands with us, Rectus and all, and we came away.

We found Priscilla sitting cross-legged on the grass outside, pitching pennies.

"That thar red-coat he want to sen' me off," said she, "but I tole him my missy and bosses was inside, and I boun' to wait fur 'em, or git turned off. So he le' me stay."

Corny, for a wonder, did not reprove Priscilla for giving the sentinel the idea that her employers hired penny-pitchers to follow them around, but she walked on in silence until we were out of the grounds. Then she turned to Rectus and said:

"I thought your name was Rectus!"

"It isn't," said he. "It's Samuel."

This was no sort of an answer to give Corny, and so I explained that Rectus was his school name; that he was younger than most of us, and that we used to call him Young Rectus; but that I had pretty much dropped the "young" since we had been travelling together. It didn't appear to be needed.

"But why did you call him Rectus, when his name's Samuel?" asked Corny.

"Well," said I, laughing, "it seemed to suit him."

This was all that was said about the matter, for Priscilla came up and said she must hurry home, and that she'd like to have her sixpence, and that changed the subject, for we were out of small money and could only make up eleven half-pence among us. But Priscilla agreed to trust us until evening for the other "hoppenny."

Corny didn't say much on the way home, and she looked as if she was doing some private thinking. I suppose, among other things, she thought that as I considered it all right to call Rectus Rectus, she might as well do it herself, for she said:

"Rectus, I don't think you're as good at talking as Will is. I move we have a new election for captain."

"All right," said Rectus; "I'm agreed."

You couldn't make that boy angry. We held a meeting just as we got to the hotel, and he and Corny both voted for me.

CHAPTER XIII.: THE CORONATION.

In the afternoon, we had our grand rally at the Queen's Stair-way. Corny couldn't come, because her mother said she must not be running around so much. So she staid at home and worked on the new flag for the coronation. We designed this flag among us. It had a black ground, with a yellow sun just rising out of the middle of it. It didn't cost much, and looked more like a yellow cog-wheel rolling in deep mud than anything else. But we thought it would do very well.

Rectus and I had barely reached the stairs, by the way of the old fort, when Priscilla made her appearance in the ravine at the head of a crowd of whooping barefooted young rascals, who came skipping along as if they expected something to eat.

"I'd never be a queen," said Rectus, "if I had to have such a lot of subjects as that."

"Don't think you would," said I; "but we mustn't let 'em come up the stairs. They must stay at the bottom, so that we can harangue 'em." So we charged down the stairs, and made the adherents bunch themselves on the level ground.

Then we harangued them, and they laughed, and hurrahed, and whistled, and jumped, while Priscilla, as an active emissary, ran around among them, punching them, and trying to make them keep still and listen.

But as they all promised to stick to us and the royal queen through thick and thin, we didn't mind a little disorder.

The next day but one was to be coronation day, and we impressed it on the minds of the adherents that they must be sure to be on hand about ten in the morning, in front of the queen's hut. We concluded not to call it a palace until after the ceremony.

When we had said all we had to say, we told the assemblage that it might go home; but it didn't seem inclined to do anything of the kind.

"Look a here, boss," said one of them,—a stout, saucy fellow, with the biggest hat and the biggest feet on the island,—"aint you agoin' to give us nothin' for comin' round here?"

"Give you anything!" cried Rectus, blazing up suddenly. "That's a pretty way to talk! It's the subjects that have to give. You'll see pretty soon——"

Just here I stopped him. If he had gone on a few minutes longer, he would have wound up that kingdom with a snap.

"We didn't bring you here," said I, "to give you anything, for it ought to be enough pay to any decent fellow to see a good old person like Queen Poqua-dilla get her rights."

"Who's him?" asked several of the nearest fellows.

"He means Jane Henderson," said Priscilla. "You keep quiet."

"Jane Henderson! Dat's all right. Don' call her no names. Go ahead, boss!" they cried, laughing and shouting. I went ahead.

"We can't pay you any money; but if you will all promise again to be on hand before ten o'clock day after to-morrow, we'll take you down to the harbor now and give you a small dive."

A wild promise rang up the sides of the ravine.

A "small dive" is a ceremony somewhat peculiar to this island. A visitor—no native white man would ever think of such a thing—stands on the edge of a pier, or anywhere, where the water is quite deep, and tosses in a bit of money, while the darkey boys—who are sure to be all ready when a visitor is standing on a pier—dive for it. It's a lot of fun to see them do this, and Rectus and I had already chucked a good deal of small change into the harbor, and had seen it come up again, some of it before it got to the bottom. These dives are called "small," because the darkeys want to put the thing mildly. They couldn't coax anybody down to the water to give them a big dive.

"You see," said I to Rectus, as we started down the ravine toward the river, with the crowd of adherents marching in front, "we've got to have these fellows at the coronation. So it wont do to scare 'em off now."

We went down to a little public square in front of the town, where there was a splendid diving-place. A good many people were strolling about there, but I don't suppose that a single person who saw those darkey fellows, with nothing on but their cotton trousers,—who stood in a line on the edge of the sea-wall, and plunged in, head foremost, like a lot of frogs, when I threw out a couple of "big coppers,"—ever supposed that these rascals were diving for monarchical purposes. The water was so clear that we could see them down at the bottom, swimming and paddling around after the coppers. When a fellow found one he'd stick it in his mouth, and come up as lively as a cricket, and all ready for another scramble at the bottom.

Sometimes I threw in a silver "check," which is no bigger than a three-cent piece; but, although the water was about fifteen feet deep, it was never lost. The fellows seemed just as much at home in the water as on land, and I suppose they don't know how to get drowned. We tried to toss the money in such a way that each one of them would have something, but some of them were not smart enough to get down to the bottom in time; and when we thought we had circulated enough specie, we felt sure that there were two or three, and perhaps more, who hadn't brought up a penny.

So when they all climbed out, with their brown shoulders glistening, I asked which one of them had come out without getting anything. Every man-jack of them stepped forward and said he hadn't got a copper. We picked out three little fellows, gave them a few pennies apiece, and came home.

A SMALL DIVE

The next day we were all hard at work. Corny and her mother went down to the queen's house, and planned what they could get to fit up the place so that it would be a little more comfortable. Mrs. Chipperton must have added something to our eight dollars, for she and Corny came up into the town, and bought a lot of things, which made Poqua-dilla's best room look like another place. The rocking-chair was fixed up quite royally. Mrs. Chipperton turned out to be a better kind of a woman than I thought she was at first.

We hired a man to cut a pole and set it up in the queen's front yard, for the flag; and then Rectus and I started out to get the crown. I had thought that if we could find some sheet-brass, I could manage to make a pretty good crown, but there didn't seem to be anything of the kind in the place. But, after a good deal of looking, we found a brass saucepan, in a store, which I thought would do very well for the foundation of a crown. We bought this, and took it around to a shop where a man mended pots and kettles. For a shilling we hired the use of his tools for an hour, and then Rectus and I went to work. We unriveted the handle, and then I held the bottom edge of the saucepan to the grindstone, while Rectus turned, and we soon ground the bottom off. This left us a deep brass band, quite big enough for a crown, and as the top edge was rounded off, it could be turned over on a person's head, so as to sit quite comfortably. With a cold-chisel I cut long points in what would be the upper part of the crown, and when I had filed these up a little, the crown looked quite nobby. We finished it by punching a lot of holes in the front part, making them in the form of stars and circles. With something red behind these, the effect would be prodigious.

At ten o'clock, sharp, the next morning, we were all at the queen's house. Mrs. Chipperton was with us, for she wished very much to see the ceremony. I think Mr. Chipperton would have been along, but a gentleman took him out in his yacht that morning, and I must admit that we all breathed a little bit freer without him. There was a pretty fair crowd sitting around in the front yard when we reached the house, and before long a good many more people came to see what was going on. They were all negroes; but I don't believe half of them were genuine native Africans. The queen was sitting inside, with a red shawl on, although it was a pretty warm day, and wearing a new turban.

We had arranged, on the way, to appoint a lot of court officials, because there was no use of our being stingy in this respect, when it didn't cost anything to do up the thing right. So we picked out a good looking man for Lord High Chancellor, and gave him a piece of red ribbon to tie in his button-hole. He hadn't any button-hole anywhere, except in his trousers, so he tied it to the string which fastened his shirt together at the collar. Four old men we appointed to be courtiers, and made them button up their coats. For a wonder, they all had coats. We also made a Lord High Sheriff and a Royal Beadle, and an Usher of the White Wand, an officer Mrs. Chipperton had read about, and to whom we gave a whittled stick, with strict instructions not to jab anybody with it. Corny had been reading a German novel, and she wanted us to appoint a "Hof-rath," who is a German court officer of some kind. He was a nice fellow in the novel, and so we picked out the best-looking young darkey we could find, for the position.

We each had our posts. Corny was to do the crowning, and I was to make the speech. Rectus had his place by the flag, which he was to haul up at the proper moment. Mrs. Chipperton undertook to stand by the old lady,—that is, the queen,—and give her any support she might happen to need during the ceremony.

We intended having the coronation in the house; but we found the crowd too large for this, so we brought the rocking-chair out-of-doors, and set it in front of the only window in the palace. The yard was large enough to accommodate a good many people, and those who could not get in had plenty of room out in the road. We tried to make Poqua-dilla take off her turban, because a crown on a turban seemed to us something entirely out of order; but she wouldn't listen to it. We had the pleasant-faced neighbor-woman as an interpreter, and she said that it wasn't any use; the queen would almost as soon appear in public without her head as without her turban. So we let this pass, for we saw very plainly that it wouldn't do to try to force too much on Poqua-dilla, for she looked now as if she thought we had come there to perform some operation on her,—perhaps to cut off her leg.

About half-past ten, we led her out, and made her sit down in the rocking-chair. Mrs. Chipperton stood on one side of her, holding one of her hands, while the neighbor-woman stood on the other side, and held the other hand. This arrangement, however, did not last long, for Poqua-dilla soon jerked her hands away, thinking, perhaps, that if anything was done that hurt, it might be better to be free for a jump.

Corny stood in front, a little at one side, holding the crown, which she had padded and lined with red flannel. I took my place just before Mrs. Chipperton, facing the crowd. Rectus was at the flag-pole, near the front of the yard, holding the halyards in his hands, ready to haul. The Hof-rath was by him, to help if anything got tangled, and the four courtiers and the other officials had places in the front row of the spectators, while Priscilla stood by Corny, to be on hand should she be needed.

When all was ready, and Corny had felt in her pocket to see that the "permission paper" was all right, I began my speech. It was the second regular speech I had ever made,—the first one was at a school celebration,—and I had studied it out pretty carefully. It was intended, of course, for the negroes, but I really addressed the most of it to Mrs. Chipperton, because I knew that she could understand a speech better than any one else in the yard. When I had shown the matter up as plainly as I knew how, and had given all the whys and wherefores, I made a little stop for applause. But I didn't get any. They all stood waiting to see what would happen next. As there was nothing more to say, I nodded to Corny to clap on the crown. The moment she felt it on her head, the queen stood up as straight as a hoe-handle, and looked quickly from side to side. Then I called out in my best voice:

"Africans! Behold your queen!"

At this instant Rectus ran up the black flag with the yellow cog-wheel, and we white people gave a cheer. As soon as they got a cue, the darkeys knew what to do. They burst out into a wild yell, they waved their hats, they laid down on the grass and kicked, they jumped, and danced, and laughed, and screamed. I was afraid the queen would bolt, so I took a quiet hold of her shawl. But she stood still until the crowd cooled down a little, and then she made a courtesy and sat down.

"Is that all?" asked the neighbor-woman, after she had waited a few moments.

"Yes," said I. "You can take her in."

When the queen had been led within doors, and while the crowd was still in a state of wild commotion, I took a heavy bag of coppers from my coat-pocket—where it had been worrying me all through the ceremony—and gave it to Priscilla.

"Scatter that among the subjects," said I.

"Give 'em a big scrahmble in the road?" said she, her eyes crackling with delight.

"Yes," said I, and out she ran, followed by the whole kingdom. We white folk stood inside to watch the fun. Priscilla threw out a handful of pennies, and the darkeys just piled themselves up in the road on top of the money. You could see nothing but madly waving legs. The mass heaved and tossed and moved from one side of the road to the other. The Lord High Chancellor was at the bottom of the heap, while the Hof-rath wiggled his bare feet high in the air. Every fellow who grabbed a penny had ten fellows pulling at him. The women and small fry did not get into this mess, but they dodged around, and made snatches wherever they could get their hands into the pile of boys and men.

They all yelled, and shouted and tussled and scrambled, until Priscilla, who was dancing around with her bag, gave another throw into a different part of the road. Then every fellow jerked himself loose from the rest, and a fresh rush was made, and a fresh pile of darkeys arose in a minute.

We stood and laughed until our backs ached, but, as I happened to look around at the house, I saw the queen standing on her door-step looking mournfully at the fun. She was alone, for even her good neighbor had rushed out to see what she could pick up. I was glad to find that the new monarch, who still wore her crown,—which no one would have imagined to have ever been a saucepan,—had sense enough to keep out of such a scrimmage of the populace, and I went back and gave her a shilling. Her face shone, and I could see that she felt that she never could have grabbed that much.

When there had been three or four good scrambles, Priscilla ran up the road, a little way, and threw out all the pennies that were left in the bag. Then she made a rush for them, and, having a good start, she got there first, and had both hands full of dust and pennies before any one else reached the spot. She was not to be counted out of that game.

After this last scramble, we came away. The queen had taken her throne indoors, and we went in and shook hands with her, telling her we would soon come and see how she was getting along. I don't suppose she understood us, but it didn't matter. When we had gone some distance, we looked back, and there was still a pile of darkeys rolling and tumbling in the dust.

CHAPTER XIV.: A HOT CHASE.

That afternoon, Rectus and I went over to the African settlement to see how the kingdom worked. It was rather soon, perhaps, to make a call on the new queen, but we were out for a walk, and might as well go that way as any other.

When we came near the house, we heard a tremendous uproar, and soon saw that there was a big crowd in the yard. We couldn't imagine what was going on, unless the queen had changed her shilling, and was indulging in the luxury of giving a scramble. We ran up quickly, but the crowd was so large that we could not get into the yard, nor see what all the commotion was about. But we went over to the side of the yard, and—without being noticed by any of the people, who seemed too much interested to turn around—we soon found out what the matter was.

Priscilla had usurped the throne!

The rocking-chair had been brought out and placed again in front of the window, and there sat Priscilla, leaning back at her ease, with the crown on her head, a big fan—made of calf-skin—in her hand, and a general air of superiority pervading her whole being. Behind her, with her hand on the back of the chair, stood Poqua-dilla, wearing her new turban, but without the red shawl. She looked as if something had happened.

In front of the chair was the Lord High Chancellor. He had evidently gone over to the usurper. His red ribbon, very dusty and draggled, still hung from his shirt-collar. The four courtiers sat together on a bench, near the house, with their coats still buttoned up as high as circumstances would allow. They seemed sad and disappointed, and probably had been deprived of their rank. The Hof-rath stood in the front of the crowd. He did not appear happy; indeed, he seemed a good deal ruffled, both in mind and clothes. Perhaps he had defended his queen, and had been roughly handled.

Priscilla was talking, and fanning herself, gracefully and lazily, with her calf-skin fan. I think she had been telling the people what she intended to do, and what she intended them to do; but, almost immediately after our arrival, she was interrupted by the Hof-rath, who said something that we did not hear, but which put Priscilla into a wild passion.

She sprang to her feet and stood up in the chair, while poor Poqua-dilla held it firmly by the back so that it should not shake. I supposed from this that Priscilla had been standing up before, and that our old friend had been appointed to the office of chair-back-holder to the usurper.

Priscilla waved her fan high in air, and then, with her right hand, she took off the crown, held it up for a minute, and replaced it on her head.

"Afrikins, behole yer queen!" said she, at the top of her voice, and leaning back so far that the rightful sovereign had a good deal of trouble to keep the chair from going over.

"Dat's me!" she cried. "Look straight at me, an' ye see yer queen. An' how you dar', you misribble Hop-grog, to say I no queen! You 'serve to be killed. Take hole o' him, some uv you fellers! Grab dat Hop-grog!"

At this, two or three men seized the poor Hof-rath, while the crowd cheered and laughed.

"Take him an' kill him!" shouted Priscilla. "Chop his head off!"

At this, a wild shout of laughter arose, and one of the men who held the Hof-rath declared, as soon as he got his breath, that they couldn't do that,—they had no hatchet big enough.

Priscilla stood quiet for a minute. She looked over the crowd, and then she looked at the poor Hof-rath, who now began to show that he was a little frightened.

"You, Hop-grog," said she, "how much money did you grab in dem scrahmbles?"

The Hof-rath put his hand in his pocket and pulled out some pennies.

"Five big coppers," said he, sullenly.

"Gim me dem," said she, and he brought them to her.

"Now den, you kin git out," said she, pocketing the money. Then she again raised her crown and replaced it on her head.

"Afrikins, behole your queen!" she cried.

This was more than we could stand. To see this usurpation and robbery made our blood boil. We, by ourselves, could do nothing; but we could get help. We slipped away and ran down the road in the direction of the hotel. We had not gone far before we saw, coming along a cross-road, the two yellow-leg men. We turned, hurried up to them, and hastily told them of the condition of things, and asked if they would help us put down this usurpation. They did not understand the matter, at first, but when we made them see how it stood, they were greatly interested, and instantly offered to join us.

"We can go down here to the police-station," said I, "and get some help."

"No, no!" said the tall yellow-leg. "Don't tell those fellows. They'll only make a row of it, and get somebody into trouble. We're enough to capture that usurper. Let's go for her."

And we went.

When we neared the crowd, the shorter yellow-leg, Mr. Burgan, said that he would go first; then his friend would come close behind him, while Rectus and I could push up after them. By forming a line we could rush right through the crowd. I thought I ought to go first, but Mr. Burgan said he was the stoutest, and could better stand the pressure if the crowd stood firm.

But the crowd didn't stand firm. The moment we made our rush, and the people saw us, they scattered right and left, and we pushed right through, straight to the house. Priscilla saw us before we reached her, and, quick as lightning, she made a dive for the door. We rushed after her, but she got inside, and, hurling the crown from her head, dashed out of a back-door. We followed hotly, but she was out of the yard, over a wall, and into a side lane, almost before we knew it.

Then a good chase began. Priscilla had a long start of us, for we had bungled at the wall, but we were bound to catch her.

I was a good runner, and Rectus was light and active, although I am not sure that he could keep up the thing very long; but the two yellow-legs surprised me. They took the lead of us, directly, and kept it. Behind us came a lot of darkeys, not trying to catch Priscilla, but anxious, I suppose, to see what was going to happen.

Priscilla still kept well ahead. She had struck out of the lane into a road which led toward the outskirts of the town. I think we were beginning to gain on her when, all of a sudden, she sat down. With a shout, we rushed on, but before we reached her she had jerked off both her shoes,—she didn't wear any stockings,—and she sprang to her feet and was off again. Waving the shoes over her head, she jumped and leaped and bounded like an India-rubber goat. Priscilla, barefooted, couldn't be caught by any man on the island: we soon saw that. She flew down the road, with the white dust flying behind her, until she reached a big limestone quarry, where the calcareous building-material of the town is sawn out in great blocks, and there she made a sharp turn and dashed down in among the stones. We reached the place just in time to see her run across the quarry, slip in between two great blocks that were standing up like statue pedestals on the other side, and disappear.

We rushed over, we searched and looked, here and there and everywhere, and all the darkeys searched and looked, but we found no Priscilla. She had gone away.

Puffing and blowing like four steam-fire-engines, we sat down on some stones and wiped our faces.

"I guess we just ran that upstart queen out of her possessions," said the tall yellow-legs, dusting his boots with his handkerchief. He was satisfied.

We walked home by the road at the edge of the harbor. The cool air from the water was very pleasant to us. When we reached the hotel, we found Mr. and Mrs. Chipperton and Corny sitting outside, in the entrance court, waiting for supper-time. A lot of arm-chairs always stood there, so that people might sit and wait for meals, or anything else that they expected. When Corny heard the dreadful news of the fall of our kingdom, she was so shocked that she could scarcely speak; and as for Mrs. Chipperton, I thought she was going to cry. Corny wanted to rush right down to Poqua-dilla's house and see what could be done, but we were all against that. No harm would come to the old woman that night from the loss of her crown, and it was too near supper-time for any attempt at restoration, just then.

"Only to think of it!" said Mrs. Chipperton. "After all we did for her! I don't believe she was queen more than an hour. It's the shortest reign I ever heard of."

"And that Priscilla!" cried Corny. "The girl we trusted to do so much, and——"

"Paid every night," said I.

"Yes," she continued, "and gave a pair of mother's shoes to, for the coronation! And to think that she should deceive us and do the usurping!"

The shorter yellow-legs, who had been standing by with his friend, now made a remark. He evidently remembered Corny, on the Oclawaha steam-boat, although he had never become acquainted with her or her family.

"Did your queen talk French?" he asked, with a smile; "or was not that the language of the Court?"

"No, it wasn't," said Corny, gravely. "African was the language of the Court. But the queen was too polite to use it before us, because she knew we did not understand it, and couldn't tell what she might be saying about us."

"Good!" said the tall yellow-legs. "That's very good indeed. Burgan, you owe her one."

"One what?" asked Corny.

"Another answer as good as that, if I can ever think of it," said Mr. Burgan.

Corny did not reply. I doubt if she heard him. Her soul still ached for her fallen queen.

"I tell you what it is," said Mr. Chipperton, who had kept unaccountably quiet, so far. "It's a great pity that I did not know about this. I should have liked nothing better than to be down there when that usurper girl was standing on that throne, or rocking-chair, or whatever it was——"

"Oh, my dear!" said Mrs. Chipperton. "It would never have done for you to have exposed your lung to such a scene of turmoil and confusion."

"Bother my lung!" cried Mr. Chipperton, who was now growing quite excited. "I would never have stood tamely by, and witnessed such vile injustice——"

"We didn't stand tamely by," said I. "We ran wildly after the unjust one."

"I would have stood up before that crowd," continued Mr. Chipperton, "and I would have told the people what I thought of them. I would have asked them how, living in a land like this, where the blue sky shines on them for nothing, where cocoa-nut and the orange stand always ready for them to stretch forth their hands and take them, where they need but a minimum of clothes, and where the very sea around them freely yields up its fish and its conchs,—or, that is to say, they can get such things for a trifling sum,—I would have asked them, I say, how—when free citizens of a republic, such as we are, come from our shores of liberty, where kings and queens are despised and any throne that is attempted to be set up over us is crushed to atoms,—that when we, I say, come over here, and out of the pure kindness and generosity of our souls raise from the dust a poverty-stricken and down-trodden queen, and place her, as nearly as possible, on the throne of her ancestors, and put upon her head a crown,—a bauble which, in our own land, we trample under foot——"

At this I shuddered, remembering the sharp points I had filed in our crown.

"And grind into the dust," continued Mr. Chipperton,—"I would ask them, I say, how they could think of all this, and then deliberately subvert, at the behest of a young and giddy colored hireling, the structure we had upraised. And what could they have said to that, I would like to know?" he asked, looking around from one to another of us.

"Give us a small dive, boss?" suggested Rectus.

"That's so," said Mr. Chipperton, his face beaming into a broad smile; "I believe they would have said that very thing. You have hit it exactly. Let's go in to supper."

The next day, Rectus and I, with Corny and Mrs. Chipperton, walked down to the queen's house, to see how she fared and what could be done for her.

When we reached Poqua-dilla's hut, we saw her sitting on her door-step. By her side were several joints of sugar-cane, and close to them stood the crown, neatly filled with scarlet pepper-pods, which hung very prettily over the peaked points of brass. She was very still, and her head rested on her breast.

"Asleep!" whispered Corny.

"Yes," said Mrs. Chipperton, softly, "and don't let's waken her. She's very well off as she is, and now that her house is a little more comfortable, it would be well to leave her in peace, to peddle what she pleases on her door-step. Her crown will worry her less where it is than on her head."

Corny whispered to her mother, who nodded, and took out her pocket-book. In a moment, Corny, with some change in her hand, went quietly up to the yard and put the money in the queen's lap. Then we went away and left her, still asleep.

A day or two after this, the "Tigress" came in, bringing the mail. We saw her, from one of the upper porticoes, when she was just on the edge of the horizon, and we knew her by the way she stood up high in the water, and rolled her smoke-stack from side to side. She was the greatest roller that ever floated, I reckon, but a jolly good ship for all that; and we were glad enough to see her.

There were a lot of letters for us in her mail. I had nine from the boys at home, not to count those from the family.

We had just about finished reading our letters when Corny came up to us to the silk-cotton tree, where we were sitting, and said, in a doleful tone:

"We've got to go home."

"Home?" we cried out together. "When?"

"To-morrow," said Corny, "on the 'Tigress.'"

All our good news and pleasant letters counted for nothing now.

"How?—why?" said I. "Why do you have to go? Isn't this something new?"

Rectus looked as if he had lost his knife, and I'm sure I had never thought that I should care so much to hear that a girl—no relation—was going away the next day.

"Yes, it is something new," said Corny, who certainly had been crying, although we didn't notice it at first. "It's a horrid old lawsuit. Father just heard of it in a letter. There's one of his houses, in New York, that's next to a lot, and the man that owns the lot says father's house sticks over four inches on his lot, and he has sued him for that,—just think of it! four inches only! You couldn't do anything with four inches of dirt if you had it; and father didn't know it, and he isn't going to move his wall back, now that he does know it, for the people in the house would have to cut all their carpets, or fold them under, which is just as bad, and he says he must go right back to New York, and, of course, we've all got to go, too, which is the worst of it, and mother and I are just awfully put out."

"What's the good of his going," asked Rectus. "Can't he get a lawyer to attend to it all?"

"Oh, you couldn't keep him here now," said Corny. "He's just wild to be off. The man who sued him is a horrid person, and father says that if he don't go right back, the next thing he'll hear will be that old Colbert will be trying to get a foot instead of four inches."

"Old Colbert!" ejaculated Rectus, "I guess that must be my father."

If I had been Rectus, I don't think I should have been so quick to guess anything of that kind about my father; but perhaps he had heard things like that before. He took it as coolly as he generally took everything.

Corny was as red as a beet.

"Your father!" she exclaimed. "I don't believe it. I'll go this very minute and see."

Rectus was right. The stingy hankerer after what Corny called four inches of dirt was his father. Mr. Chipperton came up to us and talked about the matter, and it was all as plain as daylight. When he found that Mr. Colbert was the father of Rectus, Mr. Chipperton was very much surprised, and he called no more names, although I am sure he had been giving old Colbert a pretty disagreeable sort of a record. But he sat down by Rectus, and talked to him as if the boy were his own father instead of himself, and proved to him, by every law of property in English, Latin, or Sanscrit, that the four inches of ground were legally, lawfully, and without any manner of doubt, his own, and that it would have been utterly and absolutely impossible for him to have built his house one inch outside of his own land. I whispered to Rectus that the house might have swelled, but he didn't get a chance to put in the suggestion.

Rectus had to agree to all Mr. Chipperton said—or, at least, he couldn't differ with him,—for he didn't know anything on earth about the matter, and I guess he was glad enough when he got through. I'm sure I was. Rectus didn't say anything except that he was very sorry that the Chipperton family had to go home, and then he walked off to his room.

In about half an hour, when I went upstairs, I found Rectus had just finished a letter to his father.

"I guess that'll make it all right," he said, and he handed me the letter to read. It was a strictly business letter. No nonsense about the folks at home. He said that was the kind of business letter his father liked. It ran like this:

Dear Father: Mr. Chipperton has told me about your suing him. If he really has set his house over on four inches of your lot, I wish you would let it stand there. I don't care much for him, but he has a nice wife and a pleasant girl, and if you go on suing him the whole lot of them will leave here to-morrow, and they're about the only people I know, except Gordon. If you want to, you can take a foot off any one of my three lots, and that ought to make it all right.

      Your affectionate son,   Samuel Colbert.

"Have you three lots?" I asked, a good deal surprised, for I didn't know that Rectus was a property-owner.

"Yes," said he; "my grandmother left them to me."

"Are they right next to your father's lot, which Chipperton cut into?"

"No, they're nowhere near it," said Rectus.

I burst out laughing.

"That letter wont do any good," I said.

"You'll see," said Rectus, and he went off to mail it.

I don't know what kind of a business man Mr. Chipperton was, but when Rectus told him that he had written a letter to his father which would make the thing all right, he was perfectly satisfied; and the next day we all went out in a sail-boat to the coral-reef, and had a splendid time, and the "Tigress" went off without any Chippertons. I think Mr. Chipperton put the whole thing down as the result of his lecture to Rectus up in the silk-cotton tree.

CHAPTER XV.: A STRANGE THING HAPPENS TO ME.

For several days after our hot chase after Priscilla, we saw nothing of this ex-emissary. Indeed, we began to be afraid that something had happened to her. She was such a regular attendant at the hotel-door-market, that people were talking about missing her black face and her chattering tongue. But she turned up one morning as gay and skippy as ever, and we saw her leaning against the side of one of the door-ways of the court in her favorite easy attitude, with her head on one side and one foot crossed over the other, which made her look like a bronze figure such as they put under kerosene lamps. In one hand she had her big straw hat, and in the other a bunch of rose-buds. The moment she saw Corny she stepped up to her.

"Wont you buy some rose-buds, missy?" she said. "De puttiest rose-buds I ever brought you yit."

Corny looked at her with a withering glare, but Priscilla didn't wither a bit. She was a poor hand at withering.

"Please buy 'em, missy. I kep' 'em fur you. I been a-keepin' 'em all de mornin'."

"I don't see how you dare ask me to buy your flowers!" exclaimed Corny. "Go away! I never want to see you again. After all you did——"

"Please, missy, buy jist this one bunch. These is the puttiest red-rose buds in dis whole town. De red roses nearly all gone."

"Nearly all gone," said I. "What do you mean by telling such a fib?"—I was going to say "lie," which was nearer the truth (if that isn't a bull); but there were several ladies about, and Priscilla herself was a girl. "You know that there are red roses here all the year."

"Please, boss," said Priscilla, rolling her eyes at me like an innocent calf, "wont you buy dese roses fur missy? They's the puttiest roses I ever brought her yit."

"I guess you've got a calcareous conscience, haven't you?" said Rectus.

Priscilla looked at him, for a moment, as if she thought that he might want to buy something of that kind, but as she hadn't it to sell, she tried her flowers on him.

"Please, boss, wont you buy dese roses fur——"

"No," said Rectus, "I wont."

And we all turned and walked away. It was no use to blow her up. She wouldn't have minded it. But she lost three customers.

I said before that I was the only one in our party who liked fishing, and for that reason I didn't go often, for I don't care about taking trips of that kind by myself. But one day Mr. Burgan and the other yellow-legs told me that they were going to fish in Lake Killarney, a lovely little lake in the interior of the island, about five miles from the town, and that if I liked I might go along. I did like, and I went.

I should have been better pleased if they had gone there in a carriage; but this wouldn't have suited these two fellows, who had rigged themselves up in their buck-skin boots, and had all the tramping and fishing rigs that they used in the Adirondacks and other sporting places where they told me they had been. It was a long and a warm walk, and trying to find a good place for fishing, after we got to the lake, made the work harder yet. We didn't find any good place, and the few fish we caught didn't pay for the trouble of going there; but we walked all over a big pineapple plantation and had a splendid view from the highest hill on the whole island.

It was pretty late in the afternoon when we reached home, and I made up my mind that the next time I went so far to fish, in a semi-tropical country, I'd go with a party who wore suits that would do for riding.

Rectus and Corny and Mrs. Chipperton were up in the silk-cotton tree when I got home, and I went there and sat down. Mrs. Chipperton lent me her fan.

Corny and Rectus were looking over the "permission paper" which the English governor had given us.

"I guess this isn't any more use, now," said Corny, "as we've done all we can for kings and queens, but Rectus says that if you agree I can have it for my autograph book. I never had a governor's signature."

"Certainly, you can have it," I said. "And he's a different governor from the common run. None of your State governors, but a real British governor, like those old fellows they set over us in our colony-days."

"Indeed!" said Mrs. Chipperton, smiling. "You must be able to remember a long way back."

"Well, you needn't make fun of this governor," said Corny, "for he's a real nice man. We met him to-day, riding in the funniest carriage you ever saw in your life. It's like a big baby-carriage for twins, only it's pulled by a horse, and has a man in livery to drive it. The top's straw, and you get in in the middle, and sit both ways."

"Either way, my dear," said Mrs. Chipperton.

"Yes, either way," continued Corny. "Did you ever see a carriage like that?"

"I surely never did," said I.

"Well, he was in it, and some ladies, and they stopped and asked Rectus and I how we got along with our queen, and when I told them all about it, you ought to have heard them laugh, and the governor, he said, that Poqua-dilla shouldn't suffer after we went away, even if he had to get all his pepper-pods from her. Now, wasn't that good?"

I admitted that it was, but I thought to myself that a good supper and a bed would be better, for I was awfully tired and hungry. But I didn't say this.

I slept as sound as a rock that night, and it was pretty broad daylight when I woke up. I don't believe that I would have wakened then, but I wanted to turn over and couldn't, and that is enough to make any fellow wake up.

When I opened my eyes, I found myself in the worst fix I had ever been in in my life. I couldn't move my arms or my legs, for my arms were tied fast to my body, at the elbows and wrists, and my feet and my knees were tied together. I was lying flat on my back, but I could turn my head over to where Rectus' bed stood—it was a small one like mine—and he wasn't there. I sung out:

"Rectus!" and gave a big heave, which made the bed rattle. I was scared.

In a second, Rectus was standing by me. He had been sitting by the window. He was all dressed.

"Don't shout that way again," he said, in a low voice, "or I'll have to tie this handkerchief over your mouth," and he showed me a clean linen handkerchief all folded up, ready. "I wont put it so that it will stop your breathing," he said, as coolly as if this sort of thing was nothing unusual. "I'll leave your nose free."

"Let me up, you little rascal!" I cried. "Did you do this?"

At that he deliberately laid the handkerchief over my mouth and fastened it around my head. He was careful to leave my nose all right, but I was so mad that I could scarcely breathe. I knew by the way he acted that he had tied me, and I had never had such a trick played on me before. But it was no use to be mad. I couldn't do anything, though I tugged and twisted my very best. He had had a good chance to tie me up well, for I had slept so soundly. I was regularly bandaged.

He stood by me for a few minutes, watching to see if I needed any more fixing, but when he made up his mind that I was done up securely, he brought a chair and sat down by the side of the bed and began to talk to me. I never saw anything like the audacity of the boy.

"You needn't think it was mean to tie you, when you were so tired and sleepy, for I intended to do it this morning, any way, for you always sleep sound enough in the mornings to let a fellow tie you up as much as he pleases. And I suppose you'll say it was mean to tie you, any way, but you know well enough that it's no use for me to argue with you, for you wouldn't listen. But now you've got to listen, and I wont let you up till you promise never to call me Rectus again."

"The little rascal!" I thought to myself. I might have made some noise in spite of the handkerchief, but I thought it better not, for I didn't know what else he might pile on my mouth.

"It isn't my name, and I'm tired of it," he continued. "I didn't mind it at school, and I didn't mind it when we first started out together, but I've had enough of it now, and I've made up my mind that I'll make you promise never to call me by that name again."

I vowed to myself that I would call him Rectus until his hair was gray. I'd write letters to him wherever he lived, and direct them: "Rectus Colbert."

"I WOULDN'T LIKE IT MYSELF."

"There wasn't any other way to do it, and so I did it this way," he said. "I'm sorry, really, to have to tie you up so, because I wouldn't like it myself, and I wouldn't have put that handkerchief over your mouth if you had agreed to keep quiet, but I don't want anybody coming in here until you've promised."

"Promise!" I thought; "I'll never promise you that while the world rolls round."

"I know you can't say anything with that handkerchief over your mouth; but you don't have to speak. Your toes are loose. When you're ready to promise never to call me Rectus again, just wag your big toe, either one."

I stiffened my toes, as if my feet were cast in brass. Rectus moved his chair a little around, so that he could keep an eye on my toes. Then he looked at his watch, and said:

"It's seven o'clock now, and that's an hour from breakfast time. I don't want to keep you there any longer than I can help. You'd better wag your toe now, and be done with it. It's no use to wait."

"Wag?" I thought to myself. "Never!"

"I know what you're thinking," he went on. "You think that if you lie there long enough, you'll be all right, for when the chambermaid comes to do up the room, I must let her in, or else I'll have to say you're sick, and then the Chippertons will come up."

That was exactly what I was thinking.

"But that wont do you any good," said he, "I've thought of all that."

He was a curious boy. How such a thing as this should have come into his mind, I couldn't imagine. He must have read of something of the kind. But to think of his trying it on me! I ground my teeth.

He sat and watched me for some time longer. Once or twice he fixed the handkerchief over my mouth, for he seemed anxious that I should be as comfortable as possible. He was awfully kind, to be sure!

"It isn't right that anybody should have such a name sticking to them always," he said. "And if I'd thought you'd have stopped it, I wouldn't have done this. But I knew you. You would just have laughed and kept on."

The young scoundrel! Why didn't he try me?

"Yesterday, when the governor met us, Corny called me Rectus, and even he said that was a curious name, and he didn't remember that I gave it to him, when he wrote that paper for us."

Oh, ho! That was it, was it? Getting proud and meeting governors! Young prig!

Now Rectus was quiet a little longer, and then he got up.

"I didn't think you'd be so stubborn," he said, "but perhaps you know your own business best. I'm not going to keep you there until breakfast is ready, and people want to come in."

Then he went over to the window, and came back directly with a little black paint-pot, with a brush in it.

"Now," said he, "if you don't promise, in five minutes, to never call me Rectus again, I'm going to paint one-half of your face black. I got this paint yesterday from the cane-man, on purpose."

Oil-paint! I could smell it.

"Now, you may be sure I'm going to do it," he said.

Oh, I was sure! When he said he'd do a thing, I knew he'd do it. I had no doubts about that. He was great on sticking to his word.

He had put his watch on the table near by, and was stirring up the paint.

"You've only three minutes more," he said. "This stuff wont wash off in a hurry, and you'll have to stay up here by yourself, and wont need any tying. It's got stuff mixed with it to make it dry soon, so that you needn't lie there very long after I've painted you. You mustn't mind if I put my finger on your mouth when I take off the handkerchief; I'll be careful not to get any in your eyes or on your lips if you hold your head still. One minute more. Will you promise?"

What a dreadful minute! He turned and looked at my feet. I gave one big twist in my bandages. All held. I wagged my toe.

"Good!" said he. "I didn't want to paint you. But I would have done it, sure as shot, if you hadn't promised. Now I'll untie you. I can trust you to stick to your word,—I mean your wag," he said, with a grin.

It took him a long time to undo me. The young wretch had actually pinned long strips of muslin around me, and he had certainly made a good job of it, for they didn't hurt me at all, although they held me tight enough. He said, as he was working at me, that he had torn up two old shirts to make these bandages, and had sewed some of the strips together the afternoon before. He said he had heard of something like this being done at a school. A pretty school that must have been!

He unfastened my arms first,—that is, as soon as he had taken the handkerchief off my mouth,—and the moment he had taken the bandage from around my ankles, he put for the door. But I was ready. I sprang out of bed, made one jump over his bed, around which he had to go, and caught him just at the door.

He forgot that he should have left my ankles for me to untie for myself.

I guess the people in the next rooms must have thought there was something of a rumpus in our room when I caught him.

There was considerable coolness between Colbert and me after that. In fact, we didn't speak. I was not at all anxious to keep this thing up, for I was satisfied, and was perfectly willing to call it square; but for the first time since I had known him, Colbert was angry. I suppose every fellow, no matter how good-natured he may be, must have some sort of a limit to what he will stand, and Colbert seemed to have drawn his line at a good thrashing.

It wasn't hard for me to keep my promise to him, for I didn't call him anything; but I should have kept it all the same if we had been on the old terms.

Of course, Corny soon found out that there was something the matter between us two, and she set herself to find out what it was.

"What's the matter with you and Rectus?" she asked me the next day. I was standing in the carriage-way before the hotel, and she ran out to me.

"You mustn't call him Rectus," said I. "He doesn't like it."

"Well, then, I wont," said she. "But what is it all about? Did you quarrel about calling him that? I hate to see you both going about, and not speaking to each other."

I had no reason to conceal anything, and so I told her the whole affair, from the very beginning to the end.

"I don't wonder he's mad," said she, "if you thrashed him."

"Well, and oughtn't I to be mad after the way he treated me?" I asked.

"Yes," she said. "It makes me sick just to think of being tied up in that way,—and the black paint, too! But then you are so much bigger than he is, that it don't seem right for you to thrash him."

"That's one reason I did it," said I. "I didn't want to fight him as I should have fought a fellow of my own size. I wanted to punish him. Do you think that when a father wants to whip his son he ought to wait until he grows up as big as he is?"

"No," said Corny, very gravely. "Of course not. But Rectus isn't your son. What shall I call him? Samuel, or Sam? I don't like either of them, and I wont say Mr. Colbert. I think 'Rectus' is a great deal nicer."

"So do I," I said; "but that's his affair. To be sure, he isn't my son, but he's under my care, and if he wasn't, it would make no difference. I'd thrash any boy alive who played such a trick on me."

"Unless he was bigger than you are," said Corny.

"Well, then I'd get you to help me. You'd do it; wouldn't you, Corny?"

She laughed.

"I guess I couldn't help much, and I suppose you're both right to be angry at each other; but I'm awful sorry if things are going on this way. It didn't seem like the same place yesterday. Nobody did anything at all."

"I tell you what it is, Corny," said I. "You're not angry with either of us; are you?"

"No, indeed," said she, and her face warmed up and her eyes shone.

"That's one comfort," said I, and I gave her a good hand-shake.

It must have looked funny to see a boy and a girl shaking hands there in front of the hotel, and a young darkey took advantage of our good-humor, and, stealing out from a shady corner of the court, sold us seven little red and black liquorice-seed for fourpence,—the worst swindle that had been worked on us yet.

CHAPTER XVI.: MR. CHIPPERTON KEEPS PERFECTLY COOL.

It's of no use to deny the fact that Nassau was a pretty dull place, just about this time. At least Corny and I found it so, and I don't believe young Mr. Colbert was very happy, for he didn't look it. It's not to be supposed that our quarrel affected the negroes, or the sky, or the taste of bananas; but the darkeys didn't amuse me, and my recollection of those days is that they were cloudy, and that I wasn't a very good customer down in the market-house by the harbor, where we used to go and buy little fig-bananas, which they didn't have at the hotel, but which were mighty good to eat.

Colbert and I still kept up a frigid reserve toward each other. He thought, I suppose, that I ought to speak first, because I was the older, and I thought that he ought to speak first because he was the younger.

One evening, I went up into my room, having absolutely nothing else to do, and there I found Colbert, writing. I suppose he was writing a letter, but there was no need of doing this at night, as the mail would not go out for several days, and there would be plenty of time to write in the daytime. He hadn't done anything but lounge about for two or three days. Perhaps he came up here to write because he had nothing else to do.

There was only one table, and I couldn't write if I had wanted to, so I opened my trunk and began to put some of my things in order. We had arranged, before we had fallen out, that we should go home on the next steamer, and Mr. and Mrs. Chipperton were going too. We had been in Nassau nearly a month, and had seen about as much as was to be seen—in an ordinary way. As for me, I couldn't afford to stay any longer, and that had been the thing that had settled the matter, as far as Colbert and I were concerned. But now he might choose to stay, and come home by himself. However, there was no way of my knowing what he thought, and I supposed that I had no real right to make him come with me. At any rate, if I had, I didn't intend to exercise it.

While I was looking over the things in my trunk, I came across the box of dominoes that Corny had given us to remember her by. It seemed like a long time ago since we had been sitting together on the water-battery at St. Augustine! In a few minutes I took the box of dominoes in my hand and went over to Colbert. As I put them on the table he looked up.

"What do you say to a game of dominoes?" I said. "This is the box Corny gave us. We haven't used it yet."

"Very well," said he, and he pushed away his paper and emptied the dominoes out on the table. Then he picked up some of them, and looked at them as if they were made in some new kind of a way that he had never noticed before; and I picked up some, too, and examined them. Then we began to play. We did not talk very much, but we played as if it was necessary to be very careful to make no mistakes. I won the first game, and I could not help feeling a little sorry, while Colbert looked as if he felt rather glad. We played until about our ordinary bed-time, and then I said:

"Well, Colbert, I guess we might as well stop," and he said:

"Very well."

But he didn't get ready to go to bed. He went to the window and looked out for some time, and then he came back to the table and sat down. He took his pen and began to print on the lid of the domino-box, which was of smooth white wood. He could print names and titles of things very neatly, a good deal better than I could.

When he had finished, he got up and began to get ready for bed, leaving the box on the table. Pretty soon I went over to look at it, for I must admit I was rather curious to see what he had put on it. This was the inscription he had printed on the lid:

          _____ ST. AUGUSTINE, FLORIDA." CORNY. BY WILL AND RECTUS"GIVEN TO

There was a place left for the date, which I suppose he had forgotten. I made no remark about this inscription, for I did not know exactly what remark was needed; but the next morning I called him "Rectus," just the same as ever, for I knew he had printed our names on the box to show me that he wanted to let me off my promise. I guess the one time I called him Colbert was enough for him.

When we came down stairs to breakfast, talking to each other like common people, it was better than most shows to see Corny's face. She was standing at the front door, not far from the stairs, and it actually seemed as if a candle had been lighted inside of her. Her face shone.

I know I felt first-rate, and I think Rectus must have felt pretty much the same, for his tongue rattled away at a rate that wasn't exactly usual with him. There was no mistaking Corny's feelings.

After breakfast, when we all got together to talk over the plans of the day,—a thing we hadn't done for what seemed to me about a week,—we found out—or rather remembered—that there were a lot of things in Nassau that we hadn't seen yet, and that we wouldn't miss for anything. We had been wasting time terribly lately, and the weather was now rather better for going about than it had been since we came to the place.

We agreed to go to Fort Charlotte that morning, and see the subterranean rooms and passage-ways, and all the underground dreariness of which we had heard so much. The fort was built about a hundred years ago, and has no soldiers in it. To go around and look at the old forts in this part of the world might make a person believe the millennium had come. They seem just about as good as ever they were, but they're all on a peace-footing. Rectus said they were played out, but I'd rather take my chances in Fort Charlotte, during a bombardment, than in some of the new-style forts that I have seen in the North. It is almost altogether underground, in the solid calcareous, and what could any fellow want better than that? The cannon-balls and bombs would have to plow up about an acre of pretty solid rock, and plow it deep, too, before they would begin to scratch the roof of the real strongholds of this fort. At least, that's the way I looked at it.

We made up a party and walked over. It's at the western end of the town, and about a mile from the hotel. Mr. and Mrs. Chipperton were with us, and a lady from Chicago, and Mr. Burgan. The other yellow-legs went out riding with his wife, but I think he wanted to go with us. The fort is on the top of a hill, and a colored shoemaker is in command. He sits and cobbles all day, except when visitors come, and then he shows them around. He lighted a lamp and took us down into the dark, quiet rooms and cells, that were cut out of the solid rock, down deep into the hill, and it was almost like being in a coal-mine, only it was a great deal cleaner and not so deep. But it seemed just as much out of the world. In some of the rooms there were bats hanging to the ceilings. We didn't disturb them. One of the rooms was called the governor's room. There wasn't any governor there, of course, but it had been made by the jolly old earl who had the place cut out,—and who was governor here at the time,—as a place where he might retire when he wanted to be private. It was the most private apartment I ever saw. This earl was the same old Dunmore we used to study about in our histories. He came over here when the Revolution threw him out of business in our country. He had some good ideas about chiselling rock.

This part of the fort was so extremely subterranean and solemn that it wasn't long before Mrs. Chipperton had enough of it, and we came up. It was fine to get out into the open air, and see the blue sky and the bright, sparkling water of the harbor just below us, and the islands beyond, and still beyond them the blue ocean, with everything so bright and cheerful in the sunlight. If I had been governor of this place, I should have had my private room on top of the fort, although, of course, that wouldn't do so well in times of bombardment.

But the general-in-chief did not let us off yet. He said he'd show us the most wonderful thing in the whole place, and then he took us out-of-doors again, and led us to a little shed or enclosed door-way just outside of the main part of the fort, but inside of the fortifications, where he had his bench and tools. He moved away the bench, and then we saw that it stood on a wooden trap-door. He took hold of a ring, and lifted up this door, and there was a round hole about as big as the hind wheel of a carriage. It was like a well, and was as dark as pitch. When we held the lamp over it, however, we could see that there were winding steps leading down into it. These steps were cut out of the rock, as was the hole and the pillar around which the steps wound. It was all one piece. The general took his lamp and went down ahead, and we all followed, one by one. Those who were most afraid and went last had the worst of it, for the lamp wasn't a calcium light by any means, and their end of the line was a good deal in the dark. But we all got to the bottom of the well at last, and there we found a long, narrow passage leading under the very foundation or bottom floor of the whole place, and then it led outside of the fort under the moat, which was dry now, but which used to be full of water, and so, on and on, in black darkness, to a place in the side of the hill, or somewhere, where there had been a lookout. Whether there were any passages opening into this or not, I don't know, for it was dark in spite of the lamp, and we all had to walk in single file, so there wasn't much chance for exploring sidewise. When we got to the end, we were glad enough to turn around and come back. It was a good thing to see such a place, but there was a feeling that if the walls should cave in a little, or a big rock should fall from the top of the passage, we should all be hermetically canned in very close quarters. When we came out, we gave the shoemaker commander some money, and came away.

"Isn't it nice," said Corny, "that he isn't a queen, to be taken care of, and we can just pay him and come away, and not have to think of him any more?"

We agreed to that, but I said I thought we ought to go and take one more look at our old queen before we left. Mrs. Chipperton, who was a really sensible woman when she had a chance, objected to this, because, she said, it would be better to let the old woman alone now. We couldn't do anything for her after we left, and it would be better to let her depend on her own exertions, now that she had got started again on that track. I didn't think that the word exertion was a very good one in Poqua-dilla's case, but I didn't argue the matter. I thought that if some of us dropped around there before we left, and gave her a couple of shillings, it would not interfere much with her mercantile success in the future.

I thought this, but Corny spoke it right out—at least, what she said amounted to pretty much the same thing.

"Well," said her mother, "we might go around there once more, especially as your father has never seen the queen at all. Mr. Chipperton, would you like to see the African queen?"

Mr. Chipperton did not answer, and his wife turned around quickly. She had been walking ahead with the Chicago lady.

"Why, where is he?" she exclaimed. We all stopped and looked about, but couldn't see him. He wasn't there. We were part way down the hill, but not far from the fort, and we stopped and looked back, and then Corny called him. I said that I would run back for him, as he had probably stopped to talk with the shoemaker. Rectus and I both ran back, and Corny came with us. The shoemaker had put his bench in its place over the trap-door, and was again at work. But Mr. Chipperton was not talking to him.

"I'll tell you what I believe,"—said Corny, gasping.

But it was of no use to wait to hear what she believed. I believed it myself.

"Hello!" I cried to the shoemaker before I reached him. "Did a gentleman stay behind here?"

"I didn't see none," said the man, looking up in surprise, as we charged on him.

"Then," I cried, "he's shut down in that well! Jump up and open the door!"

The shoemaker did jump up, and we helped him move the bench, and had the trap-door open in no time. By this, the rest of the party had come back, and when Mrs. Chipperton saw the well open and no Mr. Chipperton about, she turned as white as a sheet. We could hardly wait for the man to light his lamp, and as soon as he started down the winding stairs, Rectus and I followed him. I called back to Mrs. Chipperton and the others that they need not come; we would be back in a minute and let them know. But it was of no use; they all came. We hurried on after the man with the light, and passed straight ahead through the narrow passage to the very end of it.

There stood Mr. Chipperton, holding a lighted match, which he had just struck. He was looking at something on the wall. As we ran in, he turned and smiled, and was just going to say something, when Corny threw herself into his arms, and his wife, squeezing by, took him around his neck so suddenly that his hat flew off and bumped on the floor, like an empty tin can. He always wore a high silk hat. He made a grab for his hat, and the match burned his fingers.

"Aouch!" he exclaimed, as he dropped the match. "What's the matter?"

"Oh, my dear!" exclaimed his wife. "How dreadful to leave you here! Shut up alone in this awful place! But to think we have found you!"

"No trouble about that, I should say," remarked Mr. Chipperton, going over to the other side of the den after his hat. "You haven't been gone ten minutes, and it's a pretty straight road back here."

"But how did it happen?" "Why did you stay?" "Weren't you frightened?" "Did you stay on purpose?" we all asked him at pretty much one and the same time.

"I did stay on purpose," said he; "but I did not expect to stay but a minute, and had no idea you would go and leave me. I stopped to see what in the name of common sense this place was made for. I tried my best to make some sort of an observation out of this long, narrow loop-hole, but found I could see nothing of importance whatever, and so I made up my mind it was money thrown away to cut out such a place as this to so little purpose. When I had entirely made up my mind, I found, on turning around, that you had gone, and although I called I received no answer.

"Then I knew I was alone in this place. But I was perfectly composed. No agitation, no tremor of the nerves. Absolute self-control. The moment I found myself deserted, I knew exactly what to do. I did precisely the same thing that I would have done had I been left alone in the Mammoth Cave, or the Cave of Fingal, or any place of the kind.

"I stood perfectly still!

"If you will always remember to do that," and he looked as well as he could from one to another of us, "you need never be frightened, no matter how dark and lonely a cavern you may be left in. Strive to reflect that you will soon be missed, and that your friends will naturally come back to the place where they saw you last. Stay there! Keep that important duty in your mind. Stay just where you are! If you run about to try and find your way out, you will be lost. You will lose yourself, and no one can find you.

"Instances are not uncommon where persons have been left behind in the Mammoth Cave of Kentucky, and who were not found by searching parties for a day or two, and they were almost invariably discovered in an insane condition. They rushed wildly about in the dark; got away from the ordinary paths of tourists; couldn't be found, and went crazy,—a very natural consequence. Now, nothing of the kind happened to me. I remained where I was, and here, you see, in less than ten minutes, I am rescued!"

And he looked around with a smile as pleasant as if he had just invented a new sewing-machine.

"But were you not frightened,—awe-struck in this dark and horrible place, alone?" inquired Mrs. Chipperton, holding on to his arm.

"No," said he. "It was not very dark just here. That slit let in a little light. That is all it is good for, though why light should be needed here, I cannot tell. And then I lighted matches and examined the wall. I might find some trace of some sensible intention on the part of the people who quarried this passage. But I could find nothing. What I might have found, had I moved about, I cannot say. I had a whole box of matches in my pocket. But I did not move."

"Well," said Mr. Burgan, "I think you'd better move now. I, for one, am convinced that this place is of no use to me, and I don't like it."

I think Mr. Burgan was a little out of temper.

We now started on our way out of the passage, Mrs. Chipperton holding tight to her husband, for fear, I suppose, that he might be inclined to stop again.

"I didn't think," said she, as she clambered up the dark and twisting steps, "that I should have this thing to do, so soon again. But no one can ever tell what strange things may happen to them, at any time."

"When father's along," added Corny.

This was all nuts to the shoemaker, for we gave him more money for his second trip down the well. I hope this didn't put the idea into his head of shutting people down below, and making their friends come after them, and pay extra.

"There are some things about Mr. Chipperton that I like," said Rectus, as we walked home together.

"Yes," said I, "some things."

"I like the cool way in which he takes bad fixes," continued Rectus, who had a fancy for doing things that way himself. "Don't you remember that time he struck on the sand-bank. He just sat there in the rain, waiting for the tide to rise, and made no fuss at all. And here, he kept just as cool and comfortable, down in that dungeon. He must have educated his mind a good deal to be able to do that."

"It may be very well to educate the mind to take things coolly," said I, "but I'd a great deal rather educate my mind not to get me into such fixes."

"I suppose that would be better," said Rectus, after thinking a minute.

And now we had but little time to see anything more in Nassau. In two days the "Tigris" would be due, and we were going away in her. So we found we should have to bounce around in a pretty lively way, if we wanted to be able to go home and say we had seen the place.

CHAPTER XVII.: WHAT BOY HAS DONE, BOY MAY DO.

There was one place that I wished, particularly, to visit before I left, and that was what the people in Nassau called the Coral-reef. There were lots of coral-reefs all about the islands, but this one was easily visited, and for this reason, I suppose, was chosen as a representative of its class. I had been there before, and had seen all the wonders of the reef through a water-glass,— which is a wooden box, with a pane of glass at one end and open at the other. You hold the glass end of this box just under the water, and put your face to the open end, and then you can see down under the water, exactly as if you were looking through the air. And on this coral-reef, where the water was not more than twelve or fourteen feet deep, there were lots of beautiful things to see. It was like a submarine garden. There was coral in every form and shape, and of different colors; there were sea-feathers, which stood up like waving purple trees, most of them a foot or two high, but some a good deal higher; there were sea-fans, purple and yellow, that spread themselves up from the curious bits of coral-rock on the bottom, and there were ever so many other things that grew like bushes and vines, and of all sorts of colors. Among all these you could see the fishes swimming about, as if they were in a great aquarium. Some of these fishes were very large, with handsome black bands across their backs, but the prettiest were some little fellows, no bigger than sardines, that swam in among the branches of the sea-feathers and fans. They were colored bright blue, and yellow and red; some of them with two or three colors apiece. Rectus called them "humming-fishes." They did remind me of humming-birds, although they didn't hum.

When I came here before, I was with a party of ladies and gentlemen. We went in a large sail-boat, and took several divers with us, to go down and bring up to us the curious things that we would select, as we looked through the water-glass. There wasn't anything peculiar about these divers. They wore linen breeches for diving dresses, and were the same kind of fellows as those who dived for pennies at the town.

Now, what I wanted to do, was to go to the coral-reef and dive down and get something for myself. It would be worth while to take home a sea-fan or something of that kind, and say you brought it up from the bottom of the sea yourself. Any one could get things that the divers had brought up. To be sure, the sea wasn't very deep here, but it had a bottom, all the same. I was not so good a swimmer as these darkeys, who ducked and dived as if they had been born in the water, but I could swim better than most fellows, and was particularly good at diving. So I determined, if I could get a chance, to go down after some of those things on the coral-reef.

I couldn't try this, before, because there were too many people along, but Rectus, who thought the idea was splendid, although he didn't intend to dive himself, agreed to hire a sail-boat with me, and go off to the reef, with only the darkey captain.

We started as early as we could get off, on the morning after we had been at Fort Charlotte. The captain of the yacht—they give themselves and their sail-boats big titles here—was a tall colored man, named Chris, and he took two big darkey boys with him, although we told him we didn't want any divers. But I suppose he thought we might change our minds. I didn't tell him I was going to dive. He might not have been willing to go in that case.

We had a nice sail up the harbor, between the large island upon which the town stands, and the smaller ones that separate the harbor from the ocean. After sailing about five miles, we turned out to sea between two islands, and pretty soon were anchored over the reef.

"Now, then, boss," said Captain Chris, "don't ye want these here boys to do some divin' for ye?"

"I told you I wouldn't want them," said I. "I'm going to dive, myself."

"You dive, boss!" cried all three of the darkeys at once, and the two boys began to laugh.

"Ye can't do that, boss," said the captain. "Ef ye aint used to this here kind o' divin', ye can't do nothin' at all, under this water. Ye better let the boys go for ye."

"No," said I, "I'm going myself," and I began to take off my clothes.

The colored fellows didn't like it much, for it seemed like taking their business away from them; but they couldn't help it, and so they just sat and waited to see how things would turn out.

"You'd better take a look through the glass, before you dive," said Rectus, "and choose what you're going to get."

"I'm not going to be particular," I replied. "I shall get whatever I can."

"The tide's pretty strong," said the captain. "You've got to calkelate fur that."

I was obliged for this information, which was generous on his part, considering the circumstances, and I dived from the bow, as far out as I could jump. Down I went, but I didn't reach the bottom, at all. My legs grazed against some branches and things, but the tide had me back to the boat in no time, and I came up near the stern, which I seized, and got on board.

Both the colored boys were grinning, and the captain said:

"Ye can't dive that-a-way, boss. You'll never git to the bottom, at all, that-a-way. You must go right down, ef you go at all."

I knew that, but I must admit I didn't care much to go all the way down when I made the first dive. Just as I jumped, I thought of the hard sharp things at the bottom, and I guess I was a little too careful not to dive into them.

But now I made a second dive, and I went down beautifully. I made a grab at the first thing my hand touched. It was a purple knob of coral. But it stuck tight to its mother-rock, and I was ready to go up before it was ready to come loose, and so I went up without it.

"'T aint easy to git them things," said the captain, and the two boys said:

"No indeed, boss, ye cahn't git them things dat-a-way."

I didn't say anything, but in a few minutes I made another dive. I determined to look around a little, this time, and seize something that I could break off or pull up. I found that I couldn't stay under water, like the darkeys could. That required practice, and perhaps more fishy lungs.

Down I went, and I came right down on a small sea-fan, which I grabbed instantly. That ought to give way easily. But as I seized it, I brought down my right foot into the middle of a big round sponge. I started, as if I had had an electric shock. The thing seemed colder and wetter than the water; it was slimy and sticky and horrid. I did not see what it was, and it felt as if some great sucker-fish, with a cold woolly mouth, was trying to swallow my foot. I let go of everything, and came right up, and drew myself, puffing and blowing, on board the boat.

How Captain Chris laughed! He had been watching me through the water-glass, and saw what had scared me.

"Why, boss!" said he, "sponges don't eat people! That was nice and sof' to tread on. A sight better than cuttin' yer foot on a piece o' coral."

That was all very well, but I'm sure Captain Chris jumped the first time he ever put his bare foot into a sponge under water.

"I s'pose ye're goin' to gib it up now, boss," said the captain.

"No, I'm not," I answered. "I haven't brought up anything yet. I'm going down again."

"You'd better not," said Rectus. "Three times is all that anybody ever tries to do anything. If at first you don't succeed, try, try again. One, two, three. You're not expected to try four times. And, besides, you're tired."

"I'll be rested in a minute," said I, "and then I'll try once more. I'm all right. You needn't worry."

But Rectus did worry. I must have looked frightened when I came up, and I believe he had caught the scare. Boys will do that. The captain tried to keep me from going in again, but I knew it was all nonsense to be frightened. I was going to bring up something from the bottom, if it was only a pebble.

So, after resting a little while, and getting my breath again, down I went. I was in for anything now, and the moment I reached the bottom, I swept my arm around and seized the first thing I touched. It was a pretty big thing, for it was a sea-feather over five feet high,—a regular tree. I gave a jerk at it, but it held fast. I wished, most earnestly, that I had taken hold of something smaller, but I didn't like to let go. I might get nothing else. I gave another jerk, but it was of no use. I felt that I couldn't hold my breath much longer, and must go up. I clutched the stem of the thing with both hands; I braced my feet against the bottom; I gave a tremendous tug and push, and up I came to the top, sea-feather and all!

With both my hands full I couldn't do much swimming, and the tide carried me astern of the boat before I knew it.

Rectus was the first to shout to me.

"Drop it, and strike out!" he yelled; but I didn't drop it. I took it in one hand and swam with the other. But the tide was strong, and I didn't make any headway. Indeed, I floated further away from the boat.

Directly, I heard a splash, and in a moment afterward, it seemed, the two darkey divers were swimming up to me.

"Drop dat," said one of them, "an' we'll take ye in."

"No, I wont," I spluttered, still striking out with my legs and one arm. "Take hold of this, and we can all go in together."

I thought that if one of them would help me with the sea-feather, which seemed awfully heavy, two of us could certainly swim to the boat with four legs and two arms between us.

But neither of them would do it. They wanted me to drop my prize, and then they'd take hold of me and take me in. We were disputing and puffing, and floating further and further away, when up came Captain Chris, swimming like a shark. He had jerked off his clothes and jumped in, when he saw what was going on. He just put one hand under my right arm, in which I held the sea-feather, and then we struck out together for the boat. It was like getting a tow from a tug-boat. We were alongside in no time. Captain Chris was the strongest and best swimmer I ever saw.

"WE STRUCK OUT TOGETHER FOR THE BOAT."

Rectus was leaning over, ready to help, and he caught me by the arm as I reached up for the side of the boat.

"No," said I, "take this," and he seized the sea-feather and pulled it in. Then the captain gave me a hoist, and I clambered on board.

The captain had some towels under the little forward deck, and I gave myself a good rub down and dressed. Then I went to look at my prize. No wonder it was heavy. It had a young rock, a foot long, fast to its root.

"You sp'iled one o' de puttiest things in that garden down there," said the captain. "I allus anchored near that tall feather, and all de vis'tors used to talk about it. I didn't think you'd bring it up when I seed you grab it. But you must 'a' give a powerful heave to come up with all that stone."

"I don't think you ought to have tried to do that," said Rectus, who looked as if he hadn't enjoyed himself. "I didn't know you were so obstinate."

"Well," said I, "the truth of the matter is that I am a fool, sometimes, and I might as well admit it. But now let's see what we've got on this stone."

There was a lot of curious things on the piece of rock which had come up with the sea-feather. There were small shells, of different shapes and colors, with the living creatures inside of them, and there were mosses, and sea-weed, and little sponges, and small sea-plants, tipped with red and yellow, and more things of the kind than I can remember. It was the handsomest and most interesting piece of coral-rock that I had seen yet.

As for the big purple sea-feather, it was a whopper, but too big for me to do anything with it. When we got home, Rectus showed it around to the Chippertons, and some of the people at the hotel, and told them that I dived down and brought it up, myself, but I couldn't take it away with me, for it was much too long to go in my trunk. So I gave it next day to Captain Chris, to sell, if he chose, but I believe he took it back and planted it again in the submarine garden, so that his passengers could see how tall a sea-feather could grow, when it tried. I chipped off a piece of the rock, however, to carry home as a memento. I was told that the things growing on it—I picked off all the shells—would make the clothes in my trunk smell badly, but I thought I'd risk it.

"After all," said Rectus, that night, "what was the good of it? That little piece of stone don't amount to anything, and you might have been drowned."

"I don't think I could have been drowned," said I, "for I should have dropped the old thing, and floated, if I had felt myself giving out. But the good of it was this: It showed me what a disagreeable sort of place a sea-garden is, when you go down into it to pick things."

"Which you wont do again, in a hurry, I reckon," said Rectus.

"You're right there, my boy," I answered.

The next day, the Chippertons and ourselves took a two-horse barouche, and rode to the "caves," some six or seven miles from the town. We had a long walk through the pineapple fields before we came to the biggest cave, and found it wasn't very much of a cave, after all, though there was a sort of a room, on one side, which looked like a church, with altar, pillars and arches. There was a little hole, on one side of this room, about three feet wide, which led, our negro guide said, to a great cave, which ran along about a mile, until it reached the sea. There was no knowing what skeletons, and treasures, and old half-decayed boxes of coins, hidden by pirates, and swords with jewels in the handles, and loose jewels, and silver plate, and other things we might have found in that cave, if we had only had a lantern or some candles to light us while we were wandering about in it. But we had no candles or lantern, and so did not become a pirate's heirs. It was Corny who was most anxious to go in. She had read about Blackbeard, and the other pirates who used to live on this island, and she felt sure that some of their treasures were to be found in that cave. If she had thought of it, she would have brought a candle.

The only treasures we got were some long things, like thin ropes, which hung from the roof to the floor of the cave we were in. This cave wasn't dark, because nearly all of one side of it was open. These ropes were roots or young trunks from banyan-trees, growing on the ground above, and which came through the cracks in the rocks, and stretched themselves down so as to root in the floor of the cave, and make a lot of underground trunks for the tree above. The banyan-tree is the most enterprising trunk-maker I ever heard of.

We pulled down a lot of these banyan ropes, some of them more than twenty feet long, to take away as curiosities. Corny thought it would be splendid to have a jumping-rope made of a banyan root, or rather trunklet. The banyans here are called wild fig-trees, which they really are, wherever they grow. There is a big one, not far from the town, which stands by itself, and has a lot of trunks coming down from the branches. It would take the conceit out of a hurricane, I think, if it tried to blow down a banyan-tree.

The next day was Sunday, and our party went to a negro church to hear a preacher who was quite celebrated as a colored orator. He preached a good sensible sermon, although he didn't meddle much with grammar. The people were poorly dressed, and some of the deacons were barefooted, but they were all very clean and neat, and they appeared to be just as religious as if they had all ridden in carriages to some Fifth Avenue church in New York.

CHAPTER XVIII.: I WAKE UP MR. CHIPPERTON.

About nine o'clock, on Monday morning, the "Tigris" came in. When we boarded her, which we did almost as soon as the stairs had been put down her side, we found that she would make a shorter stay than usual, and would go out that evening, at high tide. So there was no time to lose. After the letters had been delivered at the hotel, and we had read ours, we sent our trunks on board, and went around to finish up Nassau. We rowed over to Hog Island, opposite the town, to see, once more, the surf roll up against the high, jagged rocks; we ran down among the negro cottages and the negro cabins to get some fruit for the trip; and we rushed about to bid good-bye to some of our old friends—Poqua-dilla among them. Corny went with us, this time. Every darkey knew we were going away, and it was amazing to see how many of them came to bid us good-bye, and ask for some coppers.

After supper, we went on board the steamer, and about ten o'clock she cast loose, and as she slowly moved away, we heard the old familiar words:

"Give us a small dive, boss!"

They came from a crowd of darkey boys on the wharf. But, although the moon was shining brightly, we didn't think they could see coppers on the bottom that night. They might have found a shilling or a half-dollar, but we didn't try them.

There were a couple of English officers on board, from the barracks, and we thought that they were going to take a trip to the United States; but the purser told us that they had no idea of doing that themselves, but were trying to prevent one of the "red-coats," as the common soldiers were generally called, from leaving the island. He had been missed at the barracks, and it was supposed that he was stowed away somewhere on the vessel. The steamer had delayed starting for half an hour, so that search might be made for the deserter, but she couldn't wait any longer if she wanted to get over the bar that night, and so the lieutenants, or sergeants, or whatever they were, had to go along, and come back in the pilot-boat.

When we got outside we lay to, with the pilot-boat alongside of us, and the hold of the vessel was ransacked for the deserter. Corny openly declared that she hoped they wouldn't find him, and I'm sure I had a pretty strong feeling that way myself. But they did find him. He was pulled out from behind some barrels, in a dark place in the hold, and hurried up on deck. We saw him, as he was forced over the side of the vessel and almost dropped into the pilot-boat, which was rising and falling on the waves by the side of the ship. Then the officers scrambled down the side and jumped into the boat. The line was cast off, the negro oarsmen began to pull away, and the poor red-coat took his doleful journey back to Nassau. He must have felt pretty badly about it. I have no doubt that when he hid himself down there in that dark hold, just before the vessel started, he thought he had made a pretty sure thing of it, and that it would not be long before he would be a free man, and could go where he pleased and do what he pleased in the wide United States. But the case was very different now. I suppose it was wrong, of course, for him to desert, and probably he was a mean sort of a fellow to do it; but we were all very sorry to see him taken away. Corny thought that he was very likely a good man, who had been imposed upon, and that, therefore, it was right to run away. It was quite natural for a girl to think that.

The moment the pilot-boat left us, the "Tigris" started off in good earnest, and went steaming along on her course. And it was not long before we started off, also in good earnest, for our berths. We were a tired set.

The trip back was not so pleasant as our other little voyage, when we were coming to the Bahamas. The next day was cloudy, and the sea was rough and choppy. The air was mild enough for us to be on deck, but there was a high wind which made it uncomfortable. Rectus thought he could keep on his wide straw hat, but he soon found out his mistake, and had to get out his Scotch cap, which made him look like a very different fellow.

There were not very many passengers on board, as it was scarcely time for the majority of people to leave Nassau. They generally stay until April, I think. Besides our party of five, there were several gentlemen and ladies from the hotel; and as we knew them all tolerably well, we had a much more sociable time than when we came over. Still, for my part, I should have preferred fair weather, bright skies, and plenty of nautiluses and flying-fish.

The "yellow-legged" party remained at Nassau. I was a little sorry for this, too, as I liked the men pretty well, now that I knew them better. They certainly were good walkers.

Toward noon the wind began to blow harder, and the waves ran very high. The "Tigris" rolled from side to side as if she would go over, and some of the ladies were a good deal frightened; but she always came up again, all right, no matter how far over she dipped, and so in time they got used to it. I proved to Mrs. Chipperton that it would be impossible for the vessel to upset, as the great weight of ballast, freight, machinery, etc., in the lower part of her would always bring her deck up again, even if she rolled entirely over on her side, which, sometimes, she seemed as if she was going to do, but she always changed her mind just as we thought the thing was going to happen. The first mate told me that the reason we rolled so was because we had been obliged to take in all sail, and that the mainsail had steadied the vessel very much before the wind got so high. This was all very well, but I didn't care much to know why the thing was. There are some people who think a thing's all right, if they can only tell you the reason for it.

Before dark, we had to go below, for the captain said he didn't want any of us to roll overboard, and, besides, the spray from the high waves made the deck very wet and unpleasant. None of us liked it below. There was no place to sit but in the long saloon, where the dining-tables were, and after supper we all sat there and read. Mr. Chipperton had a lot of novels, and we each took one. But it wasn't much fun. I couldn't get interested in my story,—at least, not in the beginning of it. I think that people who want to use up time when they are travelling ought to take what Rectus called a "begun" novel along with them. He had got on pretty well in his book while he was in Nassau, and so just took it up now and went right along.

The lamps swung so far backward and forward above the table that we thought they would certainly spill the oil over us in one of their wild pitches; the settees by the table slid under us as the ship rolled, so that there was no comfort, and any one who tried to walk from one place to another had to hang on to whatever he could get hold of, or be tumbled up against the tables or the wall. Some folks got sea-sick and went to bed, but we tried to stick it out as long as we could.

The storm grew worse and worse. Sometimes a big wave would strike the side of the steamer, just behind us, with a tremendous shock. The ladies were always sure she had "struck something" when this happened; but when they found it was only water that she had struck, they were better satisfied. At last, things grew to be so bad that we thought we should have to go to bed and spend the night holding on to the handles at the back of our berths, when, all of a sudden, there was a great change. The rolling stopped, and the vessel seemed to be steaming along almost on an even keel. She pitched somewhat forward and aft,—that is, her bow and her stern went up and down by turns,—but we didn't mind that, as it was so very much better than the wild rolling that had been kept up so long.

"I wonder what this means?" said Mr. Chipperton, actually standing up without holding on to anything. "Can they have got into a current of smooth water?"

I didn't think this was possible, but I didn't stop to make any conjectures about it. Rectus and I ran up on the forward deck, to see how this agreeable change had come about. The moment we got outside, we found the wind blowing fearfully and the waves dashing as high as ever, but they were not plunging against our sides. We carefully worked our way along to the pilot-house, and looked in. The captain was inside, and when he saw us he opened the door and came out. He was going to his own room, just back of the pilot-house, and he told us to come with him.

He looked tired and wet, and he told us that the storm had grown so bad that he didn't think it would be right to keep on our course any longer. We were going to the north-west, and the storm was coming from the north-east, and the waves and the wind dashed fair against the side of the vessel, making her roll and careen so that it began to be unsafe. So he had put her around with her head to the wind, and now she took the storm on her bow, where she could stand it a great deal better. He put all this in a good deal of sea-language, but I tell it as I got the sense of it.

"Did you think she would go over, Captain?" asked Rectus.

"Oh no!" said he, "but something might have been carried away."

He was a very pleasant man, and talked a good deal to us.

"It's all very well to lie to, this way," he went on, "for the comfort and safety of the passengers and the ship, but I don't like it, for we're not keeping on to our port, which is what I want to be doing."

"Are we stopping here?" I asked.

"Pretty much," said the captain. "All that the engines are working for is just to keep her head to the wind."

I felt the greatest respect for the captain. Instead of telling us why the ship rolled, he just stopped her rolling. I liked that way of doing things. And I was sure that every one on board that I had talked to would be glad to have the vessel lie to, and make herself comfortable until the storm was over.

We did not stay very long with the captain, for he wanted to take a nap, and when we went out, we stood a little while by the railing, to see the storm. The wind nearly took our heads off, and the waves dashed right up over the bow of the ship, so that if any one had been out there, I suppose they would have been soaked in a few minutes, if not knocked down. But we saw two men at the wheel, in the pilot-house, steadily holding her head to the wind, and we felt that it was all right. So we ran below and reported, and then we all went to bed.

Although there was not much of the rolling that had been so unpleasant before, the vessel pitched and tossed enough to make our berths, especially mine, which was the upper one, rather shaky places to rest in; and I did not sleep very soundly. Sometime in the night, I was awakened by a sound of heavy and rapid footfalls on the deck above my head. I lay and listened for a moment, and felt glad that the deck was steady enough for them to walk on. There soon seemed to be a good deal more running, and as they began to drag things about, I thought that it would be a good idea to get up and find out what was going on. If it was anything extraordinary, I wanted to see it. Of course, I woke up Rectus, and we put on our clothes. There was now a good deal of noise on deck.

"Perhaps we have run into some vessel and sunk her," said Rectus, opening the door, with his coat over his arm. He was in an awful hurry to see.

"Hold up here!" I said. "Don't you go on deck in this storm without an overcoat. If there has been a collision, you can't do any good, and you needn't hurry so. Button up warm."

We both did that, and then we went up on deck. There was no one aft, just then, but we could see in the moonlight, which was pretty strong, although the sky was cloudy, that there was quite a crowd of men forward. We made our way in that direction as fast as we could, in the face of the wind, and when we reached the deck, just in front of the pilot-house, we looked down to the big hatchway, where the freight and baggage were lowered down into the hold, and there we saw what was the matter.

The ship was on fire!

The hatchway was not open, but smoke was coming up thick and fast all around it. A half-dozen men were around a donkey-engine that stood a little forward of the hatch, and others were pulling at hose. The captain was rushing here and there, giving orders. I did not hear anything he said. No one said anything to us. Rectus asked one of the men something, as he ran past him, but the man did not stop to answer.

But there is no need to ask any questions. There was the smoke coming up, thicker and blacker, from the edges of the hatch.

"Come!" said I, clutching Rectus by the arm. "Let's wake them up."

"Don't you think they can put it out?" he asked, as we ran back.

"Can't tell," I answered. "But we must get ready,—that's what we've got to do."

I am sure I did not know how we were to get ready, or what we were to do, but my main idea was that no time was to be lost in doing something. The first thing was to awaken our friends.

We found the steward in the saloon. There was only one lamp burning there, and the place looked dismal, but there was light enough to see that he was very pale.

"Don't you intend to wake up the people?" I said to him.

"What's the good?" he said. "They'll put it out."

"They may, and they mayn't," I answered, "and it wont hurt the passengers to be awake."

With this I hurried to the Chippertons' state-room—they had a double room in the centre of the vessel—and knocked loudly on the door. I saw the steward going to other doors, knocking at some and opening others and speaking to the people inside.

Mr. Chipperton jumped right up and opened the door. When he saw Rectus and me standing there, he must have seen in our faces that something was the matter, for he instantly asked:

"What is it? A wreck?"

I told him of the fire, and said that it might not be much, but that we thought we'd better waken him.

"That's right," he said; "we'll be with you directly. Keep perfectly cool. Remain just where you are. You'll see us all in five minutes," and he shut the door.

"'KEEP PERFECTLY COOL,' SAID MR. CHIPPERTON."

But I did not intend to stand there. A good many men were already rushing from their rooms and hurrying up the steep stairs that led from the rear of the saloon to the deck, and I could hear ladies calling out from their rooms as if they were hurrying to get ready to come out. The stewardess, a tall colored woman, was just going to one of these ladies, who had her head out of the door. I told Rectus to run up on deck, see how things were going on, and then to come back to the Chippertons' door. Then I ran to our room, jerked the cork life-preservers from under the pillows, and came out into the saloon with them. This seemed to frighten several persons, who saw me as I came from our room, and they rushed back for their life-preservers, generally getting into the wrong room, I think. I did not want to help to make a fuss and confusion, but I thought it would be a good deal better for us to get the life-preservers now, than to wait. If we didn't need them, no harm would be done. Some one had turned up several lamps in the saloon, so that we could see better. But no one stopped to look much. Everybody, ladies and all,—there were not many of these,—hurried on deck. The Chippertons were the last to make their appearance. Just as their door opened, Rectus ran up to me.

"It's worse than ever!" he said.

"Here!" said I, "take this life-preserver. Have you life-preservers in your room?" I asked, quickly, of Mr. Chipperton.

"All right," said he, "we have them on. Keep all together and come on deck,—and remember to be perfectly cool."

He went ahead with Mrs. Chipperton, and Rectus and I followed, one on each side of Corny. Neither she nor her mother had yet spoken to us; but while we were going up the stairs, Corny turned to me, as I came up behind her, and said:

"Is it a real fire?"

"Oh, yes," I answered; "but they may put it out."

CHAPTER XIX.: THE LIFE-RAFT.

When we came out on deck, we saw in a moment that the fire was thought to be a serious affair. Men were actually at work at the boats, which hung from their davits on each side of the deck, not far from the stern. They were getting them ready to be lowered. I must confess that this seemed frightful to me. Was there really need of it?

I left our party and ran forward for a moment, to see for myself how matters were going. People were hard at work. I could hear the pumps going, and there was a great deal of smoke, which was driven back by the wind. When I reached the pilot-house and looked down on the hatchway, I saw, not only smoke coming up, but every now and then a tongue of flame. The hatch was burning away at the edges. There must be a great fire under it, I thought.

Just then the captain came rushing up from below. I caught hold of him.

"Is there danger?" I said. "What's to be done?"

He stopped for a moment.

"We must all save ourselves," he said, hurriedly. "I am going to the passengers. We can't save the ship. She's all afire below." And then he ran on.

When I got back to our group, I told them what the captain had said, and we all instantly moved toward the boat nearest to us. Rectus told me to put on my life-preserver, and he helped me fasten it. I had forgotten that I had it under my arm. Most of the passengers were at our boat, but the captain took some of them over to the other side of the deck.

When our boat was ready, there was a great scramble and rush for it. Most of the ladies were to get into this boat, and some of the officers held back the men who were crowding forward. Among the others held back were Rectus and I, and as Corny was between us, she was pushed back, too. I do not know how the boat got to the water, nor when she started down. The vessel pitched and tossed; we could not see well, for the smoke came in thick puffs over us, and I did not know that the boat was really afloat until a wave lifted it up by the side of the vessel where we stood, and I heard Mr. Chipperton call for Corny. I could see him in the stern of the boat, which was full of people.

"Here she is!" I yelled.

"Here I am, father!" cried Corny, and she ran from us to the railing.

"RECTUS HELPED ME TO FASTEN THE LIFE-PRESERVER."

"Lower her down," said Mr. Chipperton, from below. He did not seem flurried at all, but I saw that no time was to be lost, for a man was trying to cut or untie a rope which still held the boat to the steamer. Then she would be off. There was a light line on the deck near me—I had caught my foot in it, a minute before. It was strong enough to hold Corny. I got hold of one end of it and tied it around her, under her arms. She had a great shawl, as well as a life-preserver, tied around her, and looked dreadfully bundled up.

She did not say a word, but let Rectus and me do as we chose, and we got her over the railing in no time. I braced myself against the seat that ran around the deck, and lowered. Rectus leaned over and directed, holding on to the line as well. I felt strong enough to hold two of her, with the rope running over the rail. I let her go down pretty fast, for I was afraid the boat would be off; but directly Rectus called to me to stop.

"The boat isn't under her," he cried. "They've pushed off. Haul up a little! A wave nearly took her, just then!"

With that, we hauled her up a little, and almost at the same moment I saw the boat rising on a wave. By that time, it was an oar's length from the ship.

"They say they can't pull back," shouted Mr. Chipperton. "Don't let her down any further."

"All right!" I roared back at him. "We'll bring her in another boat," and I began to pull up with all my might.

Rectus took hold of the rope with me, and we soon had Corny on deck. She ran to the stern and held out her arms to the boat.

"Oh, father!" she cried. "Wait for me!"

I saw Mr. Chipperton violently addressing the men in the boat, but they had put out their oars and were beginning to pull away. I knew they would not come back, especially as they knew, of course, that there were other boats on board. Then Mr. Chipperton stood up again, put his hands to his mouth, and shouted back to us:

"Bring her—right after us. If we get—parted—meet—at Savannah!"

He was certainly one of the coolest men in the world. To think—at such a time—of appointing a place to meet! And yet it was a good idea. I believe he expected the men in his boat to row directly to the Florida coast, where they would find quick dispatch to Savannah.

Poor Corny was disconsolate, and cried bitterly. I think I heard her mother call back to her, but I am not sure about it. There was so much to see and hear. And yet I had been so busy with what I had had to do that I had seen comparatively little of what was going on around me.

One thing, however, I had noticed, and it impressed me deeply even at the time. There was none of the wailing and screaming and praying that I had supposed was always to be seen and heard at such dreadful times as this. People seemed to know that there were certain things that they had to do if they wanted to save themselves, and they went right to work and did them. And the principal thing was to get off that ship without any loss of time. Of course, it was not pleasant to be in a small boat, pitching about on those great waves, but almost anywhere was a better place than a ship on fire. I heard a lady scream once or twice, but I don't think there was much of that sort of thing. However, there might have been more of it than I thought. I was driving away at my own business.

The moment I heard the last word from Mr. Chipperton, I rushed to the other side of the deck, dragging Corny along with me. But the boat was gone from there.

I could see them pulling away some distance from the ship. It was easy to see things now, for the fire was blazing up in front. I think the vessel had been put around, for she rolled a good deal, and the smoke was not coming back over us.

I untied the line from Corny, and stood for a moment looking about me. There seemed to be no one aft but us three. We had missed both boats. Mr. Chipperton had helped his wife into the boat, and had expected to turn round and take Corny. No doubt he had told the men to be perfectly cool, and not to hurry. And while we were shouting to him and lowering Corny, the other boat had put off.

There was a little crowd of men amidships, hard at work at something. We ran there. They were launching the life-raft. The captain was among them.

"Are there no more boats?" I shouted.

He turned his head.

"What! A girl left?" he cried. "No. The fire has cut off the other boats. We must all get on the raft. Stand by with the girl, and I'll see you safe."

The life-raft was a big affair that Rectus and I had often examined. It had two long, air-tight cylinders, of iron, I suppose, kept apart by a wide framework. On this framework, between the cylinders, canvas was stretched, and on this the passengers were to sit. Of course it would be impossible to sink a thing like this.

In a very short time, the raft was lifted to the side of the vessel and pushed overboard. It was bound to come right side up. And as soon as it was afloat, the men began to drop down on it. The captain had hold of a line that was fastened to it, and I think one of the mates had another line.

"Get down! Get down!" cried the captain to us.

I told Rectus to jump first, as the vessel rolled that way, and he landed all right, and stood up as well as he could to catch Corny. Over she went at the next roll, with a good send from me, and I came right after her. I heard the captain shout:

"All hands aboard the raft!" and then, in a minute, he jumped himself. Some of the men pushed her off with a pole. It was almost like floating right on the surface of the water, but I felt it was perfectly safe. Nothing could make those great cylinders sink. We floated away from the ship, and we were all glad enough of it, for the air was getting hot. The whole front part of the vessel was blazing away like a house on fire. I don't remember whether the engines were still working or not, but at any rate we drifted astern, and were soon at quite a little distance from the steamer.

It was safe enough, perhaps, on the raft, but it was not in the least comfortable. We were all crowded together, crouching on the canvas, and the water just swashed about us as if we were floating boards. We went up and down on the waves with a motion that wouldn't have been so bad had we not thought we might be shuffled off, if a big wave turned us over a little too much. But there were lots of things to hold on to, and we all stuck close together. We three were in the middle. The captain told us to get there. There is no way of telling how glad I was that the captain was with us. I was well satisfied, anyway, to be with the party on the raft. I might have liked it better in a boat, but I think most of the men in the boats were waiters, or stewards, or passengers—fellows who were in a hurry to get off. The officers and sailors who remained behind to do their best for the ship and the passengers were the men on the raft; and these I felt we could trust. I think there were ten of them, besides the captain, making fourteen of us in all.

There we all sat, while the ship blazed and crackled away, before us. She drifted faster than we did, and so got farther and farther away from us. The fire lighted up the sea for a good distance, and every time we rose on the top of a wave, some of us looked about to see if we could see anything of the other boats. But we saw nothing of them. Once I caught sight of a black spot on a high wave at quite a distance, which I thought might be a boat, but no one else saw it, and it was gone in an instant. The captain said it made no real difference to us whether we saw the other boats or not; they could not help us. All the help we had to expect was from some passing ship, which might see us, and pick us up. He was very encouraging, though, about this, for he said we were right in the track of vessels bound North, which all sought the Gulf Stream; and, besides, a burning ship at night would attract the attention of vessels at a great distance, and some of them would be sure to make for us.

"We'll see a sail in the morning," said he; "make up your minds to that. All we've got to do is to stick together on the raft, and we're almost sure to be picked up."

I think he said things like this to give courage to us three, but I don't believe we needed it, particularly. Rectus was very quiet, but I think that if he could have kept himself dry he would have been pretty well satisfied to float until daylight, for he had full faith in the captain, and was sure we should be picked up. I was pretty much of the same mind, but poor Corny was in a sad way. It was no comfort to her to tell her that we should be picked up, unless she could be assured that the same ship would pick up her father and mother. But we could say nothing positive about this, of course, although we did all that we could, in a general way, to make her feel that everything would turn out all right. She sat wrapped up in her shawl, and seldom said a word. But her eyes were wandering all over the waves, looking for a boat.

The ship was now quite a long way off, still burning, and lighting up the tops of the waves and the sky. Just before day-break, her light suddenly went out.

"She's gone down!" said the captain, and then he said no more for a long time. I felt very sorry for him. Even if he should be saved, he had lost his ship,—had seen it burn up and sink before his eyes. Such a thing must be pretty hard on a captain. Even I felt as if I had lost a friend. The old "Tigris" seemed so well known to us.

It was now more dismal than ever. It was darker; and although the burning ship could do us no good, we were sorry to have her leave us. Nobody said much, but we all began to feel pretty badly. Morning came slowly, and we were wet and cold, and getting stiff. Besides, we were all very thirsty, and I, for one, was hungry; but there was no good reason for that, for it was not yet breakfast-time. Fortunately, after a while, Corny went to sleep. We were very glad of it, though how she managed to sleep while the raft was rising and falling and sliding and sloshing from one wave to another, I can't tell. But she didn't have much holding on to do. We did that for her.

At last daylight came, and then we began to look about in good earnest. We saw a top-sail off on the horizon, but it was too far for our raft to be seen from it, and it might be coming our way or it might not. When we were down in the trough of the waves we could see nothing, and no one could have seen us. It was of no use to put up a signal, the captain said, until we saw a vessel near enough to see it.

We waited, and we waited, and waited, until it was well on in the morning, and still we saw no other sail. The one we had seen had disappeared entirely.

We all began to feel miserable now. We were weak and cold and wretched. There wasn't a thing to eat or drink on the raft. The fire had given no time to get anything. Some of the men began to grumble. It would have been better, they said, to have started off as soon as they found out the fire, and have had time to put something to eat and drink on the raft. It was all wasted time to try to save the ship. It did no good, after all. The captain said nothing to this. He knew that he had done his duty in trying to put out the fire, and he just kept his mouth shut, and looked out for a sail. There was one man with us—a red-faced, yellow-haired man—with a curly beard, and little gold rings in his ears. He looked more like a sailor than any other of the men, and Rectus and I always put him down for the sailor who had been longer at sea, and knew more about ships and sailing, than any other of the crew. But this man was the worst grumbler of the lot, now, and we altered our opinion about him.

Corny woke up every now and then, but she soon went to sleep again, when she found there was no boat or sail in sight. At least, I thought she went to sleep, but she might have been thinking and crying. She was so crouched up that we could not see whether she was awake or not.

CHAPTER XX.: THE RUSSIAN BARK.

We soon began to think the captain was mistaken in saying there would be lots of ships coming this way. But then, we couldn't see very far. Ships may have passed within a few miles of us, without our knowing anything about it. It was very different from being high up on a ship's deck, or in her rigging. Sometimes, though, we seemed high enough up, when we got on the top of a wave.

It was fully noon before we saw another sail. And when we saw this one for the second or third time (for we only caught a glimpse of it every now and then), a big man, who had been sitting on the edge of the raft, and hardly ever saying a word, sung out:

"I believe that's a Russian bark."

And after he had had two or three more sights at her, he said:

"Yes, I know she is."

"That's so," said the captain; "and she's bearing down on us."

Now, how in the world they knew what sort of a ship that was, and which way it was sailing, I couldn't tell for the life of me. To me it was a little squarish spot on the lower edge of the sky, and I have always thought that I could see well enough. But these sailors have eyes like spy-glasses.

Now, then, we were all alive, and began to get ready to put up a signal. Fortunately, the pole was on the raft,—I believe the captain had it fastened on, thinking we might want it,—and now all we had to do was to make a flag. We three got out our handkerchiefs, which were wet, but white enough yet, and the captain took out his. We tied them together by the corners, and made a long pennant of them. When we tied one end of this to the pole, it made quite a show. The wind soon dried it, after the pole was hoisted and held up, and then our flag fluttered finely.

The sun had now come out quite bright and warm, which was a good thing for us, for it dried us off somewhat, and made us more comfortable. The wind had also gone down a good deal. If it had not been for these two things, I don't know how we could have stood it. But the waves were still very high.

Every time we saw the ship, she seemed to look bigger and bigger, and we knew that the captain was right, and that she was making for us. But she was a long time coming. Even after she got so near that we could plainly see her hull and masts and sails, she did not seem to be sailing directly toward us. Indeed, sometimes I thought she didn't notice us. She would go far off one way, and then off the other way.

"Oh, why don't she come right to us?" cried Corny, beating her hands on her knees. "She isn't as near now as she was half an hour ago."

This was the first time that Corny had let herself out in this way, but I don't wonder she did it. The captain explained that the ship couldn't sail right to us, because the wind was not in the proper direction for that. She had to tack. If she had been a steamer, the case would have been different. We all sat and waited, and waved our flag.

She came nearer and nearer, and it was soon plain enough that she saw us. The captain told us that it was all right now—all we had to do was to keep up our courage, and we'd soon be on board the bark. But when the men who were holding the pole let it down, he told them to put it up again. He wanted to make sure they should see us.

At last, the bark came so near that we could see the people on board, but still she went past us. This was the hardest to bear of all, for she seemed so near. But when she tacked and came back, she sailed right down to us. We could see her all the time now, whether we were up or down.

"She'll take us this time," said the captain.

I supposed that when the ship came near us she would stop and lower a boat, but there seemed to be no intention of the kind. A group of men stood in her bow, and I saw that one of them held a round life-preserver in his hand,—it was one of the India-rubber kind, filled with air, and to it a line was attached. When the ship was just opposite to us, this man shouted something which I did not hear, and threw the life-preserver. It fell close to the raft. I thought, indeed, it was coming right into the midst of us. The red-faced man with the gold ear-rings was nearest to it. He made a grab at it, and missed it. On went the ship, and on went the life-preserver, skipping and dancing over the waves. They let out lots of line, but still the life-preserver was towed away.

A regular howl went up from our raft. I thought some of the men would jump into the sea and swim after the ship, which was now rapidly leaving us. We heard a shout from the vessel, but what it meant I did not know. On she went, and on, as if she was never coming back.

"She'll come back," said the captain. "She'll tack again."

But it was hard to believe him. I don't know whether he believed himself. Corny was wildly crying now, and Rectus was as white as a sheet. No one seemed to have any hope or self-control except the captain. Some of the men looked as if they did not care whether the ship ever came back or not.

"The sea is too high," said one of them. "She'd swamp a boat, if she'd put it out."

"Just you wait!" said the captain.

The bark sailed away so far that I shut my eyes. I could not look after her any more. Then, as we rose on the top of a wave, I heard a rumble of words among the men, and I looked out, and saw she was tacking. Before long, she was sailing straight back to us, and the most dreadful moments of my life were ended. I had really not believed that she would ever return to us.

Again she came plowing along before us, the same group on her bow; again the life-preserver was thrown, and this time the captain seized it.

In a moment the line was made fast to the raft. But there was no sudden tug. The men on the bark knew better than that. They let out some two or three hundred feet of line and lay to, with their sails fluttering in the wind.

Then they began to haul us in. I don't remember much more of what happened just about this time. It was all a daze of high black hull and tossing waves, and men overhead, and ropes coming down, and seeing Corny hauled up into the air. After a while, I was hauled up, and Rectus went before me. I was told afterward that some of the stoutest men could scarcely help themselves, they were so cramped and stiff, and had to be hoisted on board like sheep.

I know that when I put my feet on the deck, my knees were so stiff that I could not stand. Two women had Corny between them, and were carrying her below. I was so delighted to see that there were women on board. Rectus and I were carried below, too, and three or four rough looking fellows, who didn't speak a word that we could understand, set to work at us and took off our clothes, and rubbed us with warm stuff, and gave us some hot tea and gruel, and I don't know what else, and put us into hammocks, and stuffed blankets around us, and made me feel warmer, and happier, and more grateful and sleepy than I thought it was in me to feel. I expect Rectus felt the same. In about five minutes, I was fast asleep.

I don't know how long it was before I woke up. When I opened my eyes, I just lay and looked about me. I did not care for times and seasons. I knew I was all right. I wondered when they would come around again with gruel. I had an idea they lived on gruel in that ship, and I remembered that it was very good. After a while, a man did come around, and he looked into my hammock. I think from his cap that he was an officer,—probably a doctor. When he saw that I was awake, he said something to me. I had seen some Russian words in print, and the letters all seemed upside down, or lying sideways on the page. And that was about the way he spoke. But he went and got me a cup of tea, and some soup, and some bread, and I understood his food very well.

After a while, our captain came around to my hammock. He looked a great deal better than when I saw him last, and said he had had a good sleep. He told me that Corny was all right, and was sleeping again, and that the mate's wife had her in charge. Rectus was in a hammock near me, and I could hear him snore, as if he were perfectly happy. The captain said that these Russian people were just as kind as they could be; that the master of the bark, who could speak English, had put his vessel under his—our captain's—command, and told him to cruise around wherever he chose in search of the two boats.

"And did you find them?" I asked.

"No," said he. "We have been on the search now for twenty-four hours, and can see nothing of them. But I feel quite sure they have been picked up. They could row, and they could get further into the course of vessels than we were. We'll find them when we get ashore."

The captain was a hopeful man, but I could not feel as cheerfully as he spoke. All that I could say was: "Poor Corny!"

He did not answer me, but went away; and soon, in spite of all my doubts and fears, I fell asleep.

The next time I woke up, I got out of my hammock, and found I was pretty much all right. My clothes had been dried and ironed, I reckon, and were lying on a chest all ready for me. While Rectus and I were dressing, for he got up at the same time that I did, our captain came to us, and brought me a little package of greenbacks.

"The master of the bark gave me these," said the captain, "and said they were pinned in your watch-pocket. He has had them dried and pressed out for you."

There it was, all the money belonging to Rectus and myself, which, according to old Mr. Colbert's advice, I had carefully pinned in the watch-pocket of my trousers before leaving Nassau. I asked the captain if we should not pay something for our accommodations on this vessel, but he said we must not mention anything of the kind. The people on the ship would not listen to it. Even our watches seemed to have suffered no damage from the soaking they had had in our wet clothes.

As soon as we were ready, we went up on deck, and there we saw Corny. She was sitting by herself near the stern, and looked like a different kind of a girl from what she had been two or three days before. She seemed several years older.

"Do you really think the other boats were picked up?" she said, the moment she saw us.

Poor thing! She began to cry as soon as she began to speak. Of course, we sat down and talked to her, and said everything we could think of to reassure her. And in about half an hour she began to be much more cheerful, and to look as if the world might have something satisfactory in it after all.

Our captain and the master of the bark now came to us. The Russian master was a pleasant man, and talked pretty good English. I think he was glad to see us, but what we said in the way of thanks embarrassed him a good deal. I suppose he had never done much at rescuing people.

He and our captain both told us that they felt quite sure that the boats had either reached the Florida coast or been picked up; for we had cruised very thoroughly over the course they must have taken. We were a little north of Cape Canaveral when the "Tigris" took fire.

About sundown that day, we reached the mouth of the Savannah river and went on board a tug to go up to the city, while our bark would proceed on her voyage. There were fourteen grateful people who went down the side of that Russian bark to the little tug that we had signalled; and some of us, I know, were sorry we could not speak Russian, so we could tell our rescuers more plainly what we thought of them.

When we reached Savannah, we went directly to the hotel where Rectus and I had stopped on our former visit, and there we found ourselves the objects of great attention,—I don't mean we three particularly, but the captain and all of us. We brought the news of the burning of the "Tigris," and so we immediately knew that nothing had been heard of the two boats. Corny was taken in charge by some of the ladies in the hotel, and Rectus and I told the story of the burning and the raft twenty or thirty times. The news created a great sensation, and was telegraphed to all parts of the country. The United States government sent a revenue cutter from Charleston, and one from St. Augustine, to cruise along the coast, and endeavor to find some traces of the survivors, if there were any.

But two days passed and no news came. We thought Corny would go crazy.

"I know they're dead," she said. "If they were alive, anywhere, we'd hear from them."

But we would not admit that, and tried, in every way, to prove that the people in the boats might have landed somewhere where they could not communicate with us, or might have been picked up by a vessel which had carried them to South America, or Europe, or some other distant place.

"Well, why don't we go look for them, then, if there's any chance of their being on some desert island? It's dreadful to sit here and wait, and wait, and do nothing."

Now I began to see the good of being rich. Rectus came to me, soon after Corny had been talking about going to look for her father and mother, and he said:

"Look here, Will,"—he had begun to call me "Will," of late, probably because Corny called me so,—"I think it is too bad that we should just sit here and do nothing. I spoke to Mr. Parker about it, and he says, we can get a tug-boat, he thinks, and go out and do what looking we can. If it eases our minds, he says, there's no objection to it. So I'm going to telegraph to father to let me hire a tug-boat."

I thought this was a first-class idea, and we went to see Messrs. Parker and Darrell, who were merchants in the city, and the owners of the "Tigris." They had been very kind to us, and told us now that they did not suppose it would do any real good for us to go out in a tug-boat and search along the coast, but that if we thought it would help the poor girl to bear her trouble they were in favor of the plan. They were really afraid she would lose her reason if she did not do something.

Corny was now staying at Mr. Darrell's house. His wife, who was a tip-top lady, insisted that she should come there. When we went around to talk to Corny about making a search, she said that that was exactly what she wanted to do. If we would take her out to look for her father and mother, and we couldn't find them after we had looked all we could, she would come back, and ask nothing more.

Then we determined to go. We hadn't thought of taking Corny along, but Mr. Darrell and the others thought it would be best; and Mrs. Darrell said her own colored woman, named Celia, should go with her, and take care of her. I could not do anything but agree to things, but Rectus telegraphed to his father, and got authority to hire a tug; and Mr. Parker attended to the business himself; and the tug was to be ready early the next morning. We thought this was a long time to wait. But it couldn't be helped.

I forgot to say that Rectus and I had telegraphed home to our parents as soon as we reached Savannah, and had answers back, which were very long ones for telegrams. We had also written home. But we did not say anything to Corny about all this. It would have broken her heart if she had thought about any one writing to his father and mother, and hearing from them.

CHAPTER XXI.: THE TRIP OF THE TUG.

The tug-boat was a little thing, and not very clean; but she was strong and sea-worthy, we were told, and therefore we were satisfied. There was a small deck aft, on which Corny and Rectus and I sat, with Celia, the colored woman; and there were some dingy little sleeping-places, which were given up for our benefit. The captain of the tug was a white man, but all the rest, engineer, fireman and hands—there were five or six in all—were negroes.

We steamed down the Savannah River in pretty good style, but I was glad when we got out of it, for I was tired of that river. Our plan was to go down the coast and try to find tidings of the boats. They might have reached land at points where the revenue cutters would never have heard from them. When we got out to sea, the water was quite smooth, although there was a swell that rolled us a great deal. The captain said that if it had been rough he would not have come out at all. This sounded rather badly for us, because he might give up the search, if a little storm came on. And besides, if he was afraid of high waves in his tug, what chance could those boats have had?

Toward noon, we got into water that was quite smooth, and we could see land on the ocean side of us. I couldn't understand this, and went to ask the captain about it. He said it was all right, we were going to take the inside passage, which is formed by the islands that lie along nearly all the coast of Georgia. The strips of sea-water between these islands and the mainland make a smooth and convenient passage for the smaller vessels that sail or steam along this coast. Indeed, some quite good-sized steamers go this way, he said.

I objected, pretty strongly, to our taking this passage, because, I said, we could never hear anything of the boats while we were in here. But he was positive that if they had managed to land on the outside of any of these islands, we could hear of them better from the inside than from the ocean side. And besides, we could get along a great deal better inside. He seemed to think more of that than anything else.

We had a pretty dull time on that tug. There wasn't a great deal of talking, but there was lots of thinking, and not a very pleasant kind of thinking either. We stopped quite often and hailed small boats, and the captain talked to people whenever he had a chance, but he never heard anything about any boats having run ashore on any of the islands, or having come into the inside passage, between any of them. We met a few sailing vessels, and toward the close of the afternoon we met a big steamer, something like northern river steamers. The captain said she ran between the St. John's River and Savannah, and always took the inside passage as far as she could. He said this as if it showed him to be in the right in taking the same passage, but I couldn't see that it proved anything. We were on a different business.

About nine o'clock we went to bed, the captain promising to call us if anything turned up. But I couldn't sleep well—my bunk was too close and hot, and so I pretty soon got up and went up to the pilot-house, where I found the captain. He and one of the hands were hard at work putting the boat around.

"Hello!" said he. "I thought you were sound asleep."

"Hello!" said I. "What are you turning round for?"

It was bright starlight, and I could see that we were making a complete circuit in the smooth water.

"Well," said he, "we're going back."

"Back!" I cried. "What's the meaning of that? We haven't made half a search. I don't believe we've gone a hundred miles. We want to search the whole coast, I tell you, to the lower end of Florida."

"You can't do it in this boat," he said; "she's too small."

"Why didn't you say so when we took her?"

"Well, there wasn't any other, in the first place, and besides, it wouldn't be no good to go no further. It's more 'n four days, now, since them boats set out. There's no chance fur anybody on 'em to be livin'."

"That's not for you to decide," I said, and I was very angry. "We want to find our friends, dead or alive, or find some news of them, and we want to cruise until we know there's no further chance of doing so."

"Well," said he, ringing the bell to go ahead, sharp, "I'm not decidin' anything. I had my orders. I was to be gone twenty-four hours; an' it'll be more 'n that by the time I get back."

"Who gave you those orders?"

"Parker and Darrell," said he.

"Then this is all a swindle," I cried. "And we've been cheated into taking this trip for nothing at all!"

"No, it isn't a swindle," he answered, rather warmly. "They told me all about it. They knew, an' I knew, that it wasn't no use to go looking for two boats that had been lowered in a big storm four days ago, 'way down on the Florida coast. But they could see that this here girl would never give in till she'd had a chance of doin' what she thought she was called on to do, and so they agreed to give it to her. But they told me on no account to keep her out more 'n twenty-four hours. That would be long enough to satisfy her, and longer than that wouldn't be right. I tell you they know what they're about."

"Well, it wont be enough to satisfy her," I said, and then I went down to the little deck. I couldn't make the man turn back. I thought the tug had been hired to go wherever we chose to take her, but I had been mistaken. I felt that we had been deceived; but there was no use in saying anything more on the subject until we reached the city.

I did not wake Rectus to tell him the news. It would not do any good, and I was afraid Corny might hear us. I wanted her to sleep as long as she could, and, indeed, I dreaded the moment when she should awake, and find that all had been given up.

We steamed along very fast now. There was no stopping anywhere. I sat on the deck and thought a little, and dozed a little; and by the time it was morning, I found we were in the Savannah River. I now hated this river worse than ever.

Everything was quiet on the water, and everything, except the engine, was just as quiet on the tug. Rectus and Corny and Celia were still asleep, and nobody else seemed stirring, though, of course, some of the men were at their posts. I don't think the captain wanted to be about when Corny came out on deck, and found that we had given up the search. I intended to be with her when she first learned this terrible fact, which I knew would put an end to all hope in her heart; but I was in no hurry for her to wake up. I very much hoped she would sleep until we reached the city, and then we could take her directly to her kind friends.

And she did sleep until we reached the city. It was about seven o'clock in the morning, I think, when we began to steam slowly by the wharves and piers. I now wished the city were twenty miles further on. I knew that when we stopped I should have to wake up poor Corny.

The city looked doleful. Although it was not very early in the morning, there were very few people about. Some men could be seen on the decks of the vessels at the wharves, and a big steamer for one of the northern ports was getting up steam. I could not help thinking how happy the people must be who were going away in her. On one of the piers near where we were going to stop—we were coming in now—were a few darkey boys, sitting on a wharf-log, and dangling their bare feet over the water. I wondered how they dared laugh, and be so jolly. In a few minutes Corny must be wakened. On a post, near these boys, a lounger sat fishing with a long pole,—actually fishing away as if there were no sorrows and deaths, or shipwrecked or broken-hearted people in the world. I was particularly angry at this man—and I was so nervous that all sorts of things made me angry—because he was old enough to know better, and because he looked like such a fool. He had on green trousers, dirty canvas shoes and no stockings, a striped linen coat, and an old straw hat, which lopped down over his nose. One of the men called to him to catch the line which he was about to throw on the wharf, but he paid no attention, and a negro boy came and caught the line. The man actually had a bite, and couldn't take his eyes from the cork. I wished the line had hit him and knocked him off the post.

The tide was high, and the tug was not much below the wharf when we hauled up. Just as we touched the pier, the man, who was a little astern of us, caught his fish. He jerked it up, and jumped off his post, and, as he looked up in delight at his little fish, which was swinging in the air, I saw he was Mr. Chipperton!

I made one dash for Corny's little cubby-hole. I banged at the door. I shouted:

"Corny! Here's your father!"

She was out in an instant. She had slept in her clothes. She had no bonnet on. She ran out on deck, and looked about, dazed. The sight of the wharves and the ships seemed to stun her.

"Where?" she cried.

I took her by the arm and pointed out her father, who still stood holding the fishing-pole in one hand, while endeavoring to clutch the swinging fish with the other.

The plank had just been thrown out from the little deck. Corny made one bound. I think she struck the plank in the middle, like an India-rubber ball, and then she was on the wharf; and before he could bring his eyes down to the earth, her arms were around her father's neck, and she was wildly kissing and hugging him.

Mr. Chipperton was considerably startled, but when he saw who it was who had him, he threw his arms around Corny, and hugged and kissed her as if he had gone mad.

Rectus was out by this time, and as he and I stood on the tug, we could not help laughing, although we were so happy that we could have cried. There stood that ridiculous figure, Mr. Chipperton, in his short green trousers and his thin striped coat, with his arms around his daughter, and the fishing-pole tightly clasped to her back, while the poor little fish dangled and bobbed at every fresh hug.

Everybody on board was looking at them, and one of the little black boys, who didn't appear to appreciate sentiment, made a dash for the fish, unhooked it, and put like a good fellow. This rather broke the spell that was on us all, and Rectus and I ran on shore.

We did not ask any questions, we were too glad to see him. After he had put Corny on one side, and had shaken our hands wildly with his left hand, for his right still held the pole, and had tried to talk and found he couldn't, we called a carriage that had just come up, and hustled him and Corny into it. I took the pole from his hand, and asked him where he would go to. He called out the name of the hotel where we were staying, and I shut the door, and sent them off. I did not ask a word about Corny's mother, for I knew Mr. Chipperton would not be sitting on a post and fishing if his wife was dead.

I threw the pole and line away, and then Rectus and I walked up to the hotel. We forgot all about Celia, who was left to go home when she chose.

It was some hours before we saw the Chippertons, and then we were called into their room, where there was a talking and a telling things, such as I never heard before.

It was some time before I could get Mr. and Mrs. Chipperton's story straight, but this was about the amount of it: They were picked up sooner than we were—just after day-break. When they left the ship, they rowed as hard as they could, for several hours, and so got a good distance from us. It was well they met with a vessel as soon as they did, for all the women who had been on the steamer were in this boat, and they had a hard time of it. The water dashed over them very often, and Mr. Chipperton thought that some of them could not have held out much longer (I wondered what they would have done on our raft).

The vessel that picked them up was a coasting schooner bound to one of the Florida Keys, and she wouldn't put back with them, for she was under some sort of a contract, and kept right straight on her way. When they got down there, they chartered a vessel which brought them up to Fernandina, where they took the steamer for Savannah. They were on the very steamer we passed in the inside passage. If we had only known that!

They telegraphed the moment they reached Fernandina, and proposed stopping at St. Augustine, but it was thought they could make better time by keeping right on to Fernandina. The telegram reached Savannah after we had left on the tug.

Mr. Chipperton said he got his fancy clothes on board the schooner. He bought them of a man—a passenger, I believe—who had an extra suit.

"I think," said Mr. Chipperton, "he was the only man on that mean little vessel who had two suits of clothes. I don't know whether these were his weekday or his Sunday clothes. As for my own, they were so wet that I took them off the moment I got on board the schooner, and I never saw them again. I don't know what became of them, and, to tell the truth, I haven't thought of 'em. I was too glad to get started for Savannah, where I knew we'd meet Corny, if she was alive. You see, I trusted in you boys."

Just here, Mrs. Chipperton kissed us both again. This made several times that she had done it. We didn't care so much, as there was no one there but ourselves and the Chippertons.

"When we got here, and found you had gone to look for us, I wanted to get another tug and go right after you, but my wife was a good deal shaken up, and I did not want to leave her; and Parker and Darrell said they had given positive orders to have you brought back this morning, so I waited. I was only too glad to know you were all safe. I got up early in the morning, and went down to watch for you. You must have been surprised to see me fishing, but I had nothing else to do, and so I hired a pole and line of a boy. It helped very much to pass the time away."

"Yes," said Rectus, "you didn't notice us at all, you were so much interested."

"Well, you see," said Mr. Chipperton, "I had a bite just at that minute; and, besides, I really did not look for you on such a little boat. I had an idea you would come on something more respectable than that."

"As if we should ever think of respectability at such a time!" said Mrs. Chipperton, with tears in her eyes.

"As for you boys," said Mr. Chipperton, getting up and taking us each by the hand, "I don't know what to say to you."

I thought, for my part, that they had all said enough already. They had praised and thanked us for things we had never thought of.

"I almost wish you were orphans," he continued, "so that I might adopt you. But a boy can't have more than one father. However, I tell you! a boy can have as many uncles as he pleases. I'll be an uncle to each of you as long as I live. Ever after this call me Uncle Chipperton. Do you hear that?"

We heard, and said we'd do it.

Soon after this, lots of people came in, and the whole thing was gone over again and again. I am sorry to say that, at one or two places in the story, Mrs. Chipperton kissed us both again.

Before we went down to dinner, I asked Uncle Chipperton how his lung had stood it, through all this exposure.

"Oh, bother the lung!" he said. "I tell you, boys, I've lost faith in that lung,—at least, in there being anything the matter with it. I shall travel for it no more."

CHAPTER XXII.: LOOKING AHEAD.

"We have made up our minds," said Uncle Chipperton, that afternoon, "to go home and settle down, and let Corny go to school. I hate to send her away from us, but it will be for her good. But that wont be until next fall. We'll keep her until then. And now, I'll tell you what I think we'd all better do. It's too soon to go North yet. No one should go from the soft climate of the semi-tropics to the Northern or Middle States until mild weather has fairly set in there. And that will not happen for a month yet.

"Now, this is my plan. Let us all take a leisurely trip homeward by the way of Mobile, and New Orleans and the Mississippi River. This will be just the season, and we shall be just the party. What do you say?"

Everybody, but me, said it would be splendid. I had exactly the same idea about it, but I didn't say so, for there was no use in it. I couldn't go on a trip like that. I had been counting up my money that morning, and found I would have to shave pretty closely to get home by rail,—and I wanted, very much, to go that way—although it would be cheaper to return by sea,—for I had a great desire to go through North and South Carolina and Virginia, and see Washington. It would have seemed like a shame to go back by sea, and miss all this. But, as I said, I had barely enough money for this trip, and to make it I must start the next day. And there was no use writing home for money. I knew there was none there to spare, and I wouldn't have asked for it if there had been. If there was any travelling money, some of the others ought to have it. I had had my share.

It was very different with Rectus and the Chippertons. They could afford to take this trip, and there was no reason why they shouldn't take it.

When I told them this, Uncle Chipperton flashed up in a minute, and said that that was all stuff and nonsense,—the trip shouldn't cost me a cent. What was the sense, he said, of thinking of a few dollars when such pleasure was in view? He would see that I had no money-troubles, and if that was all, I could go just as well as not. Didn't he owe me thousands of dollars?

All this was very kind, but it didn't suit me. I knew that he did not owe me a cent, for if I had done anything for him, I made no charge for it. And even if I had been willing to let him pay my expenses,—which I wasn't,—my father would never have listened to it.

So I thanked him, but told him the thing couldn't be worked in that way, and I said it over and over again, until, at last, he believed it. Then he offered to lend me the money necessary, but this offer I had to decline, too. As I had no way of paying it back, I might as well have taken it as a gift. There wasn't anything he could offer, after this, except to get me a free pass; and as he had no way of doing that, he gave up the job, and we all went down to supper. That evening, as I was putting a few things into a small valise which I had bought,—as our trunks were lost on the "Tigris," I had very little trouble in packing up,—I said to Rectus that by the time he started off he could lay in a new stock of clothes. I had made out our accounts, and had his money ready to hand over to him, but I knew that his father had arranged for him to draw on a Savannah bank, both for the tug-boat money and for money for himself. I think that Mr. Colbert would have authorized me to do this drawing, if Rectus had not taken the matter into his own hands when he telegraphed. But it didn't matter, and there wasn't any tug-boat money to pay, any way, for Uncle Chipperton paid that. He said it had all been done for his daughter, and he put his foot down hard, and wouldn't let Rectus hand over a cent.

"I wont have any more time than you will have," replied Rectus, "for I'm going to-morrow."

"I didn't suppose they'd start so soon," I said "I'm sure there's no need of any hurry."

"I'm not going with them," said Rectus, putting a lonely shirt into a trunk that he had bought. "I'm going home with you."

I was so surprised at this that I just stared at him.

"What do you mean?" said I.

"Mean?" said he. "Why, just what I say. Do you suppose I'd go off with them, and let you straggle up home by yourself? Not any for me, thank you. And besides, I thought you were to take charge of me. How would you look going back and saying you'd turned me over to another party?"

"YOU'RE A REGULAR YOUNG TRUMP."

"You thought I was to take charge of you, did you?" I cried. "Well, you're a long time saying so. You never admitted that before."

"I had better sense than that," said Rectus, with a grin. "But I don't mind saying so now, as we're pretty near through with our travels. But father told me expressly that I was to consider myself in your charge."

"You young rascal!" said I. "And he thought that you understood it so well that there was no need of saying much to me about it. All that he said expressly to me was about taking care of your money. But I tell you what it is, Rectus, you're a regular young trump to give up that trip, and go along with me."

And I gave him a good slap on the back.

He winced at this, and let drive a pillow at me, so hard that it nearly knocked me over a chair.

The next morning, after an early breakfast, we went to bid the Chippertons good-bye. We intended to walk to the dépôt, and so wanted to start early. I was now cutting down all extra expenses.

"Ready so soon!" cried Uncle Chipperton, appearing at the door of his room. "Why, we haven't had our breakfast yet."

"We have to make an early start, if we go by the morning train," said I, "and we wanted to see you all before we started."

"Glad to see you at any hour of the night or day,—always very glad to see you; but I think we had better be getting our breakfast, if the train goes so early."

"Are you going to start to-day?" I asked, in surprise.

"Certainly," said he. "Why shouldn't we? I bought a new suit of clothes yesterday, and my wife and Corny look well enough for travelling purposes. We can start as well as not, and I'd go in my green trousers if I hadn't any others. My dear," he said, looking into the room, "you and Corny must come right down to breakfast."

"But perhaps you need not hurry," I said. "I don't know when the train for Mobile starts."

"Mobile!" he cried. "Who's going to Mobile? Do you suppose that we are? Not a bit of it. When I proposed that trip, I didn't propose it for Mrs. Chipperton, or Corny, or myself, or you, or Rectus, or Tom, or Dick, or Harry. I proposed it for all of us. If all of us cannot go, none of us can. If you must go north this morning, so must we. We've nothing to pack, and that's a comfort. Nine o'clock, did you say? You may go on to the dépôt, if you like, and we'll eat our breakfasts, take a carriage, and be there in time."

They were there in time, and we all went north together.

We had a jolly trip. We saw Charleston, and Richmond, and Washington, and Baltimore, and Philadelphia; and at last we saw Jersey City, and our folks waiting for us in the great dépôt of the Pennsylvania railroad.

When I saw my father and mother and my sister Helen standing there on the stone foot-walk, as the cars rolled in, I was amazed. I hadn't expected them. It was all right enough for Rectus to expect his father and mother, for they lived in New York, but I had supposed that I should meet my folks at the station in Willisville. But it was a capital idea in them to come to New York. They said they couldn't wait at home, and besides, they wanted to see and know the Chippertons, for we all seemed so bound together, now.

Well, it wasn't hard to know the Chippertons. Before we reached the hotel where my folks were staying, and where we all went to take luncheon together, any one would have thought that Uncle Chipperton was really a born brother to father and old Mr. Colbert. How he did talk! How everybody talked! Except Helen. She just sat and listened and looked at Corny—a girl who had been shipwrecked, and had been on a little raft in the midst of the stormy billows. My mother and the two other ladies cried a good deal, but it was a sunshiny sort of crying, and wouldn't have happened so often, I think, if Mrs. Chipperton had not been so ready to lead off.

After luncheon we sat for two or three hours in one of the parlors, and talked, and talked, and talked. It was a sort of family congress. Everybody told everybody else what he or she was going to do, and took information of the same kind in trade. I was to go to college in the fall, but as that had been pretty much settled long ago, it couldn't be considered as news. I looked well enough, my father said, to do all the hard studying that was needed; and the professor was anxiously waiting to put me through a course of training for the happy lot of Freshman.

"But he's not going to begin his studies as soon as he gets home," said my mother. "We're going to have him to ourselves for a while." And I did not doubt that. I hadn't been gone very long, to be sure, but then a ship had been burned from under me, and that counted for about a year's absence.

Corny's fate had been settled, too, in a general way, but the discussion that went on about a good boarding-school for her showed that a particular settlement might take some time. Uncle Chipperton wanted her to go to some school near his place on the Hudson River, so that he could drive over and see her every day or two, and Mrs. Colbert said she thought that that wouldn't do, because no girl could study as she ought to, if her father was coming to see her all the time, and Uncle Chipperton wanted to know what possible injury she thought he would do his daughter by going to see her; and Mrs. Colbert said, none at all, of course she didn't mean that, and Mrs.

Chipperton said that Corny and her father ought really to go to the same school, and then we all laughed, and my father put in quickly, and asked about Rectus. It was easy to see that it would take all summer to get a school for Corny.

"Well," said Mr. Colbert, "I've got a place for Sammy. Right in my office. He's to be a man of business, you know. He never took much to schooling. I sent him travelling so that he could see the world, and get himself in trim for dealing with it. And that's what we have to do in our business. Deal with the world."

I didn't like this, and I don't think Rectus did, either. He walked over to one of the windows, and looked out into the street.

"I'll tell you what I think, sir," said I. "Rectus—I mean your son Samuel, only I shall never call him so—has seen enough of the world to make him so wide awake that he sees more in schooling than he used to. That's my opinion!"

I knew that Rectus rather envied my going to college, for he had said as much on the trip home; and I knew that he had hoped his father would let him make a fresh start with the professor at our old school.

"Sammy," cried out Mrs. Colbert,—"Sammy, my son, do you want to go to school, and finish up your education, or go into your father's office, and learn to be a merchant?"

Rectus turned around from the window.

"There's no hurry about the merchant," he said. "I want to go to school and college, first."

"And that's just where you're going," said his mother, with her face reddening up a little more than common.

Mr. Colbert grinned a little, but said nothing. I suppose he thought it would be of no use, and I had an idea, too, that he was very glad to have Rectus determine on a college career. I know the rest of us were. And we didn't hold back from saying so, either.

Uncle Chipperton now began to praise Rectus, and he told what obligations the boy had put him under in Nassau, when he wrote to his father, and had that suit about the property stopped, and so relieved him—Uncle Chipperton—from cutting short his semi-tropical trip, and hurrying home to New York in the middle of winter.

"But the suit isn't stopped," said Mr. Colbert. "You don't suppose I would pay any attention to a note like the one Sammy sent me, do you? I just let the suit go on, of course. It has not been decided yet, but I expect to gain it."

At this, Uncle Chipperton grew very angry indeed. It was astonishing to see how quickly he blazed up. He had supposed the whole thing settled, and now to find that the terrible injustice—as he considered it—was still going on, was too much for him.

"Do you sit there and tell me that, sir?" he exclaimed, jumping up and skipping over to Mr. Colbert. "Do you call yourself——"

"Father!" cried Corny. "Keep perfectly cool! Remain just where you are!"

Uncle Chipperton stopped as if he had run against a fence. His favorite advice went straight home to him.

"Very good, my child," said he, turning to Corny. "That's just what I'll do."

And he said no more about it.

Now, everybody began to talk about all sorts of things, so as to seem as if they hadn't noticed this little rumpus, and we agreed that we must all see each other again the next day. Father said he should remain in the city for a few days, now that we were all here, and Uncle Chipperton did not intend to go to his country-place until the weather was warmer. We were speaking of several things that would be pleasant to do together, when Uncle Chipperton broke in with a proposition:

"I'll tell you what I am going to do. I am going to give a dinner to this party. I can't invite you to my house, but I shall engage a parlor in a restaurant, where I have given dinners before (we always come to New York when I want to give dinners—it's so much easier for us to come to the city than for a lot of people to come out to our place), and there I shall give you a dinner, to-morrow evening. Nobody need say anything against this. I've settled it, and I can't be moved."

As he couldn't be moved, no one tried to move him.

"I tell you what it is," said Rectus privately to me. "If Uncle Chipperton is going to give a dinner, according to his own ideas of things in general, it will be a curious kind of a meal."

It often happened that Rectus was as nearly right as most people.

CHAPTER XXIII.: UNCLE CHIPPERTON'S DINNER.

The next day was a busy one for father and mother and myself. All the morning we were out, laying in a small stock of baggage, to take the place of what I had lost on the "Tigris." But I was very sorry, especially on my sister Helen's account, that I had lost so many things in my trunk which I could not replace, without going back myself to Nassau. I could buy curiosities from those regions that were ever so much better than any that I had collected; but I could not buy shells that I myself had gathered, nor great seed-pods, like bean-pods two feet long, which I had picked from the trees, nor pieces of rock that I myself had brought up from a coral-reef.

But these were all gone, and I pacified Helen by assuring her that I would tell her such long stories about these things that she could almost see them in her mind's eye. But I think, by the way she smiled, that she had only a second-rate degree of belief in my power of description. She was a smart little thing, and she believed that Corny was the queen of girls.

While I am speaking of the "Tigris" and our losses, I will just say that the second boat which left the burning steamer was never heard from.

We reached our hotel about noon, pretty tired, for we had been rushing things, as it was necessary for father to go home early the next day. On the front steps we found Uncle Chipperton, who had been waiting for us. He particularly wanted to see me. He lunched with us, and then he took me off to the place where he was to have his dinner, at six o'clock that evening. He wanted to consult with me about the arrangements of the table; where each person should sit, and all that sort of thing. I couldn't see the use in this, because it was only a kind of family party, and we should all be sure to get seated, if there were chairs and places enough. But Uncle Chipperton wanted to plan and arrange everything until he was sure it was just right. That was his way.

After he had settled these important matters, and the head-waiter and the proprietor had become convinced that I was a person of much consequence, who had to be carefully consulted before anything could be done, we went down stairs, and at the street-door Uncle Chipperton suddenly stopped me.

"See here," said he, "I want to tell you something. I'm not coming to this dinner."

"Not—coming!" I exclaimed, in amazement.

"No," said he, "I've been thinking it over, and have fully made up my mind about it. You see, this is intended as a friendly reunion,—an occasion of good feeling and fellowship among people who are bound together in a very peculiar manner."

"Yes," I interrupted, "and that seems to me, sir, the very reason why you should be there."

"The very reason why I should not be there," he said. "You see, I couldn't sit down with that most perverse and obstinate man, Colbert, and feel sure that something or other would not occur which would make an outbreak between us, or, at any rate, bad feeling. In fact, I know I could not take pleasure in seeing him enjoy food. This may be wrong, but I can't help it. It's in me. And I wont be the means of casting a shadow over the happy company which will meet here to-night. No one but your folks need know I'm not coming. The rest will not know why I am detained, and

I shall drop in toward the close of the meal, just before you break up. I want you to ask your father to take the head of the table. He is just the man for such a place, and he ought to have it, too, for another reason. You ought to know that this dinner is really given to you in your honor. To be sure, Rectus is a good fellow—splendid—and does everything that he knows how; but my wife and I know that we owe all our present happiness to your exertions and good sense."

He went on in this way for some time, and although I tried to stop him, I couldn't do it.

"Therefore," he continued, "I want your father to preside, and all of you to be happy, without a suspicion of a cloud about you. At any rate, I shall be no cloud. Come around here early, and see that everything is all right. Now I must be off."

And away he went.

I did not like this state of affairs at all. I would have much preferred to have no dinner. It was not necessary, any way. If I had had the authority, I would have stopped the whole thing. But it was Uncle Chipperton's affair, he paid for it, and I had no right to interfere with it.

My father liked the matter even less than I did. He said it was a strange and unwarrantable performance on the part of Chipperton, and he did not understand it. And he certainly did not want to sit at the head of the table in another man's place. I could not say anything to him to make him feel better about it. I made him feel worse, indeed, when I told him that Uncle Chipperton did not want his absence explained, or alluded to, any more than could be helped. My father hated to have to keep a secret of this kind.

In the afternoon, I went around to the hotel where the Chippertons always staid, when they were in New York, to see Corny and her mother. I found them rather blue. Uncle Chipperton had not been able to keep his plan from them, and they thought it was dreadful. I could not help letting them see that I did not like it, and so we didn't have as lively a time as we ought to have had.

I supposed that if I went to see Rectus, and told him about the matter, I should make him blue, too. But, as I had no right to tell him, and also felt a pretty strong desire that some of the folks should come with good spirits and appetites, I kept away from him. He would have been sure to see that something was the matter.

I was the first person to appear in the dining-room of the restaurant where the dinner-table was spread for us. It was a prettily furnished parlor in the second story of the house, and the table was very tastefully arranged and decorated with flowers. I went early, by myself, so as to be sure that everything was exactly right before the guests arrived. All seemed perfectly correct; the name of each member of the party was on a card by a plate. Even little Helen had her plate and her card. It would be her first appearance at a regular dinner-party.

The guests were not punctual. At ten minutes past six, even my father, who was the most particular of men in such things, had not made his appearance. I waited five, ten, fifteen, twenty minutes more, and became exceedingly nervous.

The head-waiter came in and asked if my friends understood the time that had been set. The dinner would be spoiled if it were kept much longer. I said that I was sure they knew all about the time set, and that there was nothing to be done but to wait. It was most unaccountable that they should all be late.

I stood before the fireplace and waited, and thought. I ran down to the door, and looked up and down the street. I called a waiter and told him to look into all the rooms in the house. They might have gone into the wrong place. But they were not to be seen anywhere.

Then I went back to the fireplace, and did some more thinking. There was no sense in supposing that they had made a mistake. They all knew this restaurant, and they all knew the time. In a moment, I said to myself:

"I know how it is. Father has made up his mind that he will not be mixed up in any affair of this kind, where a quarrel keeps the host of the party from occupying his proper place, especially as he—my father—is expected to occupy that place himself. So he and mother and Helen have just quietly staid in their rooms at the hotel. Mrs. Chipperton and Corny wont come without Uncle Chipperton. They might ride right to the door, of course, but they are ashamed, and don't want to have to make explanations; and it is ridiculous to suppose that they wont have to be made. As for Rectus and his people, they could not have heard anything, but,—I have it. Old Colbert got his back up, too, and wouldn't come, either for fear a quarrel would be picked, or because he could take no pleasure in seeing Uncle Chipperton enjoying food. And Rectus and his mother wouldn't come without him."

It turned out, when I heard from all the parties, that I had got the matter exactly right.

"We shall have to make fresh preparations, sir, if we wait any longer," said the head-waiter, coming in with an air of great mental disturbance.

"Don't wait," said I. "Bring in the dinner. At least, enough for me. I don't believe any one else will be here."

The waiter looked bewildered, but he obeyed. I took my seat at the place where my card lay, at the middle of one side of the table, and spread my napkin in my lap. The head-waiter waited on me himself, and one or two other waiters came in to stand around, and take away dishes, and try to find something to do.

It was a capital dinner, and I went carefully through all the courses. I was hungry. I had been saving up some extra appetite for this dinner, and my regular appetite was a very good one.

I had raw oysters,

And soup,

And fish, with delicious sauce,

And roast duck,

And croquettes, made of something extraordinarily nice,

And beef à la mode,

And all sorts of vegetables, in their proper places,

And ready-made salad,

And orange pie,

And wine-jelly,

And ice-cream,

And bananas, oranges and white grapes,

And raisins, and almonds and nuts,
And a cup of coffee.

I let some of these things off pretty easy, toward the last; but I did not swerve from my line of duty. I went through all the courses, quietly and deliberately. It was a dinner in my honor, and I did all the honor I could to it.

I was leaning back in my chair, with a satisfied soul, and nibbling at some raisins, while I slowly drank my coffee, when the outer door opened, and Uncle Chipperton entered.

He looked at me in astonishment. Then he looked at the table, with the clean plates and glasses at every place, but one. Then he took it all in, or at least I supposed he did, for he sat down on a chair near the door, and burst out into the wildest fit of laughing. The waiters came running into the room to see what was the matter; but for several minutes Uncle Chipperton could not speak. He laughed until I thought he'd crack something. I laughed, too, but not so much.

"I see it all," he gasped, at last. "I see it all. I see just how it happened."

And when we compared our ideas of the matter, we found that they were just the same.

I wanted him to sit down and eat something, but he would not do it. He said he wouldn't spoil such a unique performance for anything. It was one of the most comical meals he had ever heard of.

I was glad he enjoyed it so much, for he paid for the whole dinner for ten, which had been prepared at his order.

When we reached the street, Uncle Chipperton put on a graver look.

"This is all truly very funny," he said, "but, after all, there is something about it which makes me feel ashamed of myself. Would you object to take a ride? It is only about eight o'clock. I want to go up to see old Colbert."

I agreed to go, and we got into a street-car. The Colberts lived in one of the up-town streets, and Uncle Chipperton had been at their house, on business.

"I never went to see them in a friendly way before," he said.

It was comforting to hear that this was to be a friendly visit.

When we reached the house, we found the family of three in the parlor. They had probably had all the dinner they wanted, but they did not look exactly satisfied with the world or themselves.

"Look here, Colbert," said Uncle Chipperton, after shaking hands with Mrs. Colbert, "why didn't you go to my dinner?"

"Well," said Mr. Colbert, looking him straight in the face, "I thought I'd better stay where I was. I didn't want to make any trouble, or pick any quarrels. I didn't intend to keep my wife and son away; but they wouldn't go without me."

"No, indeed," said Mrs. Colbert.

"Oh, well!" said Uncle Chipperton, "you needn't feel bad about it. I didn't go, myself."

At this, they all opened their eyes as wide as the law allowed.

"No," he continued, "I didn't want to make any disturbance, or ill-feeling, and so I didn't go, and my wife and daughter didn't want to go without me, and so they didn't go, and I expect Will's father and mother didn't care to be on hand at a time when bad feeling might be shown, and so they didn't go. There was no one there but Will. He ate all of the dinner that was eaten. He went straight through it, from one end to the other. And there was no ill-feeling, no discord, no cloud of any kind. All perfectly harmonious, wasn't it, Will?"

"Perfectly," said I.

"I just wish I had known about it," said Rectus, a little sadly.

"And now, Mr. Colbert," said Uncle Chipperton, "I don't want this to happen again. There may be other reunions of this kind, and we may want to go. And there ought to be such reunions between families whose sons and daughter have been cast away together, on a life-raft, in the middle of the ocean."

"That's so," said Mrs. Colbert, warmly.

"I thought they were saved on a life-raft," said old Colbert, dryly. "And I didn't know it was in the middle of the ocean."

"Well, fix that as you please," said Uncle Chipperton. "What I want to propose is this: Let us settle our quarrel. Let's split our difference. Will you agree to divide that four inches of ground, and call it square? I'll pay for two inches."

"Do you mean you'll pay half the damages I've laid?" asked old Colbert.

"That's what I mean," said Uncle Chipperton.

"All right," said Mr. Colbert; "I'll agree." And they shook hands on it.

"Now, then," said Uncle Chipperton, who seemed unusually lively, "I must go see the Gordons, and explain matters to them. Wont you come along, Rectus?" And Rectus came.

On the way to our hotel, we stopped for Corny and her mother. We might as well have a party, Uncle Chipperton said.

We had a gay time at our rooms. My father and mother were greatly amused at the way the thing had turned out, and very much pleased that Mr. Colbert and Uncle Chipperton had become reconciled to each other.

"I thought he had a good heart," said my mother, softly, to me, looking over to Uncle Chipperton, who was telling my father, for the second time, just how I looked, as I sat alone at the long table.

Little Helen had not gone to bed yet, and she was sorry about the dinner in the same way that Rectus was. So was Corny, but she was too glad that the quarrel between her father and Mr. Colbert was over, to care much for the loss of the dinner. She was always very much disturbed by quarrels between friends or friends' fathers.

CHAPTER XXIV.: THE STORY ENDS.

Three letters came to me the next morning. I was rather surprised at this, because I did not expect to get letters after I found myself at home; or, at least, with my family. The first of these was handed to me by Rectus. It was from his father. This is the letter:

"My Dear Boy:" (This opening seemed a little curious to me, for I did not suppose the old gentleman thought of me in that way.) "I shall not be able to see you again before you leave for Willisville, so I write this note just to tell you how entirely I am satisfied with the way in which you performed the very difficult business I intrusted to you—that of taking charge of my son in his recent travels. The trip was not a very long one, but I am sure it has been of great service to him; and I also believe that a great deal of the benefit he has received has been due to you." (I stopped here, and tried to think what I had done for the boy. Besides the thrashing I gave him in Nassau, I could not think of anything.) "I have been talking a great deal with Sammy, in the last day or two, about his doings while he was away, and although I cannot exactly fix my mind on any particular action, on your part, which proves what I say" (he was in the same predicament here in which I was myself), "yet I feel positively assured that your companionship and influence have been of the greatest service to him. Among other things, he really wants to go to college. I am delighted at this. It was with much sorrow that I gave up the idea of making him a scholar: but, though he was a good boy, I saw that it was useless to keep him at the academy at Willisville, and so made up my mind to take him into my office. But I know you put this college idea into his head, though how, I cannot say, and I am sure that it does not matter. Sammy tells me that you never understood that he was to be entirely in your charge; but since you brought him out so well without knowing this, it does you more credit. I am very grateful to you. If I find a chance to do you a real service, I will do it.

"Yours very truly, "Samuel Colbert, Sr."

The second letter was handed to me by Corny, and was from her mother. I shall not copy that here, for it is much worse than Mr. Colbert's. It praised me for doing a lot of things which I never did at all; but I excused Mrs. Chipperton for a good deal she said, for she had passed through so much anxiety and trouble, and was now going to settle down for good, with Corny at school, that I didn't wonder she felt happy enough to write a little wildly. But there was one queer resemblance between her letter and old Mr. Colbert's. She said two or three times—it was an awfully long letter—that there was not any particular thing that she alluded to when she spoke of my actions. That was the funny part of it. They couldn't put their fingers on anything really worth mentioning, after all.

My third letter had come by mail, and was a little old. My mother gave it to me, and told me that it had come to the post-office at Willisville about a week before, and that she had brought it down to give it to me, but had totally forgotten it until that morning. It was from St. Augustine, and this is an exact copy of it:

"My good friend Big Little Man. I love you. My name Maiden's Heart. You much pious. You buy beans. Pay good. Me wants one speckled shirt. Crowded Owl want one speckled shirt, too.

You send two speckled shirts. You good Big Little Man. You do that. Good-bye.
"Maiden's Heart, Cheyenne Chief.

"Written by me, James R. Chalott, this seventh day of March, 187-, at the dictation of the above-mentioned Maiden's Heart. He has requested me to add that he wants the speckles to be red, and as large as you can get them."

During the morning, most of our party met to bid each other good-bye. Corny, Rectus and I were standing together, having our little winding-up talk, when Rectus asked Corny if she had kept her gray bean, the insignia of our society.

"To be sure I have," she said, pulling it out from under her cloak. "I have it on this little chain which I wear around my neck. I've worn it ever since I got it. And I see you each have kept yours on your watch-guards."

"Yes," I said, "and they're the only things of the kind we saved from the burning 'Tigris.' Going to keep yours?"

"Yes, indeed," said Corny, warmly.

"So shall I," said I.

"And I, too," said Rectus.

And then we shook hands, and parted.

Printed by Amazon Italia Logistica S.r.l.
Torrazza Piemonte (TO), Italy